PRAISE FOR
AUDREY CARLAN

"FIVE STAR REVIEW! I recommend this book to anyone looking for a sweet, fierce love story. It takes a lot to write an original story that takes twists and turns you won't see coming."

~Abibliophobia Anonymous Book Reviews Blog

"Damn Audrey did it again! Made me smile, made me laugh & made me cry with her beautiful words! I am in love with these books."

~Hooks & Books Book Blog

"A sensual spiritual journey of two people meant for each other, heart and soul. Well-crafted and beautifully written."

~Carly Phillips, New York Times Bestselling Author

A TRINITY NOVEL

Life

A TRINITY NOVEL

WATERHOUSE PRESS

WARNING

To my soul sister Dyani Gingerich.

Without you, there would be no
Maria De La Torre.

Without you, I would be a soul sister short
of my perfect friendship trinity.

Without you, this love story
wouldn't have been written.

BESOS

Bound - Eternally - Sisters - of - Souls

CHAPTER ONE

I won't cry. I *can't* cry. Showing pain would be a sign of weakness. I refuse to be seen as weak. Ten years ago, I was powerless, a product of my environment. Now, five years later, I'm a survivor. Confident and strong. I kicked my weakling side to the curb the day I chose to live.

On this day, in front of hundreds of mourners, my survival skills are ratcheting into high gear. For Tommy, I will prevail. Even though my heart is shattered, my mind is mush, and my body is a living, breathing bag of bones, tissue, and muscle functioning solely on autopilot... I have to. Tommy would want me to go on and live my life.

A life without him.

Grief is a sneaky bastard no one can hide from or abolish. It creeps like a ninja, night and day. It could even be considered an invisible monster that wraps its acid-dipped claws around a person's heart in the dead of night. They're dreaming of peace, but instead find themselves filled with devastation and gut-wrenching pain.

Pain is no stranger to me. Right now, I welcome its sharpened, lethal point. At least the dagger in my heart prevents me from drowning in the bubbled edges of numbness I want so badly to wrap myself in. The blessed relief of nothingness would be welcome during a time when everything around me is complete and utter chaos.

Everywhere I look, men in black suits and uniforms are piling into the church, their shiny badges glinting sparks of light in every direction from the midmorning sun's rays. The red, white, and blue flag draped over the casket in front of me should make me proud. A hero has fallen, and the sea of men here to pay their respects should give me a sense of closure. It doesn't. Tommy is dead because of me. Killed in the line of duty, protecting my best friend.

What's worse is that I wouldn't have it any other way. I believe in my heart that I had just started to fall for Tommy, but Gillian, my best friend, is the only family I've ever known. He knew that. If he hadn't, I don't believe he would have put himself right in the middle of the fray against a deranged killer. He saved my soul sister's life, and in exchange, he gave his own.

How do I live with that? There is no book I can read that will absolve me of my heartache, my guilt. There is no prayer I can say that will change the fact that the man I had just begun to love, to believe could be the first man I could trust with my heart, is now gone.

Gillian squeezes my hand as she holds it tightly between hers. She sits at my left—my heart side. She and my two other soul sisters are the only reason that battered organ still beats. Bree sits at my right, her hand running up and down my thigh in a soothing, sisterly gesture of support. Her other hand lies calmly on her well-rounded belly. One life gone, one life soon to be born. A superstitious person might say that's how these things work. The yin and yang. Life and death. I'd like to truck-punch the *pinchazo* who came up with that saying. Take away what he or she loves most and shove it in the face of that prick.

I stare down at my fingers—interlaced with those of my friend's—and remember the one soul sister who can't be here today. Kathleen. Still in the hospital. The other person I let down. If I had only gotten to her quicker, she might not have suffered such severe burns. Her lung might not have collapsed. She might be sitting here alongside us, sharing her support. Instead, she's in a burn center, fighting for her life.

I run my tongue over the rough surface of my dry, cracked lips and consider that night. I should have been there. Even though I tried to kick through the boards around the theatre's window to get to Kathleen, I was too late. Cuts along the bottoms of my feet itch inside the flat-soled boots I'm wearing. The discomfort is welcome. They still ache at night, and the gashes down my abdomen where I dived through the broken window to get to my friend haven't completely healed either.

Three weeks have gone by since the fire in the theatre put Kat and me in the hospital. Two weeks since the man I loved was pushed through the windows of the historical tower where he fell two hundred feet to his death. From what I was told, even as he flew through the air, my Tommy went down while releasing a hailstorm of bullets, one of them catching the perpetrator straight through the neck, ending Daniel's reign of terror and destruction once and for all.

A shiver trails through my body as I focus all my attention on the casket in front of me. Tommy's parents are sitting on the other side of the aisle alongside members of his family. When I arrived, they hugged me as if they were my own parents— not that I really know what that feels like. His mother even whispered in my ear that I was always welcome in their family. His father led me up to the front pew where a wife would sit with the family, as if I had earned that honor. Not even close.

The priest approaches the altar, bringing me back to the here and now, and starts the funeral mass memorializing Thomas Redding, San Francisco Police Detective, son, brother...the man I never had the chance to tell him I loved him. He died never knowing the truth. And that knowledge I'll have to live with for the rest of my days.

* * *

I feel a warm hand on my shoulder coming from behind as I stare unmoving at the casket. I covet the stillness. I gather the entire place has been cleared out, everyone going to Thomas's family's estate for the reception.

"Maria, *es hora de ir.*" It's time to go, Chase says in Spanish, my native language. I nod and stand, a shot of pain zipping up my legs from my feet where the cuts are bearing my weight. The doctor had issued me limited movement instructions for the better part of three to four weeks in order to let the damage to my feet heal. Unfortunately for him, I'm not a good patient, so the healing time is taking longer than anticipated.

"Can I have a few minutes alone?" I glance over my shoulder. Chase Davis is holding Gillian, my bestie, at his side. Tears track down her face in endless streams. I don't think she's stopped crying since the fire. Her skin is paler than normal, and there is an element of hollowness to her gaze. I glance down her body and take in her form. She's gained a little of the weight she'd lost during the past few months of the psycho's reign over our lives, but not much. For the most part, she's skin and bones. Hell, besides Bree and her pregnancy, the rest of us are losing more weight than we can afford. Hard knocks will do that to you.

Chase has a hand over Gillian's midsection. It's a protective and odd gesture, but he's an intensely possessive man. I learned that the hard way. Even with his faults, he's still the best thing that's ever happened to my best friend, and I'm happy they found each other. I'd hoped that all of us would live happily ever after, just like in the storybooks. Gillian with Chase. Bree with Phillip. Kat with Carson. And me with my Tommy. Not to be. I'm the loner in the crowd now.

Chase inhales and sighs. "Of course. We'll wait outside the church." He squeezes my shoulder, and I close my eyes.

Eventually, I make my way over to the casket. A life-size headshot of Tommy in his police uniform sits next to it. I place my hand over the top of the flag and hang my head.

"Tommy, I'm sorry. None of this was supposed to happen. It should have never been you," I whisper, meaning every word down to the depths of my soul. The ache of his loss is agonizing, cutting me up from the inside out.

Tears finally swell and fall down my cheeks. I give in to them, not having a chance in hell at thwarting the grief. It has dug its vile claws into me and is taking over. Holding back has finally become too much. My body shakes with the strain and effort I've expended to stop myself from falling into a pit of despair. Each tear falls down my face and drips down my chin to the floor like scalding hot magma, burning me with every pea-sized drip that releases.

"If I could, I'd take your place." I pat the casket, hoping that somewhere, somehow, my Tommy is listening.

"Ahhh, beautiful, now that would be a downright shame." A rich, gravely, all-too-familiar voice from behind startles me.

I know that voice.

That voice has come to me in my dreams every night

for the past two weeks. It's the voice I hear inside my head, soothing me when the guilt and grief are excruciating. It's *him*. Every hair on my arms and neck stands at attention. I swallow, attempting to remove the giant lump of cotton in my throat. Slowly, I inhale and close my eyes while I turn around. *Please, God...*

It's not possible.

There's just no way.

Could it be?

Tommy.

I blink furiously against what I think I see. There he is. Alive. *Esplendido.* His eyes are the same dazzling green I remember. As he looks at me, he seems to see right through me, to the brokenness within. My heartbeat goes wild inside my chest, pounding out a rhythm I'm incapable of keeping up with. I clutch at the skin above my breasts.

"Can't be..." I choke out. The tears now have a mind of their own, and they race down my face, dropping hotly onto my chest. I hold out a shaky hand. A halo of light glows around his head, but his hair is dark and layered, with the sides cut shorter. What? I blink a few times, trying to understand what it is I'm seeing. Tommy didn't have hair.

"Are you okay?" he asks, but his voice sounds deeper, not quite the same timbre I'm used to.

He grabs me under the arms and hauls me against his massive chest just as I begin to teeter and lose touch with my balance. The chest I'm plastered against is far larger than the one I'd cuddled, kissed, and hugged this past year.

"Oh my God. What's going on?" I sob while gripping his tattooed arms.

Tattooed arms? Tommy didn't have any tattoos. I trace

every inch of what I can see with an analytical eye. My body continues to shake like a leaf in the center of a windstorm.

"Tommy?" I pet his bearded jaw. Bearded jaw?

The man jerks his head back. "Tommy? No...oh, no. Miss, you've got it mixed up."

"But, but, you're him. Your eyes are the same. Your face..." I wipe at my cheeks and back out of his grip until my back collides with the casket. Just like Tommy would, it holds me up as I shake my head. "I'm losing my mind. Finally happened. I've gone *loco en la cabeza!*" I screech, barely able to hold myself up, and look at Tommy's doppelgänger.

He lifts his hands out in front of him in a placating gesture. Tommy's hands, only they seem a little bigger. Everything on this man seems larger than life. I am officially losing my shit.

"You're not crazy." He chuckles, and it's a deep rumble that pounds against my chest and squeezes my heart. It's like Tommy's laugh, but not.

"I don't understand. You're dead. And you're not you!" I cant my head to the side and try to find the exit signs or my friends. "Chase! Gillian!" I scream at the top of my lungs. Is this a dream? Another twisted nightmare I can't wake from?

A door in the back of the church opens up and light seeps in, casting the stranger in silhouette.

Feet are getting closer and closer, but so is Tommy. "You're dead." I point a finger and shake my head over and over.

"I'm not Thomas," he rushes to say, and drops his hands down to his sides.

The sound of shoes pounding against a wooden floor gets louder. "Maria!" I hear Chase's voice, and I swear it's like a healing balm over my battered wounds.

Chase reaches us, my friend's fiery red hair bouncing in

the distance behind him. "Ria!" she yells.

I fly into Chase's arms and cry—big, heaping, lung-racking sobs into his warm chest. "Tommy!" I gag out in my breakdown.

"Who are you?" Chase's voice is a lethal weapon demanding a response. "Jesus Christ, you look exactly like him!" He gasps as if he just got a good look at the man standing a few feet from us. I turn my head and take in the man before me.

Gillian arrives, teetering on her stilettos, and puts out both arms to balance herself. The man holds out a hand to steady her. She grabs his wrist and then gasps as she, too, notices his face. "Oh my God, it's you..." She reaches for her mouth, one delicate white hand covering her peachy lips.

The man shakes his head. "I was trying to tell you before you freaked out"—he addresses me where I'm still cowering into Chase—"my name is Elijah Redding, but everyone calls me 'Red.'"

"Who are you?" I manage to form the words through the fear and anxiety controlling every facet of my being.

He rubs a hand through his dark, layered hair. "I'm Tommy's twin brother."

"Twins!" I croak and push off Chase's chest. He never mentioned that he was a twin.

Elijah nods. "Identical twins."

"I'll say," Gillian adds. "You're like the Hulk version. It's uncanny."

Chase whips his head to his woman, his eyes hard on her.

"What? Look at him, baby. He's like Tommy, but with fifty additional pounds of straight muscle and badass tats." Leave it to Gigi to go straight for the hot-guy description.

Chase lets me go and moves to his wife, wrapping an arm

around her waist, bringing her close. "We'll discuss later," he grumbles, and then turns toward Tommy's brother. "Why is it that Maria hasn't met you before now?"

Exactly the question I would ask if I could form that many words at one time. As it is, I can't keep my eyes off him. Gillian's right. He is the souped-up version of my Tommy. Same height, same eyes, and same mouth. Hair's different. Tommy was bald and clean-shaven, while Elijah has a rugged jaw with some serious scruff. Although he could have shaven it off and looked the part of grieving brother, if he'd given a flying fuck. Which he likely doesn't, since he's just now showing his face.

"Been estranged the last few years. Just got back to town," Elijah says through clenched teeth. "Who are you to my brother? Saw you sitting in front. What's your relation to him?"

I squint. If he were family, why didn't he know about me? Tommy and I were an item for close to a year.

For the same reason you didn't know about him.

"Your brother was my boyfriend."

Elijah closes his eyes, smiles wryly, and shakes his head. "Of course he'd have a hot piece like you." At those words, his eyes track all over my form from the top of my black one-piece jumper to the bottom of my boots. "I should have known." He rubs his thumb across the bottom of his lip. "He always did have a way with women."

I cross my arms over my chest. Chase reaches a hand out toward me, so I take it. When I get close, he wraps an arm over my shoulders. "You ready?"

"*Listo para decir adios?* No." To say good-bye? No.

Chase nods sadly, and Gigi reaches out a hand to caress my cheek. "We never truly say good-bye to them, honey. They live on through us and those who loved them." Then Gillian glances at Elijah. "We're very sorry for your loss. Tommy died saving my life. It's a gift I can never repay, but if you need anything, anything at all, my husband and I would be honored to provide it."

Elijah's broad shoulders seem to tighten and lift right in front of our eyes. "Maybe we could meet sometime soon, and, uh, you tell me how he saved your life," he says, and clasps his hands in front of him.

My Gigi smiles so bright it's as if the heavens are shining a light directly on her face. "I'd love to share how your brother was a hero."

At that last part, Elijah winces and looks away. "Yeah, thanks."

"Do you have a business card?" Chase asks Elijah, and the question seems so absolutely absurd, I can't control the chuckle that slips out.

Elijah laughs and shakes his head. Yeah, I didn't think so.

Chase's brow deepens in a familiar way I've gotten used to. He reaches into his suit jacket and pulls out one of his own. "Here's mine. As my wife said, we'd be happy to host you for a drink or a meal. Please call. It would do my wife a great deal of good." He holds out his hand, and Elijah shakes it. Briefly, Chase leans in, far enough away that Gigi can't hear, but I can make out the words. "The guilt over his death is brutal for her," he whispers and backs up a few steps. "Again, please call."

Elijah pockets the card in the back of his dark jeans. "I will."

"Much obliged," Chase says and then holds out his arm to me. "Shall we?"

I turn to Elijah. "I'm sorry about the way I reacted..." I

lift my head and stare into his eyes, ones I know so well on a different person.

He places a hand on my cheek. "Babe, it's cool. I'm used to it."

Elijah wipes a stray tear away.

"I'm sorry about your brother." I inhale and exhale, holding the tears at bay once more.

"Yeah, me too," he says solemnly before dropping his hand away.

I lift my own hand to my cheek to replace the warmth that was there. His felt so much like Tommy's touch, yet nothing like it at all.

Chase leads me down the aisle of the church toward the large, arched, wooden double doors.

"Hey!" Elijah calls out.

All three of us turn around.

"What's your name?"

"Maria. Maria De La Torre."

"Nice to meet you, Maria De La Torre," he says before taking a seat at the front pew. I watch a moment as he leans forward, putting his elbows to his knees and his head down into his hands. He could have an anvil weighing him down with how defeated he looks in this moment.

"Come on," Gigi urges, but something makes me want to stay, to comfort him, to get to know this man who's so much like my Tommy.

His twin. I still can't believe he had an identical twin and I had no idea. Why didn't Tommy talk about Elijah? Why didn't his family? I'd been to countless dinners *en la casa familia de la* Redding. It doesn't make sense why his name wouldn't have come up. We spent Thanksgiving and Christmas together, and nothing. Not a word.

None of it makes any sense. All I know is, when he addressed me from behind, I thought Tommy was speaking to me from beyond the grave. And then I turned around, and it was like seeing a living, breathing ghost. Only he is much larger and more ruggedly handsome. Elijah looks like the type of man who wouldn't stay in one place for long. He takes good care of himself if the black T-shirt stretched over a massive wall of muscle is any indication. His dark jeans, motorcycle boots, and wide-legged stance proclaim he doesn't give a fuck what people think of his clothes, because he doesn't wear them for anyone else. Even at a funeral. Where everyone comes dressed in their Sunday finest, Tommy's own brother shows up in jeans and a T-shirt *after* the ceremony is over. I don't know whether to hug the man or flip him off.

When we get outside, Gillian stops me in front of the limo. "Holy shit, Ria. Are you okay?" She holds on to my biceps, her emerald-green eyes staring worriedly into my blue ones.

I shake my head. "I don't know. Yes. No. Maybe. That was fucked up."

Chase tugs at his sleeves, straightening them. "I'll say. You didn't know he had a twin brother?"

"No. Total messed-up surprise. Tommy and his family never mentioned him at all this past year. I'd remember if my boyfriend had told me he was a twin. An identical twin!"

Gillian pulls me into her arms. "God, this day. Wanna go drink it away at the penthouse?"

Chase tugs Gillian back against his body, whispers into her ear, and places both of his hands over her abdomen. What. The. Fuck. He doesn't usually act superhumanly possessive around me—only against males who make advances toward his woman. Even if the past few months had brought down a shitstorm of hell and damnation onto our little group, his protectiveness is reaching epic douchebag proportions.

Gillian pats his hands and locks eyes with me, but responds to him. "Oh, I'm not in the drinking mood, honey. I never drink when I'm sad. But Ria and you should definitely tie one on. How about it?" She smiles sweetly at me and pushes a lock of red hair behind her ear.

"Sounds like I'll be staying at *la casa* Davis tonight. Chase, you better break out *la buena mierda.*"

"The good shit." He smirks. "You got it. Now please get in the car and buckle up."

I pout. "Always so bossy."

"Sister, you have no idea." Gigi sighs dreamily.

"You can tell me all about it over tequila," I grumble and open the door of the limo. I glance back at the church, the one I will never enter again. "Bye, Tommy," I whisper at the same time Elijah exits. I hold my breath and watch as his eyes zero in on mine. Then he lifts a hand and waves.

A swift wind blows my hair, chilling me straight down to the bone. Gooseflesh rises on my arms, and my teeth start chattering uncontrollably. I glance once more at the church and wave at the lone figure before dipping my head and getting into the car.

CHAPTER TWO

"*Y entonces qué pasó?*" I slur into my margarita. Damn, that butler cook guy makes awesome drinks. Benty? Benito? No, no... Bentley. Yeah, that's his name. He's *increíble*.

Gigi smacks my thigh. "In English!" she scolds and giggles.

Whoops. Didn't realize that I'd spoken in Spanish. The drinks are going down too easily. "'And then what happened?,' is what I said."

My best friend crosses her legs under her while sitting on the couch next to me. Chase smirks, leaning against the back of the opposite couch. Usually, Chase is one cool cucumber, but since Daniel McBride stalked and kidnapped his beloved Gillian and murdered my Tommy, he has definitely turned more guarded, even a bit icy. Though I can see the edges around him melting the more whiskey he tosses back.

Gillian inhales, locks eyes with me, and blurts out an answer to my question. I have a feeling I know what she is going to say even before she says it.

"We got married!" she squeals, bouncing in her seat, nothing but joy plastered across her face.

I blink a few times, watching the trails of light follow her movement in blurry streaks of rainbow colors. Frizzles of heat shimmer up my body as ire fills in the gaps in each pore.

Shaking my head, I poke her thigh. "I knew it. Just knew it. You *puta*! You ran off and got married without your best friends! Without me. *No es cool!*" I pout and throw daggers over at Chase. "And you"—I move my judging finger to him—"you planned it. You realize *Karma es una puta y su nombre es Maria!*" Basically translates to Karma is a bitch, and her name is Maria.

Chase chuckles so hard he chokes on his drink. He uses his fist to pound against his sternum. "Jesus, Maria, you do not hold back."

"Never have, never will. *You eloped.* With my best friend. How could you?" My words are straightforward, but I'm not able to hide the dejected edge in my tone.

If I were more put together, I wouldn't have sounded like a whining child. Unfortunately, a handful of margaritas, a funeral, and no food to speak of... What can I say? The five-year-old makes an appearance. Chase knows Gillian means the world to me. *He knows.*

Chase's eyes are an ocean aqua-blue when he takes the chair directly opposite me and reaches for my hand. He's never done that before, but lately he's been more forthcoming physically. I'm thrilled he's making an effort to connect with me and the girls, as if we are now a real part of his life, maybe even his family.

"Maria, I think the real question is, how could I not marry her in private, after the wedding straight from hell?" He lifts one dark espresso-colored eyebrow, mocking me at the same time he speaks the truth.

Bastard has a point. A couple months ago, Gillian and Chase were supposed to be married in a beautiful seaside wedding in Cancun. What happened instead was her stalker broke into the bride's room, sliced Chase's mother's throat, and kidnapped my best friend. He had her for four full days, chained up in a concrete storm shelter, wrapped in nothing but her wedding gown. And all that happened before he started the fire in the San Francisco theatre that changed Kat's life and ended Tommy's.

I shake my head, letting those thoughts disappear along with a giant swallow of my drink. The salt from the rim and the lime-flavored tequila burn a fiery path down my throat, reminding me I'm still alive.

"I forgive you. But no more secrets." I point a finger at his chest and then at her.

Gillian widens her eyes and glances at Chase, and then at me, and then back at Chase. He's pinching his lips together with two fingers and smirking. Sexy *bastardo* is hiding something else. Gillian licks her lips and bites down on the bottom one. Shit.

"Spit it out, *cara bonita*."

She softens at my nickname for her. I've always called her "beautiful face" because she has the prettiest face I've ever seen. Even when it was black-and-blue the first day we met in group therapy over five years ago, she glowed like a battered and broken angel. Gillian has the most beautiful, pearlescent ivory skin, auburn curly hair down past her shoulders, and the brightest green eyes I've ever seen. Plus, with a set of full lips, she's every guy's fantasy. Definitely her husband's, who is constantly looking at her like he's ready to push her up against the nearest wall and fuck the daylights out of her. I like that about him. With my girl, he's blatantly obvious in his affections. She needs it. Heck, we both do.

"Baby, tell her. Dana and Jack know." He makes a cavalier

hand gesture.

Her eyes cut to him at light speed. If I didn't know any better, those eyes would be yelling, and what they would say would not be nice. She furrows her brows, and her nostrils flare with a hint of anger.

I want to laugh—the drinks I've consumed make it hard to hold it back—but I really want to know about what she's hiding. "Gigi?"

"We're pregnant," she says in a big burst of air, her chest jerking with the exertion.

"*Shitballs, putos sagrados! No puedo creer que usted guardó esto de mí!*" I stand up, flailing my hands around, speaking in rapid-fire Spanish. My body heats up as a sense of betrayal rips through me. How could she? We're best friends!

"In English!" Gigi stands. "If you're going to yell at me, make sure I can understand it!"

I glare at her and get super close. She tightens her fists and puffs out her chest, ready to take whatever I'm going to throw at her. Good girl. Stand up to me. We found that fighting nature together. Lifted one another up during those hard years.

Chase stands and puts a hand over his wife's belly again. The protective energy pumping off him could electrify anyone within a ten-foot radius. At least now the overbearing, possessive touching around me makes perfect sense.

"Maria, I don't like the stance you're taking so close to my wife, especially considering she's pregnant." His words are possessive and direct.

Protective Superman is coming out. Good. He needs to be ready all the time. Not that I'd ever in a million years lay a finger on my best friend, nor would I ever hurt her in any way. But she needs to know and understand how much this information hurts me.

Gillian bumps her booty backward, pushing Chase a step back. "Sit down. This is between me and my girl. Now, Ria, Chase and I had a lot going on. It's not like we purposely kept information from anyone, but with Danny still roaming around and then the fire, I just couldn't. Then Tommy... It wasn't the right time." Her shoulders slump, and tears roll down her cheeks.

I get close and place my hands on her shoulders and lean my forehead to hers until they touch. "You can always come to me, Gigi. You know that. You. Know. That."

She nods against me. "I do, but it's not just me anymore. I've got Chase now." Her words crack and shake under the weight of the vulnerability they carry.

Chase. She has Chase. And I'm happy for her. Sad and uncertain about my place in her life now, but still, I'd rather she have the best of everything, and Chase will give her that, once they catch a break. It's been nothing but hardship since they got together. They deserve some peace, and now that Danny is dead, they'll finally, blessedly, get it.

I sigh and wrap my arms around her shoulders. "I'm happy about that. So glad you are finally free and can live with your man and your new *bebe*."

"Babies."

I frown and pull my head back enough to make sure my liquor-saturated brain didn't misinterpret what she said.

"More than one?" I shake my head of what I thought she said, trying to focus more clearly in my inebriated state.

She nods and smiles huge, all teeth and gums. "We're having twins."

My mouth opens, and I realize I need another drink. Stat!

"You can't ever do anything boring, can you?"

Behind her, Chase laughs hard, so hard he smacks his thighs with the effort. "More drinks are in order."

"*Si, gracias!*" I shake my head and look at my best friend in the whole world. "Two babies?"

She grins and preens, tears filling her eyes again.

I put my hand over her belly, and I'm sent a zap of cold and then one of warmth. I rub a circle around her stomach, trying to ascertain what I'm sensing. I've never been wrong with guessing the sex of a baby. Not ever. Usually I feel cold for a girl and warmth for a boy. Always. This time I felt both.

"What's the matter?" Gigi places her hand over mine.

"I don't know. I'm not sure what the babies are. Boys or girls."

Gigi frowns and nibbles her lip. "What if it's one of each?"

One of each. Yes. That's it! "That's it exactly. You're going to have one boy and one girl! Oh, what fun!"

Her hands come up to her cheeks as they turn a rosy hue. "You think? Really?"

"Never been wrong." I tap her nose. "Never. You're having one of each."

Chase comes back into the room holding a glass of ice water for Gillian and a fresh margarita for me. Yum. I reach out a greedy hand and open and close my fingers until he gives over the tequila goodness.

Gillian rushes over to him. "Baby, guess what? We're having a boy and a girl!" she says, and kisses him hard on the mouth.

He kisses her back, wrapping his free hand around her waist. When she pulls away, he nuzzles her cheek. "How do you know? The book says we won't find out until the twenty-week sonogram."

Of course, possessive Chase Davis would have already read the book on his babies. He probably knows more about Gillian's pregnancy than she does at this point.

"I have a sixth sense about these things. Never been wrong. Ever," I offer.

"One of each, eh? Sounds great to me." He pecks Gillian again and then walks over to the sideboard to refill his whiskey. "I'll drink to that."

He holds up his tumbler, and I lift mine.

"Me too!"

"Me three!" Gillian claps and chimes in.

★ ★ ★

A tiny pinprick of pain nudges its way into my temple. The nudge quickly turns into an ant-sized man jackhammering against my entire frontal lobe as I attempt to open my eyes. The room is a cheery white with yellow accents. The bed is so soft, I'm sure the big man upstairs himself fashioned it on the eighth day after creating the Earth because he needed a good night's sleep. Only he forgot to mention not to drink one's weight in tequila before bed.

Good Lord, haven't you tortured me enough? I rub at the sides of my head, digging my knuckles into the sore spots. My stomach rolls and rumbles, and I'm not sure if it's the hangover or the need for food. Either way, I need a truckload of grease in my gut in order for it to stop feeling like death warmed over. I push up to a sitting position and shove my wild mane out of my eyes. The black locks tumble and fall to tickle against my lower back.

With great care, I ease out of bed, touching the ground with one toe, and then the ball, and then the heel of my foot. I sway for a few steps and finally catch my balance against the door. A silk robe hangs on the back. Gigi must have left it for me. As it was, I only got as far as my sports bra and a pair of her small cotton shorts before plummeting onto the cloud. Besides, Chase has seen me dance in less, so I don't bother putting on my funeral garb. Hell, I may burn that jumper, even though it looked killer on me. Now, I'll remember the last place I wore it and fall into a haze of grief all over again. As it is, I'm at risk for a spill as I walk on shaky feet.

I make it to the bathroom where I do my business and brush my teeth. Thank you, Chase's maid, for leaving extra toothbrushes and toothpaste for guests. I ruffle my hand through my hair, trying to work out the knots. One hand is in my hair, the other holding my forehead, when I make my way into the ginormous kitchen and stop dead in my tracks.

Sitting happily at the table are Gillian, who's already dressed in a pair of jeans and a sweater, and Chase, dressed in his golf-outing finest, with an eyebrow cocked and lips pursed. Them I expected. What I didn't plan for was staring into the eyes of Tommy's brother, Elijah, first thing in the morning. The day after the funeral.

"Did I sleep for a week and not know it?" I groan while leaning against the doorjamb. My robe is open, and I can't be bothered to care.

Elijah's eyes trace my form from bare toes to the tip of my hair and back down. "Jesus," he mumbles into his coffee cup and looks away.

"What are you doing here?" I ask, trying not to sound irritated and failing miserably.

He tips his head to the side and sets down his mug. A plate of half-eaten food is in front of him. "I was invited. Good morning, Spicy."

Spicy. What the...

"She always like this in the morning?" he asks Chase.

Chase shrugs. "Don't know. Underdressed? Yes." I glare in his direction and cross my arms and cock a hip. "Hungover? No, not usually. Yesterday was understandably a rough day for her. For us all."

Bentley the chef hands me a cup of coffee. "Ms. De La Torre. With a hint of cinnamon, heavy cream, as you like it."

I smile. "Bentley, you are too good to me. First the margaritas, and now the perfect coffee? Marry me." I wink.

The rotund little man's cheeks turn a bright cherry red as he scurries away.

"Back to you. I may have had a lot to drink last night, but when I went to bed, you were not here." I pull out a chair, and both men stand briefly until I sit down. Interesting.

Gillian beams and grabs my hand. "How did you sleep? Any more nightmares?"

I cringe and inspect the table setting, not wanting to make eye contact with anyone. "No."

"You have nightmares?" Elijah asks, as if it's normal, everyday conversation to talk about something so profound and personal.

I take a deep breath. "Sometimes."

I didn't ask for it, but Bentley sets down a plate of food in front of me. "Again, marry me?" I glance up, and he chuckles and shuffles away. Funny little man, but an amazing cook.

Eggs, bacon, sausage, potatoes, and an English muffin stare at me. My mouth waters as I fork a few bits of potato and plop the bite into my mouth.

"*Jesús dulce bebé. Tan bueno.*" Sweet baby Jesus. So good.

"So, Mr. Redding, how long are you staying in San Francisco?" Chase asks.

Elijah pokes at eggs and then sighs. "Not sure."

"Why's that?" Gillian asks, always the nosy one. Thank God.

He offers a sad smile. "Thomas left all he had to me. His house, car, fuck...everything." His chin tightens, and that scruff I saw yesterday looks even more ruggedly handsome today. Elijah rubs a hand through his hair, and I can't help but watch the action. This is what Tommy would have looked like if he had hair. Sexy as hell.

Mentally, I chastise myself for the thought. This guy is *not* Tommy.

"Do you have a family somewhere else to get back to?" Chase asks pointedly.

Elijah shakes his head. "Nah, nothin' like that. I have a few crash pads throughout the States."

I guffaw. "What are you, a drifter?"

His eyes turn sharp as knives as he focuses his gaze on mine. "No, Maria. I'm a bounty hunter. The job I have doesn't afford me a lot of opportunity to settle down. I stay where I gotta."

Immediate embarrassment heats my chest, neck, and face. I'm certain I look like a red, juicy tomato. "I'm sorry," I say softly.

He lifts one shoulder and then drops it. "No big. I get that a lot. But, I just ended a job, only it was a little too late to make the funeral on time. It's why I wasn't there."

"Doesn't exactly explain why I didn't know about you." I

poke my food so hard with my fork it clanks against the plate.

Elijah leans his elbows on the table and rests his chin on one knuckle. "No, I suppose it says more about your relationship to my brother," he fires back.

"Hey now, that isn't fair!" Gillian strikes before I even have the ability to utter a word. The hangover has made my reactions a tad slower.

"Maybe you weren't important enough to mention." I stand up and push back my chair. "Thanks for breakfast. Suddenly, I'm not all that hungry."

"Maria, wait!" Gillian says as I stomp down the hallway toward the guest room.

I turn on a dime and point down the hall where the kitchen is and raise my voice to my girl. "Who the hell does he think he is, saying that to me? He knows nothing about my relationship with Tommy!"

Gillian holds up her hands and shakes her head. "No, no, he doesn't and I agree. Both of you were out of line."

"Both of us?" Am I hearing her correctly? Is she siding with him?

She clenches her teeth, making her jaw look sharp and formidable. "Ria, you're upset because you didn't know about him. I understand. But he does have a point. Why wouldn't Tommy tell you about him? I think that's the bigger question."

I focus my gaze on her face. "You think he was keeping it from me for a reason?"

She shrugs. "Well, yeah. That's obvious. You don't date someone for nine months and then magically find out he has a long-lost identical twin. There's a big, fat reason, and the only one who knows why is sitting at my kitchen table."

I slump down onto the bed and grab my forehead. "I can't

deal with this right now. I need to go home. Be alone for a while. Think about all this."

She sits down next to me and places a hand on my back. With soothing strokes, she rubs my back up and down and then massages my neck. I groan and let my head fall forward. "I know this hurts. And it's not fair. Tommy was a great guy. The best. He saved my life, and I'll be indebted to his family forever. But he loved you. Cared about you."

I choke down the emotions and vomit pushing their way to the surface. "I never told him." The tears I've been keeping to myself march down my cheeks like tiny traitorous soldiers, fleeing the base under the shitstorm that's coming. My shoulders heave, and a sour taste hits my tongue. I'm going to be sick.

Jumping up, I rush to the bathroom and spew the entire contents of my stomach in giant heaves until there's nothing left. Gigi holds my hair back and pets me as I regurgitate my feelings, grief, and what feels like a gallon of margaritas.

When there's nothing left, I push back and lean against the edge of the toilet. Gillian hands me tissues so I can blow my nose. "I never told him, Gigi." I admit the one thing that's been needling me since it happened.

"You never told him what?" She crouches down and wipes my face with a cool washcloth.

I lick my lips and close my eyes. "I never told him that I loved him."

Her face crumbles, but she doesn't let it go. It's her turn to be strong for me. That's the way it works with us. Gigi is the only person I can show weakness because I've seen and helped her through her worst, as she has mine.

"Baby girl, he knew. Of course he knew." She pulls me

into her arms. I sink my head against her neck and soak up the vanilla-cherry scent. Home. This is my home. My soul sister. Gigi pets my hair and whispers over and over again, "He knew. He knew. I promise he did."

But I know different. Tommy asked me point-blank if I loved him the day he died, and I played it off as him being silly like I always did. I remember that moment so clearly.

★ ★ ★

I found Tommy suiting up for work when I entered his apartment.

"Maria, I gotta go. Sorry about tonight."

"It's okay, Papi. I'll be waiting when you return. How's that?"

The muscles in his face tightened as he sighed. "I've got a dangerous one tonight." He wrapped a hand around the back of my neck, urging me close. "Just want you to know I love you in case it all goes to shit."

I hugged him tight, wrapping my arms around his shoulders. I kissed his neck up to his lips. "You're going to be fine."

He shook his head. "I want to know that you love me before I go out there. Tell me."

My stomach dropped, and a sense of dread crackled at the edges of my skin. I shook my head. "No, I won't say it. Because you're coming home. To me. You're coming home to me."

"Maria...I—" I stopped him with a finger to his lips. Then I kissed him again, distracting his negative thoughts.

"Come home to me," I demanded.

He smiled softly, kissed me with everything he had before pulling away. Then he opened the door and glanced back. "You'll be here when I get home?"

I blew him a kiss. "All night long. Keeping your bed warm."

"That's how I like it. Love you," he said as he closed the door.

★ ★ ★

Love you. That was the last thing he'd said to me. And he never came home. I'd received the call from Chase to come to the penthouse in the middle of the night. Gillian was a mess of tears and bruises when I'd arrived. So much so she couldn't even tell me what had happened, but she'd held my hands while Chase reiterated the scene at Coit Tower, the night Daniel McBride took his last victim... My boyfriend, Thomas Redding.

CHAPTER THREE

My apartment is silent when I arrive. No one is there to greet me. I walk over to my voice mail. Not a single message. Only Tommy ever left messages. I click on the message button, knowing what the last message is I'll hear, but needing it anyway.

"Hey gorgeous, sorry I missed you. Heading over to the pub after the game. It will be a late night, but text me if you want me to come over and give that sexy body a snuggle." He laughs, and the sound shreds my heart. *"Love you."*

Again, it's the last thing he said to me. And I never returned it. Even that night, I let him have his evening and didn't ask him to come over. We hadn't slept together for a month prior to his death. A full month and a half since I've felt his love. I'd rehearsed at the theatre every night, needing to make up for the missed time I'd been out due to Danny kidnapping my best friend. Then, of course, the fire happened, and a week later, he was gone. It feels like ages since I felt another man's touch.

I blow out a long breath of air as I enter the kitchen to pour a huge glass of water. This body needs some serious liquids to battle the dehydration of a night of drinking, crying, and, half an hour ago, vomiting.

I wish I'd had him come over that night. After everything

I've been through, it's hard now to remember his touch. In the bedroom, Tommy was *muy caliente,* but he couldn't keep up with my libido. I chuckle when I think back to how he tried. Oh, how he tried. Still, I didn't care, because when he was making love to me, he meant it, and it was always satisfying. God, I miss him.

Leaning against the counter, I work on the yoga breathing Bree taught us. In for five seconds through the nose, out for five seconds through the mouth. Let it go. *Let it all go, Maria. You can either sit and mope or do something, anything.*

My best bet is a shower. Wash off yesterday and start over. Literally. I need to start over.

Once I've removed my clothes and set the temperature on the shower, I step in. My knees and thighs smart once the heat hits them. The pain has been increasing with the endless hours of rehearsal, reminding me of the broken femurs that took a full year of hard-core physical therapy and heaping doses of determination to heal as well as they have. Doctors were amazed I could dance again.

The problem is, those old wounds ache and are showing signs of strain these past few years. As much as I hate to think about it, I'm not going to be able to dance forever. I'm twenty-eight—in dancer years, that's closer to fifty. The average dancer is retired by thirty-five and only if they've been perfectly healthy. I definitely need to start considering what's next.

Frustrated anew, I snap off the water, not feeling an ounce better. My headache's gone, but the tension, the steady ache of loss, is still pumping inside of me. Every step has my nerve endings tingling. Spending my teen years with my ailing grandmother after my parents died was hard. More so when my grandmother died and I had to spend two years bouncing from foster home to foster home. Some were nice. Most were awful, disgusting places any sane, knowledgeable social worker would put out of commission. Not the case in my experience.

I open the towel and wrap it around my long, wet hair. When I stand up, I catch a glimpse of myself in the mirror. Big breasts, not too saggy for their double-D size. My body is in great shape. Dancing on stage for a thousand people most nights of the week, not to mention rehearsals, ensures my fit status. Still, the hourglass shape and the Italian-Spanish genetics give me a Bubblicious ass I can't tame no matter how hard I work on it.

With each hand I run my fingers over my waist. Most of the cuts on my abdomen have healed. The five jagged ones, however, still have the stitches. I touch a couple of them to make sure they're staying put and the skin around them is healing. It is. That should be a comfort. It's not. I'd rather have the physical reminders. Proves I tried to save Kat.

Thinking about Kat reminds me I need to jet down to the burn center and pay her a visit. I didn't make it there yesterday, but I'm not going to go more than a day without checking in.

A knock on my front door startles me. This is strange, because I have a doorman who announces visitors prior to letting them up. When Gigi moved in with Chase, I moved here. From my perspective, the change would allow me to pay a lower rent. Since Chase refuses to accept payment, I've kept the money in a savings account. Now I could put it toward their kids' college fund or something—not that they need it. Honestly, I don't even know why I'm saving it. Years of needing to take care of myself must have ingrained that trait in me.

The banging starts again. I grab an embroidered black and red Japanese silk robe. It has cherry blossoms in bursts of bright white with red trim tracing each petal against a solid black background. Something I picked up for myself in Chinatown. I rush to the kitchen where I left my purse and grab my phone. I press 9-1-1 and then keep my finger hovered over the green call bubble.

"Who is it?" I say through the door, too afraid to even look through the peephole.

"Uh, hey, it's me. Elijah Redding. I wanted to talk to you."

Elijah Redding. Why the hell is he here? Instantly the flame of anger starts small in my gut but quickly builds as I swing the door open.

"What are you doing here? Better yet, how the hell did you find out where I lived?"

He doesn't respond. Instead, his eyes take in my attire the same way he did at breakfast. They spend a little longer on my silk-covered breasts, which causes my nipples to tighten and become erect under his lusty gaze. He's into me. My boyfriend's brother is into me.

"Jesus." His jaw tightens, and he rubs a hand through his hair.

I stare stupidly at him staring at me. Insanity. This is my life.

"*No hay manera de mierda,*" I grumble and tap the wooden door with my index finger.

"What do you mean by 'o fucking way'?"

It's as though my head is separated from my body as it jerks back and I clock it into the door. "Ouch! Fuck me!"

Before I know it, I'm pressed into the house, the door is kicked shut, and I'm in Elijah's arms. His green eyes seem concerned as he pushes the towel off my head with one hand and rubs his other big paw over my scalp. I groan at the feeling of his fingers massaging my aching head. I lose myself to the moment, holding on to the lapels of his leather jacket as he manipulates my entire head with supremely talented fingers. He smells of leather and spice, two scents I adore.

"You okay? That was quite a knock on the noggin," he whispers, his face so close I can feel the heat of his breath against my cheek.

"Yeah." I practically moan as he works those fingers down to my neck where he exerts more pressure. I'm putty in his arms, almost completely a limp noodle as he works the tension out of my shoulders and neck.

One of his hands trails down my back, sending a jolt of excitement right between my thighs, reminding me exactly how long it's been since I've been intimately held by a man.

Realizing what's happening, I push off and away from him. *"Lo sentimos, que no era una buena idea,"* I respond, pushing my hand through my wet hair before tightening the belt on my robe.

He grins and leans against the closed door. "Why isn't it a good idea? You seem to be enjoying it. Needing it even."

I wince and walk into my kitchen, attempting to find something to do with my now shaking hands. I can't even wrap my head around the way I responded to Elijah, and I don't want to think about it. Ever. Because it won't happen again.

"Tea? Water?"

"I'll take a cup of coffee if you have it." He follows me into the kitchen and sits on the stool at the island.

I nod. *"Café, si."* *Insert pod into machine. Fill cup of water and pour into top.* Got it. *Press start.* I talk myself through the motions, still reeling from the embrace, even though it was completely innocent. *Right?*

It dawns on me he responded to my questions even though I'd asked them in Spanish. "Oh, you understand Spanish?"

He smiles, and on his rugged unshaven face, it's more than handsome. The man is sex incarnate, and if he wasn't my boyfriend's brother, I'd have definitely chased after him or had a great one-nighter with him prior to Tommy.

"In my business you need to know a little of most languages. Since I do a lot of work on the West Coast, Spanish is a job necessity."

I nod and purse my lips. "So, care to enlighten me on why you're here?"

"I told you, my brother's passing. Had to pay my respects."

I set about pouring two cups of coffee. "Cream and sugar?" I ask, because that's the way Tommy took it.

He shakes his head. "Nah, black is fine."

They take their coffee different. An unintentional harrumph slips from my lips.

"What?"

"Nothing. It's nothing."

He lays a warm hand over mine. "What is it?"

I grin, thinking about Tommy. "You and Tommy don't take your coffee the same. He liked cream and sugar."

"Well, Spicy, he definitely preferred things in life to be a little sweeter. Not that you're not sweet, because looking at you, any man within his right mind would want a taste, but you have a serious edge to you."

One side of his mouth curves up, and he makes a point to ogle the deep open V in my robe and wink. My breasts are pushing up and out, helpless to the male pheromones he's giving off.

"What is going on here, Eli?" I ask while slapping the

counter in front of him.

"Red," he says, deadpan.

I scrunch up my nose and cock my head. "Red what?"

"Just Red. My name. People call me Red."

I roll my eyes. "What people?"

He grins. "All people."

"That's unfortunate. I'm not one of your 'people,' and since I'm me, I'll call you what I want, which is Eli."

"See, hot as hell and spicy as fuck." The man has absolutely no filter. He says what's on his mind and means it.

"So that's why you call me Spicy? Not sure if it's a compliment or a thinly veiled smart-ass remark."

"Both. You're quick to run your mouth, and the heat you leave in your wake isn't diminished by a quick sip of water. Plus, look at you. Every man's wet dream." Once again, his eyes trace all over my curves. I wonder what he sees.

"Ha ha. Are you going to tell me why you're here?" I point to the counter. "As in, my apartment. Last I saw you, you were with Chase and Gigi."

His shoulders lift and fall slowly, as if the weight of what he wants to say is enormous. Just as he's about to speak, the buzzer on my apartment goes off.

I lift up my hand and show him my index finger. "*Un momento.*" I rush over to the intercom and press the button. "Yes?"

"A package arrived for you, Ms. De La Torre. Okay to have it brought up?"

"Sure. Thank you."

Moments later, the elevator dings and the doorman hands me a long, skinny white box. One you'd normally receive if you were getting roses. I know for a fact because Gillian received several bouquets of roses from her stalker. A shiver of fear tingles at my nape as I accept the package and thank the doorman.

I set it down on the kitchen table and stare at the box as if it's a ticking bomb, completely forgetting about my unwanted visitor.

"You gonna open it?" His voice jars me out of my quiet reverie.

The room suddenly feels cold, and I wrap my arms around myself, wishing I'd had the time to get dressed. "No."

Eli walks over to me and puts a hand on my shoulder. "Looks like you have a secret admirer."

I glare at him and step farther away from the box.

"Hey, it's okay. I can leave. Come back another time to finish our chat." He moves to grab his coat off the other stool's chair.

Leave? God, no! He can't leave me alone. Not until I know what's in the package. What if it's the roses, and I don't have time to get away before he gets to me? My mind starts going a hundred miles a minute, flashes of the roses Daniel sent to Gigi, the dead ones he sent after he killed that girl in the yoga studio, the ones that arrived at the hospital after she'd been kidnapped.

Once again, my body is pulled into a pair of large solid arms. Eli rubs my back and head repeatedly. "Hey, hey, now. It's okay. I'm right here. Jesus. You're shaking."

For long moments he holds me close, and I revel in his heat and security. Tommy used to hold me, and when he did, I felt pretty safe. The man was a cop, carried a gun. But for some reason, in Eli's arms, it's like Fort Knox. The man is huge and built to punish and capture bad guys. Nothing could get through this wall of muscle and man. Again, like his brother, only different. I have got to stop comparing the two men. It's not healthy, nor is it going to help me get over Tommy's death.

I take a few deep breaths and pull back. "I'm sorry. It's just they could be roses and..." I shake my head and pull at my robe strings. "Can you open it, please?"

"Sure, babe. Not a problem. Have a seat on the stool."

I follow his directions as though I'm a marionette being positioned by its puppet master.

He lifts the lid of the box and frowns. Every millisecond that goes by in which he doesn't respond shoots arrows of anxiety into my chest. I clutch at the neck of my robe and rub my lips against the silken fabric. "What is it?" My voice is small and shakes, as though it is coming from the mouth of a child.

His expression turns into one of confusion when he pulls out a dull silver object. It's long and looks almost like a metal...

Oh my fucking God.

I open my mouth and stare at the offending thing, not knowing what the hell I'm seeing, and yet knowing exactly what it means.

Eli turns to me, holding it up. "A baseball bat? Someone sent you a baseball bat."

Those are the last words I hear when the entire room sways, ebbs, and then turns completely black.

★ ★ ★

"Maria, babe, you gotta wake up. Come on now," a voice so similar to Tommy's says as a cool cloth is placed over my forehead.

I blink a few times and see someone, a blurry shadow

hovering over me. I reach up and wrap my hand around the front of his throat. "Don't fucking touch me!" I grit through clenched teeth, still stuck in the clutches of fear.

"Maria, babe. It's me. Eli. It's Eli!" he calls, wrapping two giant paws around my wrist and removing my hand.

I sit up fast and then sway. "I'm, uh... I'm sorry." I remove my hand. "I didn't hurt you, did I?"

One of his eyebrows arches in query. "Hardly. Scared me? Yes. You dropped like a rock into shallow water. I barely caught you before you hit the tile."

Slowly coming to, I rub at my head and then remember. The bat. Skittering back, I look around restlessly, trying to make sure everything looks as it should. "Has he been here?" I whisper as I jump off my bed and look under the lamps, in the closets, and around my bedroom. He's the type who would break in and watch me for a while before he attacked. Plant bugs, or cameras, definitely listening devices. He was always good with electronics.

"Has who been here?"

"Him!" I groan and keep looking.

Eli grabs my arms and pushes me toward the bed where I'm forced to sit. "Let's start with the basics. Who's him?"

"Antonio! He's back!" I grit my teeth together.

"And what's his significance?"

Attempting to jump up, I'm thwarted by his much stronger hands.

"Let me up." The three words come out as a demand, one I mean from the tips of my toes to the top of my hair.

"Not until you tell me why you were so scared you passed right out. And who this Antonio fella is who put that fear there."

I suck in a huge breath and blast him with it. "Antonio is

my ex. He used to knock me around a bit. The bat is special. Confirms he's back."

"I thought my brother was your ex?"

"Keep up." I groan. "Before Tommy, I was with a guy for a few years." I force his arms off mine. "Happy? Now let me go. I have to do something. Go somewhere. Anywhere!"

He lets me up, but instead of leaving me alone, he leans against the wall, crosses his arms, and then rests one ankle over the other. "You're not going anywhere until we figure this out."

"I don't have time! If he's back, that means he's coming after me. Don't you see?" I screech right up into his face. "*¡Hombre estúpido!* Get out of my way!" I yank my suitcase out of the closet and toss it onto the bed.

Eli wraps a hand around my bicep, stopping me in my tracks. "You think this man is going to hurt you?" His tone is far too kind and sweet for this moment. I can't handle nice right now.

I blink, wondering if this idiot can be any dumber. "Are you not listening? Clean out your ears! Yes, he's going to hurt me. More than that, the last time I saw the *bastardo*, he promised he'd murder me! Now let me go so I can get the hell out of town!"

"You're not leaving town." He half-chuckles.

"Oh, yes I am! Who's gonna stop me?"

"Me."

I snort. "You? I don't even know you, and frankly, I don't want to."

He laughs heartily. "Yeah, well, that never stopped me before. I'm not going to let anyone harm you."

"And why would you want to protect me? Out of some misguided favor to your dead brother?" The words are scathing and hurt me more than their intended target.

"Something like that, yeah. But first, we're going to sit down and you're going to tell me everything about this Antonio and why he threatened to murder you."

I choke out a gasp. "That's not happening."

"Oh, but it is. And you wanna know why?"

"Because you're an alpha asshole that thinks you can control women? Make them do what you want? You know what? You're nothing like your brother."

"Well, true. And no, it's because you don't have any other choice."

Like sucking on a lemon, I can feel my expression shifting into my sour, pinched, angry one. The one that scares most people, men included, but apparently not this one. "Oh yeah?"

He smiles. The bastard *smiles*. "Yeah."

I head into the kitchen and pick up my phone and hit memory number five.

"Davis here. *¿En qué puedo ayudarle, Maria?*" He asks how he can help me.

I smile while sending daggers in Eli's direction. He thinks he can take care of me. Not in this lifetime.

"Hey, Chase. I've got some trouble I need help with."

Chase tells me to come over whenever I want to discuss, and as Eli watches me I thank him and hang up.

"Your girlfriend's billionaire husband. Cute. I'm still not leaving you. I will figure this out and make sure you're safe. Tommy would want it. I want it."

"Why you? Tommy, I get. He'd have moved heaven and earth to save me. Hell, he did once," I admit solemnly.

Eli's eyes widen at the same time I realize the truth I've spilled.

"Oh yeah, how so?" he asks.

"None of your business." I firm my chin and upper lip and have a stare-off with him.

"Spicy, I'm making it my business."

CHAPTER FOUR

"Okay, this is what I've been able to ascertain from the police chief," Chase says as he exits his study, notebook in hand.

"You have a personal line to the San Francisco police chief?" Eli asks, breaking into our conversation. He'd been holding up the wall in the corner until Chase got off the phone, much to my chagrin. He's like a flu bug I can't shake. A sexy, six-foot-two, ruggedly handsome flu bug.

Chase grimaces. "Mr. Redding. I understand that you were there when the bat arrived, but this is a family matter, and my associates and I can handle the situation. Your services, frankly, are not needed." Chase's voice is hard and direct.

Score one for Chase. Maybe now Tommy's brother will leave and get out of my business.

Eli walks over to Chase, his back to where Gigi and I are now sitting on the couch in their sitting room. Without even attempting to lower his voice, he addresses Chase. "Mr. Davis, Chase. Ms. De La Torre was in my company when the object arrived. I was there to witness how frightened she became. In fact, she passed out."

The muscles in Chase's jaw harden and a steady tic flickers at his cheek.

"Were you there to take care of her? Carry her to bed, ensure she was safe? Interrogate the doorman who received the package? No. All me. And when a woman is threatened in my presence, I make it a point to involve myself."

Chase purses his lips and puts a hand in one pocket. "I see. Am I to assume you've taken a personal liking to our Maria?"

"There a problem with that?" Eli clenches his jaw and tightens his hands into fists. Chase glances down at Eli's hands and smirks.

"Do you have any idea how fast my bodyguards are?" Chase's eyes shift to the right, where Jack is standing, hand on his gun in his breast pocket, and then he looks to the left where Austin, Gillian's assigned guard, is mimicking Jack's stance.

"Does it look like I'm afraid? I clocked your men when I came in. Military men, one high up in the ranks. I can tell by the subtlety in the way he stands and scopes a room. He's used to protecting you. Would take a bullet for you."

I'm certain he's referring to Jack Porter, Chase's long-time bodyguard, driver, and whatever else he does.

"The other is far newer, but has a gleam in his eye, something to prove. So yeah, I can imagine they'd take me down, but not without a fight. A bloody one. Instead of us pissing a circle around ol' Spicy over there"—he jerks his head in my direction—"how's about we work together to catch this scumbag, yeah?" Eli finishes.

Chase's lips twitch, and I know from that simple movement, he is going to cave. He loves a man who's protective of a female. Damnit. Why me?

"Eli, really. We're fine. Chase and Jack can handle this quietly and between us. You don't have to assist," I attempt for the umpteenth time.

He turns around and puts both hands on his denim-clad hips. The jeans fit snug, outlining a serious bulge and a pair of tree-trunk-sized thighs. "Let me ask you this. Either of you tried to catch a criminal?"

Everyone in the room nods.

"And how long did that take? Months, if the police reports I read were accurate, and only after several lives were taken and others equally destroyed, one of them being my brother. I guess you'd say I have an interest in seeing his woman taken care of in his absence."

Again, he hits the nail right on the head.

Chase crosses an arm over his chest and rubs at his chin thoughtfully.

"My capture rate is one hundred percent. Go ahead, have your people check it out. I'm surprised they didn't call me to catch McBride." He turns his head toward me, and his green eyes brighten as he assesses me. "Makes sense now that I know my brother was on the case. He'd call the devil himself before asking me for help."

Now that was an interesting bit of information I'd be bringing up to him at a later date. Not knowing Tommy had a brother the whole time we dated feels as if he were betraying my trust. Makes me think all the time I thought we were getting closer to something everlasting was a total and complete joke. Guess the joke was on me.

Chase sighs. "Be that as it may, I'd rather have this dealt with swiftly. I'll allow your assistance, mostly because I want this dealt with quietly and without incident. We've been through enough. All of us. Maria, do you agree?"

I bite my tongue and tip my chin in acceptance. Something about agreeing to this feels like I'm going to regret it, but he's right, and I'm woman enough to admit it and wise enough to back down when a good man is trying to help. Even a misguided one. "Fine."

"Okay then. Now back to what I've found out. Turns out one Antonio Ramirez was released from San Quentin after serving only five years of his ten-year term. Originally, he pled guilty to second-degree attempted murder. He was a model prisoner for the past five years with gold stars for rehabilitation. The parole hearing was held two weeks ago where there was a unanimous vote for early release. According to the chief, he hasn't missed his weekly meeting with his parole officer and has already gotten a job at a local big-box furniture store where he works in the warehouse."

"Which one? I'll check it out and pay the scumbag a visit," Eli offers.

Chase nods. "Austin will assist while Jack runs down some additional angles from here. Jack, you're on my wife at all times. Maria, you should stay with us until this is settled."

I shake my head and stand. "No way. I can't."

Gigi stands and grabs my hand. "Ria, please."

"No. I'm sorry. I can't have any harm come to you, Chase, or your *niños*. Besides, I've overrun my stay for the past several months. I need space. We all do."

Gillian's lips compress into a thin line, and her eyes darken in what I can only assume is sadness. "I never need space from you."

I tip my head back and laugh, hard. "*Cara bonita,* that's sweet, but you know that's not true." I pet her shoulder and hug her into my side. "Promise. I'll be fine in my building. There's a doorman, and Antonio doesn't know which apartment I'm in, just the building. How he even knows that is a mystery since

I'm unlisted."

"Doesn't matter. You'll stay with me." Eli's voice is close and grating, like a saw blade cutting into metal.

Again, laughter bubbles up and out as I adjust the girls in my tank and cant my head to the side. Chase, Jack, and Austin look at me as though I've gone loco. Maybe I have. All of this is too much. It's too damn much.

"Okay look, *Red.*" I emphasize the name he prefers. "I am not your problem. This desire to ensure the safety of *mujercita* on behalf of your brother is admirable, but not necessary. I've dealt with Antonio before and survived."

"Barely," he huffs.

The single word strikes a chord so hard in me I lash out.

"Screw you! You don't know me. You don't know my past. And from what I gather, you probably didn't even know Tommy!"

He doesn't even wait a beat before running off at the mouth. "In some ways you're right. But I knew my brother. In case you're forgetting, we're twins. We shared everything up until a few years ago. I think twenty-five years of being inseparable counts for something. Definitely more than a nine-month fling."

Can the blood inside a perfectly healthy human being actually boil? I lose it. And when I say lose it, I mean I am about to go batshit crazy on his ass.

"How *dare* you? I cared about Tommy!"

Eli steps closer to me. One step and then two, until we're face-to-face, only inches away from one another. "I know he loved you. That's easy. Even I can see through the bravado and grit. I've known you half a day, and I'd jump in front of a bullet to make sure not one hair on your head was touched. But babe, you wouldn't know what true love is if it slapped you in the head with a sledgehammer."

My eyes sting as his words hit their target. The hairs on my neck stand at attention, and my nose runs.

I will not cry. I will not cry. I will not cry.

"You don't know me." My comeback is fast and raw with emotion.

He flinches and then shifts his head so his mouth is a scant inch or two away from my ear. "I know you better than you think. We're the same, you and me. And it's going to be a helluva lot of fun proving it."

I lift my arms up and push against the solid wall of muscle. He steps back a few feet. "Do you want to head back to your pad and get your stuff, or do you want to stay here? Those are your only options, Spicy. Pick one."

In a few quick strides, I grab my purse, kiss Gigi on both cheeks, and then hug Chase. "*Gracias por tu ayuda.*" I thank him for his help.

"Always. Anytime. You know that, right?"

I smile briefly. "I do. Take care of my girl."

"With my life," he promises.

Such an honorable man. I wink and fling my coat over my arm.

"Ready?" Eli asks.

"For the record, I hate you."

He snickers. "That's what they all say."

"Does not surprise me at all."

★ ★ ★

Eli drives us through the middle of downtown San Francisco

until we're across the street from Golden Gate Park. I've made it a point to avoid any and all conversation with the overbearing, annoying, and infuriatingly demonstrative man, preferring instead to look out the window and brood. This is not at all what I'd planned to do with my time after I'd buried my boyfriend the day before. Most people would be wallowing in their own self-pity. Sitting back looking through pictures trying to remember the good ol' days. No, not me. I get thrown right back in the middle of assholes wanting to control my life or end it. One brand-new and the other a ghost.

Eli clicks a button on the visor of his black, tricked-out GMC SUV. Up ahead, about four houses down, the smallest garage door I've ever seen rises on an iconic home.

"Seriously?" I take in the beautiful Victorian house. It has to be at least a hundred and fifty years old with its cone-shaped roof and circular castle-like towers. The color is the palest yellow, reminding me of a baby chick just hatched. The trim around each window and special decorative features are all a stark white. Between the yellow and white, the black shingles of the roof stick out like the lead of a number two pencil pointing to a perfectly dark starry sky.

The home is absolutely beautiful and the exact opposite of what I'd expect a rugged, bounty-hunter type to live in. Honestly, I thought he'd bring me to Tommy's place since he now owns it. Though I'm glad he didn't. I'm certainly *not* ready to enter his apartment yet.

"*¿Está soplando humo por el culo?*" I gasp, taking in more of the historical beauty.

He chuckles. "I'm not blowing smoke up your ass. I can think of a dozen better things to do to that fine ass, but blowing smoke isn't one of them."

I flick my hair to one side. "Watch it. You so much as touch my ass and I'll break your fingers."

He grins. "Have it your way, Spicy. Eventually, I'll be getting it my way. Regularly."

"You realize I was sleeping with your brother six weeks ago?"

Eli flies into the driveway, cutting off a gray Mercedes in the process, turns off the ignition, and boxes me in with his arms. The space of the car suddenly becomes miniscule when surrounded by a behemoth. "A month? He let it go a month without fucking you? Trouble in paradise?"

I let out an irritated sound he ignores. "No. Not that it's any of your business."

He looks at me, just stares at every facet of my face before he drags those eyes of his over my form like a physical caress. My nipples pucker and elongate under my blouse knowing what a lusty gaze like that means.

"All I know is, if you were my woman, I wouldn't be able to keep my hands off you. A month is far too long. Hell, a day would be unbearable."

Heat fills my veins and my pussy becomes swollen, my clit aching for attention. I swallow and lick my lips, not the slightest bit sure what to do with the desire rising to the surface in this man's presence.

"Jesus," he mumbles under his breath before taking one last lusty look, and then he's gone. He opens his door and gets out of the car so fast I don't even have time to blink.

Before I know it, I hear him open the trunk of the SUV and roughly grab my bags from the back and toss them over his shoulder as if they were light as a feather.

The silence is deafening after the heavy, awkward

conversation in the car when we enter his house. With Eli, I don't know what's up, down, front, or back. My emotions, libido, and my common sense are spinning like a vortex around a man that is so familiar, but not.

I walk in, and I'm shocked stupid. The home is impeccably decorated. Magazine worthy. Leather couches in the living room are lush and urge the user to cuddle up and stay awhile. The kitchen is a chef's dream. Not that I cook, but I can appreciate amazing décor when I see it. Gray granite slab countertops with top-of-the-line black appliances. Black, frosted glass drop lamps and track lighting give the space an open, classy feel.

"Do you live here?"

Eli drops his keys into a bowl on the kitchen counter. "Yes. Does that surprise you?"

I glance around and hold my arms out. "Uh, yeah. You said you have crash pads, but nothing you call home. This looks like a home to me."

He smirks. "Just because I crash here when I'm on the West Coast doesn't mean it can't be comfortable."

"You're a bounty hunter."

Eli walks toward the stairs, and I follow him up. "Yeah."

"A bounty hunter who catches criminals for a living."

"Yeah, babe. So?"

"So, how can you possibly afford a home in the heart of San Francisco in one of the most classic neighborhoods?"

I follow him down a hall. A set of double doors are open on the right leading into what could only be called a command center. I stop and enter the room as if I were invited in. On one entire wall are monitors in varying sizes. Several computers are set up on a sleek, smoked glass surface. The left wall holds a huge touch screen whiteboard they only have on those high-tech investigative shows.

"*Mierda*. You're Batman!" I whisper while running a finger down the glass desk surface. "What is this place?"

Eli leans against the doorjamb, a relaxed pose he seems to take often. A small smile slips across his lips, and it makes him seem more kind, softer somehow.

"Maria, I have twelve guys working under me across the globe. I have to be able to check in on them no matter where they are."

"Twelve? Bounty hunters?"

"And then some. Couple of guys are into the tech stuff. They work out of their homes until I need them on-site for something top security."

I worry my lip. "What would constitute top security?"

"If I told you, I'd have to kill you," he deadpans.

I roll my eyes and groan. "Come on. I'm not leaving this room until you tell me."

"What if I made you?" One dark slash of an eyebrow arches in question.

Eli does not seem like the type of guy to bluff. "Tell me," I say nicely.

He takes a deep breath. "A top security job would be a high-level kidnapper, terrorist, mafioso, a cartel man. High-ranking criminals. But I only take those jobs if I have the time and the men. And I only do them because they pay for shit like this." He gestures to the equipment and then spins a finger in the air suggesting the home. "Bread and butter are medium-to high-level lawbreakers. The ones who have eluded the FBI, CIA, and other chains of law enforcement and military, but they have a name and description."

"Seems strange they'd need the help when there are so many law enforcement officers that could work together."

He points a finger. "Ah, but that would cost the taxpayers enormous amounts of cash and put a heavy burden on manpower. We're a one-stop shop. When there's a set bounty on their heads, we bring them in. And then of course, there are the outside jobs."

I cringe. "Outside jobs?"

"The jobs that are not quite within the parameters of the law."

"You pick up bad guys for bad guys?"

He shrugs. "When necessary, yeah."

"And when is it necessary?"

"When the price tag is high enough."

I shake my head. "Just when I think you might be a good guy, you prove me wrong. Congratulations. Where's my room?"

For long moments, Eli stares at me, and a flicker of sadness crosses his eyes—an expression I can't place nor do I want to. When Tommy used to look at me like that, it was during the times he'd said he loved me and I didn't respond. He'd always have a sorrowful plea in his gaze that I did everything in my power to avoid seeing.

"Come on." He jerks his head out to the hall.

He leads me to another room that has a simple queen-size bed, a dresser, and suitcase stand. He plops my duffle on the stand.

"Bathroom is across the hall. My room is at the end. There's not much in the kitchen. I haven't been able to stock it yet. We'll do that tomorrow. How does pizza and beer sound?"

My mouth waters at the simple suggestion. *When was the last time I ate?*

"Pizza heavenly, beer a solid no. *Gracias.*"

"*De nada.* Why don't you get settled and I'll order up dinner."

I nod and watch as he leaves. Sighing, I sit on the bed and test its bounce. Like Chase and Gillian's spare bed, it's really comfortable. Maybe I need a new bed? Everyone else seems to have better ones than I do.

While I'm getting my stuff situated, my cell phone pings. I dig it out of my purse and read the message.

To: Maria De La Torre
From: Caller Unknown
You can run and hide, mi reina. But I will find you. ~T

Blood-curdling fear rushes through me. My stomach tightens and seizes into a painful clinch. I glance around, my vision flickering as I try to remember these surroundings. Out. I have to get out. Before he finds me. Antonio *always* finds me.

I take the stairs at a dead run.

Eli is speaking as I'm hitting the last few steps, but I can't decipher what he's saying. My goal is clear. Get to the door, get in a cab, and bail. Now.

"Hey, Spicy, I ordered pepperoni on one half and combo on the other. I didn't know what you'd..."

I rush to the front door. "I've gotta go. I have to run!" My fingers slip and slide over the multiple locks on the door, trying frantically to get them open.

"Babe, what's wrong?" A strong arm wraps around my waist and hoists me into the air and away from the door. I scream at the top of my lungs.

His hand wraps around my lips. I bite down on the flesh

until the coppery taste of blood fills my mouth.

"Motherfucker!" He roars like a wounded animal and drops his hand.

"Let me out!" I try for the door once more.

Everything around me is blurring and mixing together. My heart is pumping so loud it's deafening. Then there are sirens.

"Stop! Just stop and breathe. Maria, breathe goddamnit!"

No sirens. It's a man. It's Elijah's voice yelling at me a few inches from my face. His hands are holding my hands up against the door, and something wet is dripping down my forearm. I glance at it. It's blood, but not mine. His.

"That's it, baby. Breathe. In and out."

I follow his breathing pattern until I realize where I am. Eli's hard body has mine pinned against the door. He holds my wrists above my head. His eyes are on mine.

"There you are. Welcome back to the land of the living. Care to tell me what the fuck triggered this episode?"

CHAPTER FIVE

I swallow down the bile rising up my throat. Eli's face is only a few inches from mine. His breath is hot against my misty skin.

He eyes me as though I'm a wounded animal. I flinch. That is not how I want him to see me. Taking a few blessed moments, I breathe in and out, focusing on pulling my strength to the surface bit by bit. I am not weak. Antonio should not get to have this control over me. The simple problem is that fear is winning, and I can't deny I'm scared. Scared out of my mind he is going to find me and finish what he promised he'd do all those years ago. I close my eyes and search for the remaining scraps of pride nudging at my psyche.

"What happened?" His voice is soft, gentler than I've heard from him before. "You can talk to me. Better yet, you can trust me."

Trust.

Such a simple, one-syllable word that means more than any other. Could I trust this stranger? Just because he is Tommy's brother doesn't mean he automatically gets carte blanche status in the circle of trust. Technically, he's Tommy's *estranged* brother. I hold on to that bit of information and duck under his arms to put space between us. When his body is surrounding mine, I become downright *estúpido*. I've always been a sucker for a handsome face, and Eli takes the prize for sexy-as-fuck faces—and bodies, for that matter.

I cross my arms over my chest and lean against the back of the sofa. "Tell me why you and your brother haven't talked for years."

Eli chuckles. "This isn't I share, you share. I'm not the one who's got a violent ex threatening me. That would be you, Spicy. How's about you tell me what spooked you so I can set about handling the situation, yeah?"

I roll my eyes and glance at the bookcase across from the couch. The shelves are filled to the brim with books—so many that some are stacked sideways on top of the upright titles. He has quite the collection, too. A mixture of everything.

"You like to read," I state.

He sighs and runs a hand through his dark hair, making it fall into even messier layers. One lock falls over his forehead. I itch to shift the hair aside and let my finger graze across the worry lines appearing there.

"Yeah, babe, I read. A lot. What of it?"

"Just, you know, making an observation. You like suspense and autobiographies?"

"So?" His voice is tinged with irritation, but I press on.

"Nothing." I sigh.

"How is this helping you come clean about what had you making a doubleheader to the door as if your feet were on fire?"

This time I inhale and let out a long breath. "I'm trying to know you better, okay? You want me to open up the diary of my past and let the demons bleed out into the open, but you're not willing to share anything of yourself."

He scoffs. "Is that what this is about? You wanting more information about me? There's not a whole lot to tell. I work.

Sleep. Fuck. Eat. Read and then work some more."

I glare at him. "You're not that boring. Everyone has something they are into. Like, I enjoy dancing. Hanging out with my soul sisters, seeing movies, that kind of thing. What are you into?"

"Dancing?" he repeats.

"Really?" I wouldn't have pegged him for a guy that likes to shimmy, but the world is full of surprises. "What kind of dancing do you like?"

He laughs and takes a seat in the chair near the couch where I'm sitting. I follow his movements with my eyes and make myself busy, curling my feet under my bum and settling in.

"I'm not into dancing, babe. Though I'm interested in what kind you do." His eyes gleam a darker shade of green.

I tamp down my frustration. "You truly don't know anything about me, do you?"

He shakes his head. "Nope. Not a thing."

"And yet you willingly drop everything—your working, sleeping, fucking, eating, and reading—to protect me from a man you also know nothing about. *¿Por qué?*" Awe and surprise coat my tone as I nervously twine a lock of hair around my finger.

He purses his lips. "There's something about you I can't stay away from. Don't even want to try. Maybe it's that you were close to the one person I cared for more than any other before his last days. Maybe it's because when I saw you looking at my brother's casket, you looked like the entire world had been set on your shoulders with absolutely no one to help lighten the load."

Tears prickle against my eyes, but I suck in a slow, deep

breath to keep them at bay.

"Also, you're fucking beautiful. Not just pretty. I *know* pretty. I *fuck* pretty. Nah, you, you're the type of woman a man would spend every dollar in his bank account to make happy, the kind he'd break his back and work his fingers to the bone in order to keep. Thought I had that once. Been lookin' for it ever since."

Holy shit. "Eli...*Dios mío*, what game are you playing?" I whisper around the ball of shock clogging my throat. This man does not pull any punches. He says what he wants to say and is one hundred percent serious when he lays it down.

"Who says I'm playin'?" He grins right as the doorbell rings. "Stay here. I don't want you anywhere in sight."

I couldn't move if I wanted to. His words stun me into thoughtful silence.

After a few minutes, Eli comes back in with three pizza boxes in his hands.

"*¿Tres pizzas?*"

He shakes his head. "Nah, one has boneless chicken wings."

I'm pretty sure if I look in a mirror right now I'll see my eyes bulging out of their sockets!

He sets down the three boxes, opens a lid, and pulls out a cheesy, toppings-loaded slice before eating half in one bite.

"So, no plates?"

He frowns. "You high maintenance, Spicy? That's going in the con column."

I jerk my head back and stare at the man as if he'd told me he was married, had a wife, a child, and a dog named Sparky.

"The con column? What's in the pro column?"

He grins the sexiest grin I've ever seen on a man to date.

And I am a self-proclaimed professional when it comes to logging men's sexual attributes. His grin is special. The corner of his mouth lifts up, making his lower lip puff out enticingly. A tiny bit of moisture glistens on the edge. His left cheek rises, allowing a wink of a dimple to appear. For me, that dimple's appearance has the same result as a meaty steak to a hungry dog. Lust city.

I wiggle in my seat and grab a slice. "Cat got your tongue?"

"Nope." He keeps chewing and grinning. "How 'bout I tell you when I've added them all up, yeah?"

I adjust my seat next to him to ensure not a speck of my body is touching his. No need to poke the beast, though I kind of want to. Desperately even. Anything to take away the sick, twisted feeling in my gut that came with a text from my vile ex, Antonio. Finally, I break down and slide my phone toward Eli, showing him the text message.

He scans the text, his jaw tightening. I can almost hear his teeth grinding before he asks me a completely random question. The last possible thing I'd assume he'd ask after reading what Antonio sent.

"Why did he end the text with a T?" he asks.

I pick up a slice of pepperoni, giving myself a few moments to think about lying or being honest. "I used to call him Tony the Tiger." Honesty wins.

Eli stops mid-chew and stares at me before he swallows, tips his head back, and laughs. Hard. So hard he starts coughing and hacking. He lifts a napkin to wipe his mouth. Even his eyes have a sheen of wetness from the intensity of his laughter.

"Really? *No es cool.*"

He continues chuckling and then finishes by slapping his muscled thigh. The damn thing strains against his pants, outlining some impressive quads. I glance away and take a huge bite of my pizza. Unfortunately, I'm too hasty in my desire to stuff my face, because the bite lodges itself in my throat and I start to gag. Eli notices my issue when I curl over myself.

"Shit, you choking? Fuck!" He pats my back hard until the piece is dislodged, and I spit it into my napkin.

He rubs up and down my back in slow, mesmerizing sweeps, lulling me into a comfortable silence. I need a man's touch like I need air to breathe. My defenses begin to crumble along with my posture. The weight of holding myself up after a grueling two days of loss, fear, and anxiety is beyond what I can manage anymore.

Without preamble, I curl toward Eli's warmth. He closes his arms around me where I nuzzle right into his neck. Being in his embrace is so right, more right than I've ever felt in any man's arms, even Tommy's.

God...Tommy.

What would Tommy think of me now, taking comfort in his brother's arms? Would he be angry, disgusted, devastated the way I would be if I found him being held by another woman? But that's never going to happen because Tommy is gone. Dead. And he's never coming back. He'll never hold me again. Never kiss me. Make love to me. Everything we had fell out the window with him.

The tears and pain rip through me like a chainsaw into the trunk of a tree. I sob against Eli. The sobs then turn to anger as the tears slip down my cheeks. I pull back. "It's not fair! Tommy was good. Kind. Everything I'm not. He shouldn't have even been there. He did it for me. For me! Because he knew I couldn't live without the only family I have left," I croak as he pulls me back against his warm chest.

"Thomas was a good man. The best there was. I agree. But he wouldn't want you blaming yourself. He chose the life of a cop because he had honor and grit. He wanted to help make the world a better place. And he took out that killer with his last breath. There is no sorrow or disgrace to be had. He died doing what he loved. Protecting who he loved. You."

I blink several times, trying my damnedest to stop the flow of tears, but they won't go away. "And now what? Now, Antonio is back. To claim his revenge? He's been gone for five years! Why now?"

Eli shakes his head. "Babe, I don't know. All I can promise is I'm going to do everything in my power to protect you. But you have to be honest with me. Tell me what started all of this."

I swallow and push my hands through the waves of hair that have fallen in my face. "Does it matter? He wants me dead, and he's patient. He's waited *cinco años* after all. What's another few days, weeks, months?"

"Something tells me he's not going to wait that long." Eli's jaw tightens and squares. The scruff on his chin going down to the very top of his neck gives him an even stronger bad-boy appeal. The twin sleeves of tattoos complete the look a hundredfold.

Those tats hypnotize me, and I run a finger over a thick tribal branch that weaves from his wrist up his forearm. "Why do you think that?"

His nostrils seem to flare as I lift my gaze to his face. He rubs a hand over his chin and mouth.

"Because, babe, if I'd had you, I don't think I could stop wanting you, either."

On those words, I skitter away toward the other end of the couch. "Tell me about you and Tommy. Why didn't I know about you?" My voice shakes like a dead leaf on a branch. "If you tell me, I'll talk. *¿Bueno?*"

He leans back against the leather couch, looking like a man who's comfortable in his own skin. He stretches out one arm along the back of the couch and lifts up one of his legs, crossing the other at the knee. Eli is wearing pristine white socks. There isn't even a smudge on the bottom of them. Must keep his boots clean. For some odd reason, his feet fascinate me.

"All right. Growing up, Thomas and I were inseparable. We were the Redding twins. Made a point to look alike, talk alike, do the same things. This afforded us the ability to screw with adults. You know, pure fun for two boys."

I smile, lift my knees up to my chest, and rest my chin on the crevice in between them.

"'Cept when we were teenagers, it became clear we were not into the same things. I loved motorcycles, rock music, working on cars, getting into girls' pants, you know..." He smirks.

"Yeah, I can imagine. And what about Tommy?"

He smiles huge at the mention of his brother as a teen. "Straitlaced as they come. Honor Roll all through school. Never so much as touched a girl until prom. I blew off prom to go drinking with some high school buddies of mine and bang sorority chicks. Not Tommy. He'd been with the same girl all through school, and at seventeen, he'd saved up his cash, booked a fancy hotel room where he took his longtime girlfriend to give her the night of her life. They both lost their cherries and were solid as a couple all through school."

"Wow." I think back to how long it took Tommy to take me to bed. Weeks of dating before he even so much as attempted to bed me. I'd made several advances, but he'd always pushed me away. He said he wanted the moment we took our relationship further to be special. And it was. "I can see how Tommy would be sweet like that. Then what happened?"

Eli grabs a slice of pizza and eats half in one bite. He takes his time chewing and looking off into the distance before he sucks back most of a beer. The bottle dangles between his fingers as he swirls it around. "Girl ended up going off to college in another state. He was destroyed. Didn't trust women for a long time after that. But then he got me to sign up for the police academy with him."

"You were a cop?" I ask, absolutely shocked.

He snickers. "What? I don't look like cop material to you?"

I scan his tats, his rough exterior, his supremely fit body, and shake my head. "*No, en absoluto.*"

"Not at all, eh? Fair enough. Turns out I wasn't cut out for traditional law and order either." He teeters his head to the side, and his mouth tightens into a fine line.

Before he can continue, I butt in. "Why weren't you cut out for it?"

He swallows and, once again, avoids eye contact. "Just wasn't. Let's leave it at that. But during that time, Thomas and I had a...uh...disagreement over a situation between us. He didn't agree with the way I handled it. I didn't agree with his response. So we fought. I left the force and went off on my own. We exchanged only a few e-mails over the past few years. Last e-mail I got from him was a few months ago, and he didn't mention you. Sorry, Spicy."

He didn't mention me? What does that mean? Did he say he loved me and not mean it, or was his relationship with his brother such that he didn't want to give him any information? All questions I'll never get answers to. Not that they matter anyway.

"Your turn. Spill," he demands.

"My story isn't pretty."

His lips twitch with a hint of mirth. "They rarely are."

I clutch my knees tighter against my chest. The phantom ache at my thighs increases with the hold, but I don't lessen my grip.

"When I was eighteen, I was accepted into a prestigious dance company. I'd worked my ass off to audition, and I was chosen. Antonio was as well. They brought in young dancers from around the world, and he came from Brazil. It was the opportunity of a lifetime and set my career up."

"Ah, so you're that kind of dancer. The kind on the big stage, not the kind that swings around a pole."

I frown. "Did you think I was a stripper?"

"Think? No. Hope? Maybe." He gives one of those Cheshire Cat grins.

"*Cerdo repugnante*," I mumble under my breath.

He chuckles. "A disgusting pig? I guess if the boot fits, I might as well put it on. Continue your story. None of this answers why this fucker is after you. Everything you've said sounds dandy to me."

I smile around the memory. "For the first year, our relationship was everything I'd ever dreamed of. I didn't have a lot growing up. Nothing, if I'm being honest. Anyway, Antonio took a liking to me and I to him. We became a couple pretty quickly. I was in heaven. I had the dream job, flying around the world from place to place with the handsome foreign boyfriend who whispered sweet things to me in Portuguese when we made love."

Eli rolls his eyes. "And?" He makes a speed-it-up gesture with his hand.

I glare at him. "Do you think this is easy for me? To relive my past? It's not."

He turns more fully on the couch and places a hand over my knee. "I'm sorry. I was being rude. Continue. Please."

"What I was going to say was that after a year is when it all turned to shit. It was only little things at first. He'd look at me with a nasty gleam in his eye. That quickly morphed into verbal yelling matches where he'd shove me a little. When pushing wasn't enough, he started smacking me, only swollen cheeks were easy to see. Normal fights between regular couples would include slamming doors and storming out of a room. Not for me." My voice sounds warbled and shaky as I respond. I tighten my grip on my shins and close myself up even more.

"It's okay. I'm right here. No one is going to hurt you." Eli moves closer, tunnels his big hand through my hair, and wraps his warm hand around my nape. "Go ahead."

I stiffen my upper lip and look right into his eyes. "Then he started hitting me. I thought punching me in the gut was the worst thing that could ever happen to me. Not so. He had a whole slew of ways to hurt me physically and mentally."

"Like how?"

A flash of a memory rushes to the surface.

★ ★ ★

"Tony, no. No, I swear. He didn't touch me inappropriately during that lift! The dance required he palm my thigh."

Antonio's ebony eyes glinted with rage, and his voice shook.

"¿Você amou cada segundo. Sim?" *he sneered in Portuguese, his native language. I'd picked up enough of his words in order to communicate with him fluidly to know what he'd said.*

I shook my head and backed up and away, heading toward the flat tile wall of the bathroom. I stood in only a towel. Rehearsals that day had been brutal, and all I wanted to do was take a soak in the old claw-foot tub that came stock in the British condos the dance company rented out during this portion of our tour.

Antonio and I had our own condo since we were a couple. Usually, it was four to a place, but since Tony was one of the lead dancers, and I wasn't half bad myself, we scored one alone. In that moment, I wished more than anything else we had roommates.

"Tony, I did not like him touching me. I promise. I swear on all that's holy. Work. He had to lift me."

He ground his teeth, spat in my face, and pushed me up against the wall. "His hand strayed, mi reina." *He called me his queen in Spanish. I loved how he'd made an effort to learn Spanish on top of English. Only, right then, he spewed the endearment like an accusation. "That* garoto *touched a part of you which should only be mine. Yes?"*

I shook my head. "I don't think he did. I don't." I scrambled to say anything that would diffuse Tony's anger. Thinking quickly, I wrapped my arms around his neck lovingly, the way he liked. "Tony, my tiger, I only want your touch. Always. Forever."

His mouth twisted into a white-lipped snarl. "Yes. And I shall prove how this body is mine and only mine."

I swallowed and widened my eyes. Usually this type of proprietary talk spoke of a session in the sheets that would blow my mind, but the way he said it did not lend to tidings of romance and rough sex.

Just as I was about to ask what he had in mind, he gripped my arm, tugged the towel off my body, and flung me toward the bath. He toppled me into the water and then held my body under. I thrashed and kicked, holding my breath for as long as I could. All I could see above me through the ripples of the water was his ugly scowl. The hate and fire in his eyes burned as much as the water did as I gulped heaps into my throat and lungs.

The pain was excruciating. Water filled my mouth, nose, and throat like a tidal wave crashing to shore. I felt the moment my body started to go limp, and blackness surrounded my vision before I was yanked out of the tub and thrown over the edge, where Tony lifted me up and pounded my back until I vomited water across the tile floor.

"There you go. You see, mi reina?*" He held me close and placed kiss after kiss against my wet skin as I heaved the last bits of water from my stomach and lungs. "Look at you. Needing me. Don't you see? I hold your life in my hands."*

★ ★ ★

"Jesus fucking hell!" Eli stands up and paces the floor. "He nearly drowned you that time?"

I shrug and wipe my eyes. Tears are flowing again, and I realize I've told the story out loud.

"That time?" I chuckle lamely.

"You mean he did it more than once?" His eyes are twin green circles of anger.

I glance over the couch to the bookcase. Abraham Lincoln. Hellen Keller. Dr. Martin Luther King. Pieces of what this man I know very little about likes to read. He must enjoy reading about people who made a difference in our lives. Those who shaped American civilization. Maybe he planned to one day shape the way we see the world.

"Answer me," he thunders.

"Why? So you can go all macho man crazy?"

He frowns and then comes back to sit next to me. Right next to me. His thigh touches me where I have my feet splayed in front of me. I wiggle my toes and tuck them under his leg to warm them.

"No, because the more I know, the better I will be at catching this twisted motherfucker."

I lick my lips and look down at my fingers. The nail polish I'd put on the other day is chipping at the edges, the soft pink revealing the dry, brittle nails beneath. "Yeah, he liked water games," I respond dryly.

"Why?"

This man sees a lot. He catches criminals for a living. How he cannot understand a man's desire to control a woman by whatever means necessary is beyond me. Then again, maybe Antonio is a special breed of evil.

I blink a few times and then purse my lips. "Obvious reasons."

"Which are?"

"The number one being because water torture didn't leave any visible marks."

CHAPTER SIX

A deep rumbling sound wakes me. I open my eyes to a room still dark, even though it feels like I've been asleep for a full ten hours. The blackout blinds over the windows are phenomenal. Definitely need to get me a pair for my bedroom windows. Once I get my bearings, I lift up and strain to hear what's being said in the office across from the guest room I'm currently occupying. The clock on the side table shows it's only seven. Eli must be an early riser.

Pushing back the covers, I tiptoe on bare feet to the wooden door cracked open about an inch. I usually sleep with the door completely closed. He must have looked in on me while I slept last night, even though I don't recall going to bed. I should be creeped out by him spying on me while I am vulnerable and asleep, but all I can come up with is a feeling of warmth and happiness that he cared enough to check on me.

I open the door a few inches and listen near the opening.

"My team scored me the police report from the last time Maria saw Antonio Ramirez. I'm faxing it now." Eli's voice is curt and stern.

Even the mere speck of a reminder of that awful night grates on my anxiety, stirring my fear into a thick roux.

A few beeps ring through the space, which is probably him

faxing whatever document his mystical team of misfit crime fighters found.

"Got it? Good. It's not pretty, man. Downright fucking ugly." He sighs. "My brother put two bullets in the guy. Hip and knee, after the scumbag broke both of her legs with a baseball bat and tried to drown her in a bathtub, which I understand was nowhere near the first time. Thomas barely got to her in time. She was damn lucky not one, but *two* neighbors called in a disturbance, one mentioning they thought the woman of the house was in grave danger." Eli rubs a hand through his hair. "This guy is dangerous."

A few moments of silence tick by as I shift closer. Eli is pacing the room with a cordless phone to his ear, wearing only a pair of plaid pajama pants.

Dios mio. El es guapo.

His pants are slung low on the finest pair of hip flexors I've ever seen. Hands down. No contest. And those sleeves of tats go all the way to his shoulders, wrapping around sinew and muscle as though they are etched into cut granite. He turns toward me, and I'm gifted with a sight that could make angels fall to their knees and weep for mercy. A square breastplate and a set of abdominals so finely honed they mirror a set of bricks two across and four down.

I bite my lip while inspecting further. It's not that I don't want to look away, I do. I genuinely do, but it's not every day I see something so honestly beautiful.

"He did five years total. Of that, one was spent in prison physical therapy recuperating and learning how to walk again before he spent the rest of his time placing slop on inmates' trays three times a day. Says here he got in a couple scuffles while in the clink with a couple gang members known to be part of the Red Devils." He paused for a few moments. "Davis, they're an Oakland-based street gang. Anyway, looks like they made amends, because he came out of prison alive."

So Antonio got in a few fights in jail. No surprise there. He always did have a sense of entitlement that had a knack for getting him into trouble.

"Yeah, I'm going to head down there today. Pay him a visit at his workplace, talk to his boss. Shake the ground for him a bit. Let him know exactly who he's fucking with."

Eli nods and sits down in his office chair. He looks like a golden, tatted, real-life superhero working his command center. I push open the door to my room and lean against the jamb, mimicking the pose he often takes. He doesn't notice me right away, giving me a few more moments to enjoy watching him in his element.

Watching a man work can either be gratifyingly sexy, almost a precursor to a wild romp in the hay, or the opposite. It helps me figure out what kind of man they truly are, which in my experience, aside from Tommy, has not been pleasant. Elijah moves, speaks, and holds himself with the utmost confidence and strength. He's precise, leaving no room for interpretation when something is important to him.

Why I'm now the recipient of all that focus is a mystery. Sure, he said he thinks it's because I was close to his brother, but then he followed it up last night by making it clear he is definitely attracted to me on a physical level. He seems to have no concerns whatsoever about the reality that I was once his brother's girlfriend. In fact, if anything, I'd say he was rather sweet on me. Not that I plan on returning his attention.

"All right, Davis. Thanks." Eli lets his head fall forward and he rubs his hair once again. "Yeah, she's doing as well as can be expected. I'll take care of her, man." He listens for a few seconds. "*I said*, I'll take care of her." His voice is a low rumbling sound that means business. That's when he looks up and his gaze finds mine. Recognition blazes in the rise in his eyebrows and the flare in his nostrils. He could easily be compared to a ferocious wild animal staking his claim on his mate.

"Fine. Will catch up with you later." He hits a button on the phone and sets it on the desk. "You sleep good?"

I smile. "Like a rock. I don't even remember going to bed." As a matter of fact, I don't recall anything after I sobbed into his chest like a lame damsel in distress.

"Yeah, you cried yourself to sleep on me. I carried you up. Made sure you were solid."

I cringe. "You carried me up a flight of stairs, and I didn't even wake? *Mierda*. I must have been out of it."

He grins. "Better today?"

I shrug. "Not exactly sure how I feel anymore."

"Well, I feel hungry. You?"

At that precise moment my stomach gurgles. I didn't eat much of the pizza he'd purchased last night and had very little to eat yesterday. Hell, I don't remember the last time I had a full meal.

"Guess that answers that. Come on, Spicy. Let's put some meat on those bones."

I scoff. "Like I don't have enough."

He stops midstride, turns his head to look at my ass, and then back around where he blatantly ogles my chest.

"Nah, I like my women with plenty of cushion. Don't like to grind bone on bone. You could gain a few and still be every man's wet dream."

"*Cerdo*! Are you always this piggish?"

He grins and leads me down the stairs toward the kitchen. "Why am I a pig for calling it like I see it?"

"Look, *Cazador*, regardless of what you might think, not all women want to hear they are every man's wet dream. Frankly, it's crass and suggests the woman you are speaking to is less than a lady."

Eli chuckles. "*Cazador*? Hunter? That's what you're calling me now?"

I tip my chin forward. "Yeah, what of it?"

He shakes his head and pulls out a frying pan from the cupboard, and then eggs and bacon from the fridge. "Nothing. Guess it fits just fine."

"You cook?" I gesture to the pan.

"I've been taking care of myself for thirty-one years. A man's gotta eat. Why? You offering?"

I shake my head so fast it could very well pop off my neck. "*Yo no cocino.* I'm skilled at burning water."

He sighs. "Beauty, brains, a body that doesn't quit...but you can't cook. I knew there had to be something wrong with you aside from that smartass mouth. That's going in the con column."

"But the other things, they're in the pro?" I quip.

He clucks his tongue and rubs at the hair on his chin. It makes a grating noise that forces shivers up my back. Dead sexy. I love a bit of scruff on a man. A clean shave is nice, but a bit of edge to my man makes my heart go pitter-patter and my pussy jump with joy.

"Oh yeah. Your pro list is climbing too," he offers.

I push back my hair and settle onto a stool to watch him work. "Well, that's a relief. And here I was worried you wouldn't think I was pretty."

"We already established you're fucking beautiful, but you know that already and use it to your advantage. A lot. Don't try to play the coy card with me or bat those baby blues. I've got your number, babe."

I glare at him and then trace the veins in the granite countertop. Eli has a point. I've been known to use my looks to my advantage a time or two. When you grow up with nothing, you use whatever is in your bag of tricks to get ahead without stepping on toes and making waves. My athletic ability paired with my face and curvy body have gotten me into countless auditions. I've also never paid for a drink at a bar in my life.

Instead of agreeing with him, I change the subject. "So I heard you on the phone with Chase. You're planning to go see Antonio today?"

He cracks a few eggs into the pan. They sizzle and pop instantly. Quick as a wink, he turns over the bacon, browning the one side to absolute crispy perfection, and then pushes down a couple pieces of toast.

"Yup."

"I want to go with you."

He stops with the spatula held in the air and turns around as slow as honey dripping down the bark of a tree. "You are going nowhere near that man. Nowhere near. You got me?" His tone is a low timbre that seeps through my pores, delving deep into my bones.

"Eli, this is my battle..."

Before I can say another word, he's turned down the flame on both burners, whipped around the island, opened my thighs, and planted himself directly between them. He curls both hands around my cheeks, tipping my head back. His eyes seem to bounce all over my features as if he doesn't know where to focus his attention. Finally he settles on a firm stare. "Nowhere. Near. Got it?"

I scowl, but once again I'm unable to speak, because he places his thumb over my lips.

"You may have been my brother's girl once upon a time, but babe, you admitted he hadn't had you in a month. That, to me, means things between you were changing whether you wanted to admit it or not. Now, I'm willing to give you time to understand what's starting up here between us, but not forever. Regardless, let's get one thing clear. When it comes to your safety, I call the shots."

I snort right into his face. "You call the shots? *You*. Call. The. Shots." I shake my head. "Us? Let's get one thing perfectly clear right now. I take care of me. Secondly, there is no us. *Comprende*?"

"Babe, there is." His eyes soften, and his face moves closer to mine.

I swallow around the lump forming in my throat at his proximity, as a trickle of anticipation tingles against the curve of my lower back. The one place on my body that always takes notice when I'm turned on.

"Just two days ago, I buried your brother."

Eli plants his hands on the counter behind me and leans his face near my neck. I can feel his breath as he dips his face closer. "Christ. Normally, I catch the scent of flowers but damn. Right now, you smell like cherries in the dead of summer. So sweet. Ripe. I'd like to take a juicy bite right out of you, babe."

With effort, I place my hands on his bare chest. He still hasn't put a shirt on. Everything in me says to lean into the haven I found there last night, wallow in the safety he is providing, but the independent woman in me is balking and bitch-slapping her way to the surface. Using my best effort, I push hard against his chest. He barely moves back an inch.

"Did you not hear what I said?"

He nuzzles my neck, and I close my eyes, enjoying the flesh-on-flesh contact.

"I heard you, Spicy. Those two things are not mutually exclusive."

"Are you insane?"

"Not the last time I checked, although I have been knocked on the head a time or two."

"*Dios mio. Voy a matarte,*" I say right as his lips touch down on the tender column of my neck. As much as I want to deny it, that single touch sends a bolt of desire ripping through every nerve ending, landing with a bout of arousal at the apex of my thighs.

He chuckles against my neck where he places another wet press of his lips. "You are not going to kill me. The sooner you realize I'm not going to back off, the sooner we can get to the good part."

"Which would be?" I sigh and then lock my lips together. No, no, no. This is so wrong.

Do not encourage him, Maria.

"Us. Naked. You flat on your back with me pounding every inch into you, over and over until you scream out my name. Not *his*. Because when I lay you down, there will be no substitutes, nothing between the sheets but me and you, Spicy."

"*Detener.* Stop. *Por favor.* I can't take it." I dig my fingers into his muscled pecs.

Eli drags his lips up the side of my neck until I gasp. Then he lifts my chin with both hands. If I were psychic, I would announce he was planning to kiss me. With my last shred of dignity, I shake my head a few millimeters. Just enough to get my point across.

Not here. Not now.

"Soon, Spicy. You'll take everything I give and beg for more." He leans forward and kisses my forehead. Then he's gone, already back around the counter and tending to the food. My body still feels him, yearns and aches for him to be right back where he was, between my legs, pressing up against my heat.

I suck in a loud, ungraceful breath. *"Señor, dame fuerzas,"* I whisper under my breath, attempting to quell my body's lustful response.

Eli plates the food and sets it in front of me.

"Eat. You're going to have a long day of twiddling your thumbs while I deal with your ex."

★ ★ ★

Long day my *culo.* If Elijah thinks a couple of harsh requests and a manly man grumble are going to keep me in his bounty hunter Batcave, he's smokin' something righteous. But I'm not stupid. I realize there's a serious threat out there, so instead of hailing a taxi and heading where I needed to be, I call Gigi to pick me up. I expect Austin, now that he's healthy enough to be back at work after being taken down in Mexico by Danny. That dose of etorphine Danny gave him almost killed the guy. Thankfully, he was found in time and given the antidote. Only Austin wasn't who showed.

The black stretch limo looks like black oil gliding along concrete as it pulls up to the curb. Jack Porter, the guy Gigi calls Chase's "linebacker," exits the car. He comes to the entrance of Eli's home, looking left and right as he ascends the stairs. I fling open the door, having watched him through the window. When I am about to exit, Jack grabs my arm and tugs me toward the car and down the steps quicker than my feet can carry me. Before I know it, I'm hustled into the limo wondering what the heck happened.

Gigi's sitting prettily in the back of the limo. Chase prefers her closest to the driver, especially when he's not in the vehicle with her. Overprotective nut.

"Where's Austin, *cara bonita*?"

She rolls her eyes. "Protecting my husband. Unfortunately."

"Why unfortunately?"

Gillian flattens her lips and speaks through clenched teeth. "Because Austin allows me a bit of privacy. Jack is all up in my business, all the time. It's exhausting."

I smile, loving I'm finally back where I want to be. Where I can just be me. With *mi familia*. "That man of yours is wildly protective. And now that you've got the *niños* to think about...I can only imagine what you have to look forward to."

She sighs and leans her cheek on her hand. "Ria, you have *no* idea. Chase doesn't want me working, going to yoga, doing anything strenuous, basically anything I want to do. He says it's not good for the babies." Again she rolls her pretty green eyes.

"At least he cares. That counts for something."

"Has a woman ever killed her husband because he was too nice to her?" She taps her bottom lip with one manicured index finger.

I shake my head. "No, *lo siento*. I think most women pray

to God for that kind of man every night."

"Pity." She yawns and smiles.

"Tired?"

"Right now? Always. Doc says it's normal toward the end of the first trimester, especially with twins. Joy." She yawns again.

"How's Kat?" I ask, afraid to hear. Right before the funeral she was undergoing extremely painful skin repair surgery of some kind. At the time, I couldn't string two words together let alone understand what type of treatment my soul sister was getting in the burn center.

"She'll be better when she finally sees you," Gigi says.

"I was there every day until the funeral. She just wasn't awake." I pout and cross my arms.

Gigi pats my knee. "I know, honey. And she knows, too. She asked about you yesterday. Wished she could have been at the funeral, even though she was in so much pain."

Just thinking about how I couldn't get to her, how the smoke was billowing out of the theatre window where I smashed my bare feet into the wooden beams that shouldn't have been there. My feet are still sore. That sick bastard Danny knew exactly what he was doing. He ensured doing the most damage by locking Kat in her wardrobe closet and boarding up the window so that we couldn't get to her, and she couldn't get herself out. Even though I went in, she still suffered severe burns to her right arm and side. The prognosis at this time is still uncertain.

"I have faith she'll make it through this an even stronger woman. After what we've experienced in our pasts, what Danny did..." Her voice trembles as she speaks. "If not, there is no hope for any of us now, is there?"

I lay my head back against the leather seat. "I don't know, Gigi. How can we be certain of God's plan? Why is it we've endured so much and yet so many others live easy with not a care in the world?"

She smiles and intertwines her fingers with mine. "We can't be certain. The only thing we can do is live every day to the fullest. Give our best self to those we love and never forget that what we've survived has made us who we are today, but it doesn't define us. That's a lesson Chase has spent countless hours trying to instill in me. And you know what?"

"What, *cara bonita*?"

"He's right. You, me, Bree, Kat, Phillip, Chase...we're all survivors. It's something that bonds us, and I for one wouldn't take it back."

"Any of it?"

She smiles and looks off into the distance. "I guess I could have lived without seeing all the deaths. Chase's mom, Tommy, those people in the gym explosion, Charity the yoga mentee." Gigi covers her abdomen where her twins rest, growing bigger every day. "Then we realize there is always a yin and yang, a high and low, good versus evil. If all of this hadn't happened, I might not have found Chase, married him, and I wouldn't be carrying his children. Perhaps even the most vile things happen for a reason, and this past year was all to see these two human beings come out of it."

"I hope so. But now there's this thing brewing with Eli."

"Eli?"

"Did I say, Eli? I, uh, meant Antonio."

Gillian smiles so huge her entire face glows. "You definitely said Eli. So, there's more to this situation with Tommy's brother than I would have guessed. Care to share?"

"No. Not particularly."

"Ria, don't you dare leave me hanging. I'm pregnant, I've survived a crazy hard year, you have to share because we're soul sisters, and we don't keep anything from one another. Not the good stuff anyway."

I cringe. "There's nothing to tell. I mean it's weird. He's into me." Her nose crinkles up, which—after knowing her for five years—means she's not following. "He keeps making these comments as though he's attracted to me and not at all worried about it."

She gasps. "You're kidding. Tommy's brother is putting the moves on you?"

"Not exactly, but kind of...yeah. What's worse—and the reason I know for a fact I'm going to hell in a handbasket—is I'm attracted to him too. Isn't that sick?"

"Sick? My goodness no. Ria, you can't help who you're attracted to. It's not like you woke up one day and said, 'I'm going to be attracted to my Tommy's brother.' I mean, I almost would be surprised if you weren't. He's like the super sexy, bad boy version of Tommy. No offense to Tommy, you know I cared deeply for him, and I know you did as well. But, honey, it was always strange to me how you and Tommy fit. I mean, you're so different and you've always gone for the bad boys. Tommy was the exact opposite of a bad boy, down to the style of jeans he wore. Still, he was hot, and as far as looks go, your type. As is his identical twin brother."

"So you don't think it's weird?"

She shakes her head. "Not at all. I'd find it weird if you didn't. I mean, the man is his identical twin, only he's the super duper, smokin' hot, motorcycle-riding-type version."

"He did say he was into motorcycles."

Gigi dances in her seat. "See!"

I laugh and lean my head on her shoulder. "I'm not ready to let Tommy go. I don't know when I will be, but that doesn't mean my libido isn't working overtime. Tommy and I had a dry spell right before he passed."

"How long of a dry spell?" Her voice lowers into a gentle murmur.

"A full month."

Gigi's head whips back so fast I worry she's given herself whiplash.

"What? I'm sorry. You went a month without getting laid? Were you fighting? Not getting along?"

Why does everyone think that?

"No, just busy, and all the stuff with Danny took its toll."

"Huh. How do I put this without coming off as a mean bizatch? Honey, I've never known you to go a full month without a tumble in the sack. Ever. I mean, I had a dry spell, and you hounded me relentlessly to go out and pick up guys with you so my vagina wouldn't be covered in cobwebs. Hell, you gave me the same spiel when I met Chase in that bar in Chicago. Remember?"

"Oh, *diablos*. You're right." I push my fingers through my hair, trying to figure out why we hadn't been intimate that last month before he was killed. Sure, there was the work for him, rehearsals for me, but that had never stopped me before. I have an outrageously active libido on a good day. So much so, in the nine months we dated, Tommy and I would go weeks where we had sex every single day. We couldn't get enough of one another.

Now that I'm thinking back, was it longer than the last month? Were we drifting apart? Before I can dig into this line of thought, the limo stops in front of The Bothin Burn Center at St. Francis Memorial Hospital. Our soul sister Kathleen Bennett has spent the last couple of weeks here since being released from the ICU after the fire. I look up at the glass doors and the white exterior. The building looks like pristine white Legos with dark windows stacked on top of one another.

Yin and yang. Black and white.

Now what side will our Kat be sitting on when I finally see her? Taking a deep breath, I lock hands with Gigi and let the linebacker lead us into the building.

CHAPTER SEVEN

"Just go. You're suffocating me!" Kat's voice is a grating screech as Gigi and I approach her room. "Carson, I need some space. Let me deal with what's going on. I can't even lift my fucking arm let alone sign my name! Stop asking me what's wrong. Everything's wrong. Everything!" she yells. The sound of our girl sobbing has both Gigi and me rushing in to comfort her.

Kat's boyfriend, Carson, is pulling at the ends of his blond hair and pacing the small space. "Kat, I have to be here! I want to help," he says before realizing we've intruded on their private moment.

"Make him go!" Kat sobs.

My girl wants him out. He's fucking gone. Period. She comes first. My soul sisters always will. I walk over to Carson where he's shaking his head. His face is a mask of frustration and anger.

"Car, *mi amigo*, she needs a little time to process."

His lips turn pale as he stares at Gigi, who is holding Kat while she cries.

"It's been a month. I'm tired of her avoiding talking to me!" he grits between clenched teeth loud enough for Kat to hear. Her crying jag gets louder.

I grab his bicep and tug him toward the hallway.

"Maria, that woman"—he points at the door we exited—"means everything to me. I need to be there for her."

"Even if she doesn't want you there?" I say exactly what I know he doesn't want to hear.

He glares at the door. "I don't understand why she keeps pushing me away. Before all of this, we were fine. Better than fine. We were amazing. I want to be with her forever, Maria. Forever. I want to marry her, have children with her. The whole nine. Why is she doing this?" His eyes glisten, and he turns away from me, once again yanking at the layers of his hair.

I slowly put a hand on his back as he faces away from me. "You have to give her time to wrap her head around this. She's losing everything. The use of her arm, her ability to sew, her career. She doesn't know what's up or down right now."

"So pushing me away is the answer?" His body visibly shakes with the amount of adrenaline I imagine is pumping through his veins.

I shake my head. "No, no, it's not. But right now, she needs some time to figure things out. Give her a few days. Can you do that?"

He sucks in a deep breath, tightens his mouth and nods curtly. "Fine. But you sisters better talk some sense into her because she's pushing too hard. I don't know how much more I can take from her. She won't talk to me." His breath leaves his body in a whoosh of misery.

I close my eyes and nod. "I will, I promise. And, Carson, you can talk to me. I lost big too, you know."

He drops his head and shoulders in a defeated posture. Then he wraps his arms around me and pulls me into a tight hug. "I'm sorry, Maria. Tom was a good guy. The best. He didn't deserve what happened to him. None of you deserve any of this. God, I wish... I wish things were different."

I listen to his heartbeat for a few moments, enjoying the steady rhythm. "Me too, Carson, me too."

Carson pulls back and tucks his hands into his back pockets. "Take care of her for me, will ya?"

I smile. "Of course. Always."

He nods, turns, and heads down the hospital corridor. I take a calming breath and head back into Kat's room. She's wiping away her tears with her left hand. Her right is covered from a spot under her neck down past her fingertips.

"How's my *gatito*?"

She smiles briefly. "Losing it. Obviously."

Gigi sits down on the edge of the bed and places her hand over her stomach.

"Oh! I know something that will cheer you up!" I grin and sashay around the bed.

Her caramel-brown eyes seem to light up. "Please. I could use some good news right about now."

"Gigi?" I glance down at her belly and then at Kat, and back to her belly, and then again at Kat.

She crinkles her nose in that cute, innocent way she does. "What?"

"Something you want to tell Kat about"—I hold up two fingers—"two big surprises." I nudge her shoulder.

Her eyes go wide. "Oh my, yes." She clasps Kat's hand in hers and focuses all her attention on our friend. Poor thing looks like hell warmed over. Her normal blond curls are lifeless against her shoulders, her light brown eyes sunken in. Even her skin tone seems to lack the normal tanned luster she usually has. Then again, she's been cooped up behind the walls of a hospital for over a month.

Gigi sits up straight and looks at Kat. "Well, you know Chase and I got married while we were in Ireland."

Kat glowers. "Yes, I'm still mad about that, but I understand why you did it. What's that have to do with whatever news you have now?"

"News? What news?" Bree bustles in, belly first, carrying a huge bouquet of sunflowers. She sets them down and then turns around. If I hadn't seen her the other day, I would have thought her belly had grown another inch or two.

"Gigi apparently has some news," Kat says.

"Yeah, the bitch got married without her best friends. Old, irritating news." She offers a fake smile. "We're still going to have a party or something to celebrate when Kat's healed. There is no way we're not going to be a part of our best friend getting married," she complains.

"*Cara bonita...*" I remind Gigi to spill the beans.

"How about instead of a wedding party, we plan a baby shower?" Gigi offers.

"Well, duh, this baby is going to need a lot of shit, and since you're best friends with both Phillip and me, you have to throw it!" She grins and rubs her giant bump.

Bree's rounded belly is like a homing beacon calling me to it. I walk around the bed and put both of my hands on her belly. Bree puts up with it as usual. She knows she can't keep any of us away from the bump. It's fascinating. I can't wait to see Gigi and her belly swelling with twins. I wonder if we'll be able to feel each baby independently.

Gigi giggles. "No, I meant a baby shower for me and the twins I'm carrying, but I'd be happy to throw your shower... Ouch!" Gigi tugs her hand away from Kat and waves.

"You're pregnant? Twins?" Kat's lower lip shakes, and her eyes water.

I glance over at Bree, and the girl is already a puddle of tears. They're coming so fast and furious they are wetting her shirt.

Gigi nods. "We found out shortly after the fire and then... well, you guys know."

Bree practically tackle-hugs Gigi. "Our babies are going to grow up together and be best friends!" she declares, tears clogging her voice. "I'm so happy!" she cries, as more tears fall.

I wrap my arms around my girls. The four of us huddle as best we can, taking comfort in the one thing that's going to give us the strength to carry on. New life.

★ ★ ★

Once Gigi and Bree leave to go get some lunch at the cafeteria, I sit in the chair next to Kat's bed and grab her good hand. "What's going on with Carson?"

She groans and turns her head away. "I don't know."

"Don't play that card with me. I invented it." I smirk, but it falls flat on my friend.

Kat turns her head back, leaning her left, unburned side into the pillow and bed, bringing her body position to face me more fully. "You promise not to be mad?" she whispers.

I shake my head. "No."

She gives a bitter attempt at a weak smile. "I can't have him here going through this with me."

"Why?" I ask, not even a hint of accusation in my tone.

"He doesn't love me." Her response is simple and absolute.

Now that was not what I expected to hear. "What makes

you say that?"

She blinks and sniffs while her eyes tear up again. I lift my hand and trace her face, trying to comfort her while she shares what's obviously hard for her to say.

"In all these months, he's never told me. I've said those words to him countless times, yet he's never once told me he loved me."

Her upset hits me like a two-ton truck. I never told Tommy, either, but I did love him. In my own way. Maybe not the same way I love these girls, or the way I thought I loved Antonio all those years ago, but I definitely cared deeply for him.

"Have you asked him why?"

"Yeah, I finally did. Right before I had the skin grafting surgery where they scalped my ass and thighs to cover some of the most severe burns."

I shiver uncontrollably and squeeze her hand at the thought of what she's already undergone.

"You know what he said?"

I hold my breath, not able to respond.

Kat continues on, breathless. "He said he cares for me more than any other woman he's been in a relationship with, but not once has he said those three little words. And worse, he won't tell me why."

"Kat..."

She shakes her head as the tears fall. "No. I know exactly why he couldn't say them. Because he's not a liar, and if he doesn't feel them, he would never go so far as to say them if he didn't believe it himself. He's a commendable guy like that."

I look down at her body, the bandages seemingly everywhere. "Maybe he just couldn't utter the words." I swallow and pet her hand.

"If you love someone, truly, are *in love* with them, there's something inside you that burns like white-hot fire to get out. The need to share that love is so strong, lit by a thousand matches. If you really love someone, the way I love him, you wouldn't be able to hold back. Like how Gigi loves Chase and Bree with Phillip. They can't contain it and neither can their men."

Her words sear a hole straight through my heart. Tommy couldn't contain it with me. But I never said a word.

"I won't be his consolation prize, Ria. The scarred woman he takes care of out of some sense of loyalty or pity."

Fuck. I close my eyes and attempt to focus while my heart is breaking for her. Hell, it's breaking for Tommy as well.

"What are you going to do?" I finally croak through the emotion.

She closes her eyes and leans her head back on the pillow. "I don't know. I love him, but I can't have him here right now. I just can't. Maybe down the road..."

Down the road. Oh no. "You're going to break it off with him, aren't you?"

She firms her lips but doesn't open her eyes. A tear slips down each side of her face. "Yeah, I am."

"*Gatito, no, mi amiga.* Don't do this now. You're not thinking clearly, and this isn't something you can easily take back."

Kat firms her chin, wipes her eyes, and steels her resolve. "I have to."

"You have to what?" Bree asks as she bounces in, her long blond hair a perfectly golden sheet down her back. The woman is seven months pregnant, and she looks like she could be doing a beauty pageant.

"Get some sleep. Kat needs some shut-eye, girls."

"Oh, okay. You'll call if you need anything?" Gigi asks, forever the mommy of the group checking in on her chicklets. She's going to be an amazing mother.

"I'll be fine. Surgeon comes tomorrow for another gander at the burns. We're hoping I can leave in the coming weeks if the grafts take well."

I lean over and kiss Kat on the forehead and then lean back far enough to look directly into her eyes. "I love you, Kathleen. *Besos.*"

She smiles and raises her good hand to my face. "I love you too. Call me tomorrow?"

"You bet."

★ ★ ★

Jack walks me up the steps to Eli's home and opens the door like he owns the place. Once I'm inside, he shuts the door without saying a word.

"*Gracias! Tirón,*" I scream through the door.

"Where the fuck have you been?" Elijah's voice booms only a few feet from where I was yelling at the door.

I jump back and spin around. "Dude! You could have warned me."

"Don't make me say it again," he says, practically growling.

What's with him and the growly responses? He needs to learn some new expressions if he thinks he's going to get me to respond accordingly.

I adjust my boobs up with my forearms, tilt my head, and rest a hand on a cocked hip without saying a word. It's my signature "suck it" move.

He takes a step closer to me. "Where." Another step. "The fuck." Another step. "Were." Step. "You!" he roars, pushing me up against the wall. His body doesn't stop until he's plastered against my body from neck to knee.

Well, hello there.

My heart starts pounding in my chest, and my body heats to what feels like a million degrees instantly. I lick my suddenly dry lips. "Uh, the hospital."

He squints. "Why?"

"*Dios mio*, you read the reports, right? My best friend and I were in a theatre fire set by Danny McBride, the man who killed your brother."

"Kathleen is a friend of yours?" he asks. It is obvious that he read the report because I never told him her name.

I roll my eyes. "Yeah, she's a friend. There are three of them, for your information. Gigi you've met, and Bree and Kathleen. We're soul sisters, and Danny fucked with all of us trying to get to Gigi. Kat's undergoing several burn treatments, not that it's any of your business."

"If it involves you, it's my business." He inches his face closer. I can smell his minty breath he's so close. I'm trying desperately not to react, but for some insane reason, when it comes to Elijah Redding, my body and libido are Judas.

I purse my lips. "Back off, please."

He focuses all his attention on my face before pushing off the wall behind me and walking to the living room.

"What happened with Antonio?" I ask, needing to know whatever he found out about my ex.

Eli's back is to me. He tightens his hands into fists as he rotates around stiffly. "You sure know how to pick 'em, Spicy."

I scowl. "What's that supposed to mean?"

He clucks his tongue. "Let's see." He lifts a hand and presses one finger down. "One, he looks like a prissy boy douche." He grabs another finger. "Two, he says he hasn't seen you in five years since, and I quote, 'the *cadela* locked me up and stole my freedom with her lies.'"

"He denied what he did and called me a bitch?" I snap.

"Oh yeah. Says he hasn't reached out, either. Shared his phone number with us so we could verify the numbers in and out."

"That's impossible!" I stomp my foot. Yes, I stomp my foot like a frickin' child.

"No, it's not, babe. A burner phone can't be traced, and what I gathered from this prick, he's far from stupid. Conniving, but not stupid. For now, he's covering his tracks and playing along."

I fall down on the couch. The weight of this day, the last week, and now this is enough. I've had it.

"What else did he say?" I'm afraid of the answer.

Eli sits down next to me and puts his hand on my knee. "He promised he wouldn't go near you. Knew there was an order from the court stating he couldn't be within five hundred feet of you."

I laugh. Straight up laugh in his face. "And you believe him?"

Eli squeezes my knee. "Fuck, no."

"That's something then. Antonio promises a lot of things." I huff and shake my head. "Promised me every day he wouldn't hurt me right after he'd shoved me against a wall. Or after each time he tried to 'teach me a lesson' about respect. Or perhaps when he thought I needed a good water treatment." I stand up and pace the floor. "I need to go down there myself! Look that *bastardo* in the eye."

"Oh hell!" Eli makes noises like an angry animal again.

I head toward the door, but before I can get there, an arm curls around my waist, lifts me off the floor, and places me back on the couch. Only I'm not on the couch exactly. More like I'm in Eli's lap while he sits on the couch, holding me as I struggle.

"Let me go!" I scream directly in his face like a flailing banshee.

"No way, Spicy. Not a chance! I'm not letting you near that slimy fucker."

After spending an inordinate amount of time struggling, I finally realize he's not budging even a little bit. "Are you going to let me go?"

"Are you going to slow your California roll?"

I fake a smile.

"You think I don't know what you look like when your smile's genuine? Babe, don't confuse me with your dumb ex."

"Are you referring to your brother?" I seethe.

He glares. "No."

"Didn't think so. Watch what you say to me."

"Fair enough. Now can we talk about this without you going off half-cocked?"

"I don't have a cock!" I bite back, my wit in full form.

"You could have one in about two point five seconds if you wanted, babe. I've made it absolutely clear I'm at your service."

"*Cazador...*" I warn.

"Yeah, babe?" He smiles.

"You disgust me." My voice is low and full of malice, making it obvious exactly how I feel about being restrained and not allowed to do or go where I want.

"That's fine. I'll wear you down."

I sigh and go completely limp in his arms.

"Ah, now there's my nice girl. See, I knew there was a nice side to you. Listens to authority figures. Pro column," he says before standing up and righting us both. "Now to make dinner. Hope you like chicken and rice. You can make the salad."

I snarl my reply. "I don't cook."

He yanks my arm, pushes me ahead of him, and smacks the rounded part of my ass cheek and thigh. Enough to sting and entice. "Hey!" I jump out of the way, moving toward the kitchen.

"Nobody can fuck up a salad. Not even you."

Yep. Doesn't know me at all. "If it involves food of any kind, you'd be surprised."

"I'm rarely surprised."

"Give me time." I smirk, trying to make a point and catch him off guard.

Instead, I'm the one caught off guard by his next reply.

"Plan to, babe. That's what I'm doing here, and I've got all the time in the world to make you mine."

CHAPTER EIGHT

A little over a week has flown by with nothing remarkable happening with Antonio. Eli and Chase's men have been keeping an eye on him, but for all intents and purposes, Antonio's been a good little parolee. Reports from the guys are he gets to work on time, goes straight home, and meets up with his parole officer as mandated by the court. To any law enforcement officer, it would appear he was following the rules. And Eli's scare tactic of visiting him at work must have hit the mark. However, I did not buy it, because I know exactly what Antonio is capable of. He's a meticulous, calculating, and most importantly, patient man. And no way was I going to share that with Batman and his comrades.

Nope. Instead, when Eli leaves today to do a drive-by of Antonio's workplace, I'm going to pack my shit and get the hell out of dodge.

No one deserves to be cooped up in a house—albeit a large house—with a grumpy, testosterone-filled bounty hunter with nothing but getting laid on the brain. All week, I made it a point to wear more clothing than was actually comfortable so he wouldn't ogle. Of course, he did not follow that same courtesy. No, Eli liked to walk around clad only in a pair of basketball shorts or his flannel pajama bottoms. I swear the man has those thin cotton things in every variety of plaid under the sun. And each and every single one of them is so sexy I have to practice Bree's yoga breathing techniques in order to ward off the fire burning inside me. But I do it. For Tommy. Because it would be wrong to hop into bed with his brother within three weeks of burying him.

Siete semanas.

Seven dickless weeks of absolute celibacy altogether. It's the longest I've gone since my legs were broken by Antonio a little over five years ago. That time, I went a full year just to see if I could. Technically, the broken legs, healing wounds, group therapy with other domestic violence victims, and meeting and becoming best friends with Gillian definitely helped fight the hormone and libido battle back then. I could not say the same now. Getting out of his place ASAP was mandatory. My sanity warranted it.

I sigh as I enter my empty apartment. The air is stale and stuffy, but as I glance around, I'm welcomed by the fact that everything is in its rightful place. And it's all mine. My memories of life beyond Antonio and the good times I've had with my girls overflow in frames on the small mantel. Even my cushy fabric furniture and multicolored throw pillows renew my sense of peace and tranquility.

This is my home now. Mine. Not some burly bachelor pad with leather couches that are too cold to sit on or that stick to my thighs if I wear shorts. What is it with men and leather anyway? Is leather somehow the quintessential fabric that says, "I am man—smell my leather couch as proof," or something?

Blowing off those thoughts, I set about opening the windows and the patio door to let in some fresh air. I light a few candles and turn on the soundtrack to the newest show I'll be working on in a few months. In the meantime, I need to get back to my regular exercise routines and connect with the few dancers I've taken on to help teach some of the harder choreography.

The dancers just coming out of the academy haven't had a lot of real-world experience and need to be challenged and taught some new things in order to succeed. In this business, a person has to be the best, all the time. Knowing one style of dance is not going to keep a roof over our heads in most cases, unless the dancer happens to be the most famous in a specific style of dance, such as ballet dancers like Baryshnikov or Markova, or heck, the queen, Anna Pavlova, the first ballerina to ever tour internationally.

Me, I'm great at jazz, Latin, ballroom, and hip-hop, but my sweet spot—what I'm best known for—is contemporary and modern dance. Still, at twenty-eight, I'm aging out fast and not likely to ever become famous. Unquestionably, though, fame never once entered my sights. I've only ever wanted to dance and be a part of theatre, the big-screen entertainment equivalent in my chosen profession.

Hiding out at Eli's this past week and a half has taken me off my routine and put the dancers who need me in a sour position. Sure, I could have told Eli I was moving back to my *casa,* but it's no longer any of his business, and I had to get away. I had to. I could not stay in that home one more day and not jump his bones. And for me, as well as for Tommy, I've abstained. It's the right thing to do, no matter how much my body aches for Eli to press me into the nearest wall and fuck my brains out. I won't do it. I can't.

Decision once again firmly beaten into my mind, I make a

few calls and schedule my sessions with a couple of the dancers using Bree's I Am Yoga studio in Davis Industries across the street. She allows me use of the extra room she normally keeps for private sessions or meditation classes. It's smaller than her normal yoga room but plenty big enough to work with my clients on their craft. As long as my sessions are during normal yoga hours or after hours when no one's there, she doesn't mind me using the place. And the best part, it's rent-free. BFF status at its finest.

Wait, *clients*. Huh. I never thought of my peers as clients before. Colleagues, sure, but they are paying me to work with them, and I do pay taxes on the money I make, so I guess they are clients of mine. That's when it hits me. I am serving as a dance instructor or consultant—a *choreographer* of sorts.

Choreography has always been a part of my everyday life, coming up with new moves, new stories to tell to the music being played. I've helped countless instructors and choreographers over the years solidify the routines and movements to some pretty large pieces. And I love doing it. I almost love it more than being on the stage myself. I definitely appreciate that it's easier on my legs.

Performing on stage twice a day for a packed house for months on end is hurting me more than I've been able to admit to anyone. The ghost ache of those broken bones has brought me to my knees in the past few weeks more times than I care to admit, but I've ignored it because of everything else that's been going on. The sorry truth is I'm not going to be able to ignore it for long. This new show I'm supposed to do in the fall is set to run for six months, provided the opening month does well. If so, I'll be traveling with the crew for months all over the globe.

I clutch at my quads, my legs reacting already to the

exhaustion, the wear and tear on my body, and the old injury that will inevitably ensue. While taking a deep breath, I put on my clothes and think about the clients I have today and what facets of dance I'm going to teach them.

Even though no one's around to hear me, I chuckle to myself. Clients. It's an interesting concept. Could I work with more people? Not the everyday dance class a child takes, but actual dancers already well into their craft. Maybe teach some classes at the local dance school? I wonder what a person needs to teach there. Probably a degree in education and dance—neither of which I have.

I could go back to school, get a degree in dance or teaching. Though it seems so ass-backward to go to school *after* I've already lived the real-life experience of being a professional dancer for the past ten years.

My phone buzzes on the dresser across the room. I glance at the display and ignore it. I'm not picking up his calls. I need some damn time to myself. Five seconds later, my phone buzzes again. This time it's Gigi. Of course, I pick up right away.

"Hey, *cara bonita*. What's shaking, baby?"

"Ugh. Did you ignore your bodyguard's call?" she asks, annoyance sitting acidly on the tip of her tongue.

A prickle of irritation flutters over my skin. "Maybe. What's it to you?"

"Because he's right here standing next to me with a pissed-off macho-man face that— Hey! Give that back." I hear Gigi's voice get farther away.

"Spicy, where have you run off to?" Elijah's rumble soaks straight through to my bones.

This time I groan. "Can't you take a breather, *Cazador*? I'm at my place getting ready to meet up with my clients. I've moved back home."

"The hell you have." He grumbles his usual distaste for my actions.

"Whatever, Eli. Antonio hasn't so much as made a peep. I'm not staying with you anymore. The coast is clear. He's leaving me alone. Your job with me is done."

"When it comes to protecting you, *Maria*, my job will never be done."

The way he says my name sends a lightning bolt of lust barreling straight to my core. I sit down on my bed and clench my thighs tightly together. He rarely uses my full name, and when he does, I turn to jelly.

I suck in a long, slow breath, allowing him to hear how frustrated I'm getting. "Eli, thank you. Thank you for being so kind the past ten days, but I'm telling you, I no longer need your help. I'm not afraid anymore. You and Chase's men have proven Antonio is not coming after me. End of story."

"It's not the end."

"Oh yeah, why not? Do you know something I don't? Something you're keeping from me?" I goad him, wanting to know if he truly is keeping something important from me in some type of valiant effort to ensure I'm not scared.

"No."

"Then why?"

"If I put myself in the man's shoes, there's no way in hell I'd leave you alone for long. I'll be at your place in five minutes."

"I'll be gone," I say as I hang up and grab my rehearsal bag that's already preloaded with music, protein bars, towelettes, and bottles of water. "Peace out, sucker!" I say to the empty apartment as I fly to the elevator.

★ ★ ★

Note to self—when someone calling you is directly across the street from the same building you need to be at, you can't exactly escape them. When I arrive at Davis Industries a few minutes later, Eli is leaning next to the elevator, arms crossed, head cocked, and a dirty smirk worth a thousand words. I want nothing more than to smack that face, or worse... Kiss it. I'm still not sure what to do when I get right up in his personal space.

"Admit it. You're stalking me."

He grins that deadly sexy one where his lip curls up enticingly. I glance away and press the up button, oh, about a hundred times. Eli follows me onto the elevator, and the door closes us in alone.

"Why can't you leave me alone? I don't get it. I honestly do not get it."

Eli smirks and shakes his head.

"Seriously. Do you like to go after women who are not interested in you? Am I some kind of a challenge you feel the need to break?"

"Oh, you're a challenge all right."

I clench my jaw and grind my teeth. The heat of irritation rushes up my chest and neck and inflames my cheeks. Great, now I'm going to look like a pissed-off tomato. Perfect.

The elevator dings, and he follows me down the hall past the Davis gym Chase put in for the yogis and the building employees. Gillian and all her girls have full access to it, too. Again, free of charge. It's super awesome to have friends in high places.

I open the door for I Am Yoga and wave at the receptionist.

Bree is moving up in the world. The second she opened the new office, all her old clientele were happy to move to the new location, and now she has all the Davis Industry employees taking advantage of the new studio at a serious employee discount. All enough for her to hire some staff. Win-win.

"Hey, Ceej, how's it going, *chica*?"

The petite woman with the wicked cool name runs around the desk and throws her arms around me. "Oh my goodness! It's so good to see you, Maria!" During my time as BFFs with Bree, I've come to find out the average yogi is very touchy-feely. Something I'm not altogether used to but accept as part of the package when I'm surrounded by a bunch of tree-hugging hippies. Bree encourages me to roll with it, so I do. For her.

"*Gracias*. I'm glad to be seen." I wink, knowing that she means since the accident and funeral, but see no reason to bring that up. "You guys been busy?"

Ceej nods, and her long, curly black hair bounces with her. I love that Bree found such a genuinely happy soul to come work for her. "You teaching any classes yet?"

The woman smiles so wide, I'm pretty sure the room brightens with her presence. Her light brown skin positively glows from her Chamorro heritage. She holds up her fingers, showing about an inch of space. "I'm this close to getting my Registered Yoga Instructor credentials, so I've been assisting Bree during the harder classes to get my practical hours. But when she goes on maternity leave..." Ceej points a thumb to her chest, showing off her forearm covered in eclectic tattoos. "I'm her girl. I can't wait!"

I tap Ceej on the shoulder. "That's awesome, *chica*. Keep up the good work. Make Bree proud."

"I will. I promise I will," she says eagerly.

"Cool."

Ceej looks behind me and up, way up from her five-foot-two stature. "Um, hi. Welcome to I Am Yoga. Is this your first time taking yoga?"

It takes everything in my power not to fall to the floor and roll around while kicking my feet with insane laughter. The image of Elijah doing yoga is enough to have me snort-laughing and holding my gut.

Eli, who's too damned cool for school, cants his head to the side and says in the manliest tone possible, "Sweetheart, do I look like the type of guy that does yoga?"

Ceej blinks her long lashes prettily, not at all deterred. I think I like her more for not being affected by the extreme manliness and sex personified oozing from his every pore. I wish I could say the same for myself.

"Yoga is for everybody, Mister..." She uses the formal pronoun, giving him an opportunity to say his name.

"Just call me Red. Everybody does."

"Okay, Mr. Red. Can I interest you in a schedule and services offered pamphlet?"

He grins and licks his lips, and I positively swoon at the glistening moisture sitting on his plump bottom lip. Again, Ceej waits for his reply like the consummate professional she is, completely unaffected. I'm going to tell Bree to give her a raise. Even a small bump for having to deal with people like Eli is worth another dollar an hour. Never mind, I'll tell Chase. That man loves to play with his money.

"No. I'm with T and A over there." He nods to me.

Ceej furrows her brow, the area above her nose crinkling. "T and A. What's that—"

"Oh never mind!" I turn my back to the sweet girl and grab Batman's bicep, glaring and presenting my teeth the same way a dog would snarl before a scuffle. "Come on. I need to get set up, and we need to finish this little *chat* we're having so you can get on with your day.

"Thanks, Ceej, catch you later. Great seeing you."

"It's good seeing you too, Maria! Bye."

"*Adios,*" I holler over my shoulder while dragging the big guy down the other hallway to the private room I'll be using. Once we get inside, I slam the door.

"T and A? Seriously? Are you trying to piss me off?"

Eli leans a hand against the wall, loops an arm around my waist, and plants one big paw on my ass, bringing me flush against his hard body. He grips a handful and squeezes while grinding me against his muscular form. I moan automatically. My body is starved for male attention in the worst way. Leather and spice fill the air, and I can't help sucking in a full breath of it, dipping my head closer to the silky patch of tanned skin visible through the opening at his collar.

Just one taste is all I need...

"You got a lot of nice ass, and based on the reaction of every man that comes into contact with you, you've got a great pair of tits."

He nudges my neck with his nose, the heat of his breath sending shivers of lust down my spine. He hasn't so much as made a move on me since he got close at breakfast on one of the first days I was with him. Now he knows it's been seven weeks since I've had a man intimately, and he's making his play.

Shit. Fuck. *Shit.*

He slides his hand from my ass, up my hip, and cups my breast. "Make that a world-class fucking rack. Sweet Jesus, you're spilling out the top of your shirt. Fuck."

"Eli..." I make one last ditch effort at stopping this train wreck, knowing things are moving to a place so fast we won't be able to turn back.

"You're fucking killing me, Spicy." His voice is strained and filled with desire.

I suck in a harsh breath, wrap my arms around his neck, and nudge my pelvis against one deliciously impressive erection. "*Dios mio.*" I'm imagining that thick column sliding deep inside me.

"I can't wait any longer." Eli's voice rumbles like an incoming storm against my neck, sucking on the tendon there before biting down.

A burst of arousal rips through me, settling right between my thighs. Without further thought, I lift a leg to get closer, and in a second, he crushes us back against the nearest wall.

An objection is on the tip of my tongue when he presses his denim-clad erection perfectly against my clit, and slants his mouth over mine.

Madre de Dios.

The man can kiss. Sensation after sensation blasts through me. His exquisitely placed cock rubs me into submission while his tongue delves into my mouth, the two separate parts of him so beautifully in sync. I run my fingers through the layers of his hair and cry out at the desire shredding my psyche. Everything around me disappears, and all I can do is feel.

His searching tongue, tasting of peppermint, tangles with mine.

Eli moves his hands all over me. One curls around my breast, a thumb moving over my nipple in dizzying circles I never want to stop.

My heart pounds like a bass drum in my chest as I kiss him and kiss him and kiss him, as though I might never have another chance.

Eli sucks on my bottom lip and pulls back. I groan at the loss before he's back, nipping, sucking, pecking at my lips, leaving no area untouched. He can't seem to get enough.

I hold his head and turn it sideways, wanting, needing to swallow him whole. "My turn," I whisper before nibbling on his lips, plucking at the top one, teasing his tongue with mine until he lifts my other leg up so both legs are wrapped around his waist.

"Christ, I knew it would be good with you, babe, but I never knew it would be this fucking explosive."

I mewl into his mouth, and he grinds his hips against my pussy. His jeans provide extraordinary resistance, catapulting me from turned on to seconds away from my release.

It's been so long...

The room is intensely hot as we kiss and dry hump against the wall. I scratch my nails down the back of his shirt and tug the fabric up until I get to the smooth, warm skin below. He moans and thrusts harder.

"Need inside you, Spicy. Right. Fucking. Now."

"Mmm, yeah," I say, losing myself to the moment.

Every touch sends me higher. Each kiss makes me see the light. The rigid press of his dick against my center turns my mind to mush. Pleasure ripples through my pores and soaks my panties. "I'm gonna..." I gasp into his mouth, pushing my tongue in to taste him when he sends me into orbit.

"Oh no you don't." He pulls his hips back and lets my legs drop to the floor.

I'm catapulted into the here and now on shaky legs and

sopping wet undies. "Wha... Uh, what happened? Why did you stop?" I tug on his neck, bringing his mouth to mine.

He only lets me have his luscious lips for a brief second. My heart pounds against my chest like a battering ram as I blink away confusion and the haze of need. "Eli..."

Eli curls a hand around my nape and up into my hair where he grips it tight at the roots and pulls my head back so I'm forced to look directly into his eyes. Tingles of pain and pleasure coalesce from the roots of my hair at his dominant move.

"When you come the first time, Spicy, it's going to be when your cunt is wrapped around my cock and squeezing the life out of my dick. Got me?"

My knees shake as his words pierce right through my libido and light a bonfire of excitement I have no hope in hell of putting out.

"Fuck me sideways," I gasp.

"Will do, but not the first time," he confirms.

I swallow. "Deal," I answer, not realizing that one word would seal my fate in a way I never thought possible.

CHAPTER NINE

Just as I'm about to go for gold and take what I want, the door only a few feet from where Eli has me pinned opens, and my first clients, Jessica Locke and her dance partner Meghan Butler, walk in. With Eli's hands and mouth on me, I had completely forgotten the entire reason I came to the studio—to work on a contemporary piece they're trying to perfect for an upcoming audition. The two women stop midstride, one with her hand still on the doorknob, the other with eyes wide and cheeks pinking.

"Um, uh, we'll come back," Jessica offers.

Her friend doesn't move. Her gaze is all over the six-foot-plus hunk of tatted sexiness with messy bedroom hair that I've been yanking on in my effort to get more of him all over me. One look at Eli and I get it. He's hard not to look at. Jessica tugs on Meghan. "Come on!" she urges.

I pull away from Eli as if I've been splashed with hot coffee. "No, ladies, *lo siento*. I'm sorry. We were, uh..."

"Making out," Jessica says rather directly.

I cringe. "Yeah, about that..." I blink a few times, trying to get my bearings, and fail miserably.

Eli puts an arm around my shoulders, tugging me closer to his body. "Ladies, I'm Red. I'm going to be sitting in on today's session."

Wait. What? "You're going to what?" I shake my head, thinking I must have missed something between the moment we were bickering to the span of time we were grinding up against one another like horny teenagers. My clit is still throbbing at the wicked pressure he denied at the last possible second.

And what the heck were we doing, anyway? Did I agree to fuck him? Would I if they hadn't showed in the nick of time?

The answer is a resounding, mind-altering yes. Yes, I would have. God, I'm such a *puta*. Ready to fuck my dead boyfriend's brother against a wall in my best friend's workplace. I push my hand through my hair and try to focus on the here and now. I can't go wallowing in the hole of my own self-pity right now. I have two paying clients who need assistance with their craft, and I'm going to be the one to help them.

Focus on the work, girl. Deal with the mierda *later. You've got this.*

"Ladies, why don't you go ahead and get situated in the center of the room facing the mirror. We'll work on the synchronized sections first."

Both women hustle over to the far side of the room, set their bags down, and shed their outer clothing until they are down to their sports bras and booty shorts. Basically half-naked.

Eli's gaze goes from me to them. He tilts his head and checks out each girl's attributes fully. "Nice workplace. I think I'm going to like hanging out here." He smirks, and I want to punch the expression right off his handsome face.

I squint and furrow my brow. "You are not staying here." My tone is back to harsh and unrelenting.

"Babe, I'm not leaving you alone," he states simply, as if he has just remarked it's sunny out. What he doesn't realize is it's about to be storming in the yoga studio if he doesn't carry on about his day...somewhere else...*rapido!*

Perhaps it was the banging of my head against the wall while being pressed into sexual oblivion that brought out my softer side in order to help me respond without malice. "Davis Industries is more secure than your house in Golden Gate Park. Try to tell me it isn't," I insist, cocking my hip and taking my standard *I'm serious* pose. Chase Davis has ramped up security of his building times a thousand in the wake of Danny and finding out his wife is carrying his children. The man is psycho Papa Bear. We're probably safer here than in Fort Knox.

He rubs his hand against the morning scruff he didn't bother to shave. After staying with him for ten days, I've learned he shaves about every three to four days. So he's either sleek and sexy or scruffy and sexy. The in-between is just as smokin' hot as the former and latter. Which basically means he's sex on legs walking around San Francisco for all women to gawk at.

"I'll concede that. But for now, I'm staying. We're not done with our little chat, and of course, there's the other big problem we've got." He reaches down and adjusts his rock-hard erection. It hasn't gone down, and the outline of his hefty package through denim makes my mouth water. *Jesucristo, I need to get laid.*

I close my eyes and count to ten, not caring at all that I may look *estúpido.*

"Fine," I grunt through my teeth. "But you have to promise not to disturb me. Once we get into the routines, I call the shots." I get close to him and prod my index finger hard against his chest. "Do. Not. Interrupt. Me. Got. It?" I accentuate each word with a point to his sternum.

Eli chuckles and puts his hands up in a placating gesture while smiling. "Got it, babe. You won't even know I'm here."

"Your giant self is a little hard not to notice."

He leans close, wraps a hand around my waist, and plasters me up against him again. "Like that you think that, babe. Means there's hope."

I scowl and push back as much as he will allow in his superhuman hold. Damnit, this man is nothing like Tommy. He doesn't move the same, touch me the same, speak, walk, or think the same. He's almost the exact opposite, and I can't help melting at his every touch and word.

I'm going to hell in a handbasket.

"Hope for what?" I finally whisper, not sure I want to know but dumb enough to ask.

"For the future. For more than a fan-fucking-tastic roll in the hay. Because I know we're going to set the sheets ablaze."

I sigh. "You're so confusing," I murmur while struggling against his hold.

"So are you, Spicy. So are you. Now get on with your work so we can continue where we left off."

Once he lets me go, I turn and look over my shoulder. "I make no promises. Before, I wasn't thinking clearly."

Eli smirks. "With what I plan to do to you later, the only things you'll be thinking are *more and harder.*"

An image of the two of us horizontal, naked, me tangled all around his massive muscles and slick tattoos, him thrusting hard and deep, assaults my brain. I clutch at my chest and suck in a harsh breath. "Eli..."

He winks and leaves me there, dumbstruck, as he pulls up one of the chairs at the other side of the room and settles into the seat. He stretches his long legs out and crosses them at the ankles before clasping his hands over what I suspect is a softening erection.

The girls giggling in the center of the room snap me out of my daze. "All right, all right, show's over, ladies." I make my way to the sound system and set up the music for their routine.

"Let's start in position one."

While the strains of a moody classical piece fill the room with its heady dose of penetrating violins and hard hitting piano chords, I take up position in front and to the side of both women. When the drum beat flares up, the three of us move into a squatted lunge and then fly into the air in a synchronized kick split when the cymbals in the music crash. A manly gasp fills the air, adding to the intensity of the piece. In my peripheral vision, I notice Eli is sitting up, his elbows to his knees, hands clasped in front of him as he shifts forward following our movements with his gaze.

Maybe there's hope for him yet.

★ ★ ★

My back hits the door to my apartment with a resounding crack. "*Dios mio.*" I am clutching at Eli's hair. His tongue is trailing down my chest, licking at the sweat still there from dancing.

"You taste so good," he murmurs against my skin, both of his large hands curled around my rib cage, plumping my breasts up so he can get to more of me. "Open the door, Maria. I can't be responsible for what I'm about to do to you in public if you don't hurry and open the damn door."

I'm panting as I turn around and fumble in my purse to find my key. His mouth is on my neck instantly as his right hand moves down my abdomen, past my navel, directly into the front of my spandex shorts and panties. He cups my sex firmly and rolls all four fingers around in the wetness he finds.

"I'm going to fuck this cunt in so many ways you won't be able to teach dance tomorrow." He pushes two fingers deep and my vision goes black, stars popping behind my eyelids, while I roll my hips into each thrust of his fingers. He moves his thumb and swirls it around my clit.

"You're going to come up against this door, Spicy. You want all the neighbors to hear you scream in ecstasy as I finger fuck this sweet cunt? Hmmm?" His words are filthy, coated with a lust so intense I fear the flames about to rain down, but I'm still unwilling to put out the fire. No, I want to burn under his hand.

"Yes!" I hiss between my teeth as those thick, long digits of his slip deep. I lean my forehead against the door, panting like a bitch in heat, not caring who may see me getting finger fucked in the hallway. I just don't care. As long as he never stops. "Never stop," I repeat out loud.

Eli grabs the handle. "Unlock the door," he groans, but the door opens without the key and we stumble in.

His fingers slide out of me, and I would cry at the loss, if I wasn't so horrified at what I am seeing. Like a sick slideshow of natural disaster pictures, my mind shoots me a barrage of disturbing images. "My place... It's...it's destroyed!" I cry out and clasp a hand over my mouth.

Eli grips me around the waist, trying to push me out into the hallway with one hand while the other lifts his cell phone to his ear.

"Yeah, Porter, it's Red. I'm at Maria's. Before I call the cops, you're going to want to see this. It's bad, man. I'm going to fucking kill him." His voice is coated in poison and sounds lethal.

I pull away from his hold and look around, trying to assimilate what I'm seeing. My couches have been cut and the stuffing shredded. Puffs of cotton trail all over the floor where the cushions have been tossed. All my pictures and figurines—the ones that mean the world to me—are shattered, the broken pieces strewn throughout the living room.

Slowly, I walk to the kitchen and peer over the island. All the drawers have been dumped and food mixes with broken cutlery and stemware in varying stages of disarray all over the tile floor and granite countertops. The fridge door is open and milk, fruit, veggies, and everything in between are spilling out onto the floor, leaving a sour scent permeating the air.

With as much stoicism as I can muster, I walk through the apartment to my bedroom. Eli, hot on my heels, is still speaking in a low tone into his phone. He's already taken a cursory look and has come back, so I know the coast is clear. At this point, though, I can't hear what he's saying. It's a jumble of words until I reach the master bedroom.

I step a single foot into my room, my sanctuary, the place I let all the injustices of the world go and focus on the good as I lay my head down to sleep each night. It's a fucking nightmare come to life. No other way to sugarcoat the catastrophe that occurred here tonight.

Tattered remnants of my clothes are everywhere. My bras and undies have been cut and tossed on the bed like multicolored confetti in piles of ripped lacy fabric. The jewelry box the girls got together and bought me for my twenty-fifth birthday is broken and lying on its side. All the drawers are now wooden chunks with jewelry scattered everywhere as though he pulled out handfuls and tossed them all over willy-nilly.

But that's not the worst of it. Spray-painted in bright crimson red, mimicking blood, complete with wet drips of paint marring the text, is a message written on the entire wall where my headboard rests. A message for me. One I cannot deny is a threat from my ex.

Three words.

Three little words that, together, and using only six letters, are arranged in such a way as to end any semblance of a healthy reality I'd been working so hard to achieve for these last five years. I know now that no matter what, regardless of who threatens him, or whether he gets put in jail again, it will never end. Never. The message is clear in those three words. And I know with my whole heart and being he means every last one of them down to the depths of his vile, demonic black soul.

I OWN YOU

★ ★ ★

Flashing lights. Boots on the floor. Murmuring voices. Whispered words of anger and fear surround me as I sit on one of my dining room chairs in the far corner of the room, as far away from it all as I can get.

Jack Porter, Chase, Eli, and three members of Eli's secret league of bounty hunters tromp all over my private space taking pictures, looking for clues, all while San Francisco's finest poke and prod me for information.

"No, I don't know who did this, but I suspect Antonio

Ramirez."

"Yes, he's been violent to me in the past."

"No, I haven't seen him personally."

"Yes, I'm aware I should stay somewhere else."

"No, I haven't provoked him or seen him at all in the past five years."

"Yes, I know this looks like the person is mentally unstable."

"No, I didn't leave my door unlocked."

"Yes, I'll let you know if anything more happens."

"No, I don't know if anything has been taken. It's impossible to determine right now."

Eventually, the police leave me alone to sit in silence while they do their thing. A voice booming through the door catches my attention.

"Ria! Where are you? Maria!" Phillip, Bree's boyfriend and Gillian's longtime best guy friend, enters the room on a roar. His voice is strained with worry.

"Phil! Over here," I call out and wave him over.

He rushes over to me and pulls me into his arms. I clutch on to him like he's a life raft and I'm stranded at sea.

"Oh my God. Is this shit ever going to end?" He is petting my hair and then curls his hands around my cheeks. "Are you okay?"

His eyes are tired and crinkled at the edges. "Gigi called Bree, and you know what happened then." He sighs.

"My girl lost her shit." I state only the facts. When Bree and Gigi heard my place had been broken into, especially after what's happened this past year, they probably flipped out. Big time. Poor Phillip and Chase. At least Chase can restrain his wife by sticking her with a bodyguard who will refuse to let her leave their penthouse across the street. Of course, that didn't stop my girl from calling out for reinforcements. Damn, I love my soul sisters. Best. Friends. Ever.

Phillip smiles briefly. "That about sums it up. Why didn't you call? We're family now. I can take care of you," he says, offering up the world, like he does to our Bree.

Before I can respond, I'm catapulted out of Phil's arms and locked to a wall of man. His leather and spice scent hits my nose, and I calm instantly, as much as I hate he has that effect on me. Mostly because it's too soon and doesn't seem rational since we've only known each other for less than two weeks.

"Who the hell are you?" Eli demands in his usual alpha-badass-I-don't-have-time-for-this-shit rumble.

"Holy shit! What the fuck..." Phillip's eyes widen, and he slams back against the wall, knocking over the other dining chair. No matter, it just adds to the pile already there. "You... You're, you're... What the fuck?" Apparently, he hasn't been told about Eli.

"I'm Elijah Redding. Thomas's twin brother. Now I will repeat. Who are you?" Eli speaks slowly but with a hint of impatience.

Phillip spaces out for a few moments, his gaze seeming to move all over Eli's face and body, probably cataloguing the similarities and differences the same way I did at first. Then he glances at me and back at Eli and the protective way he's holding me.

"Maria, you and this guy?" His accusation is warranted and exactly what I am trying to avoid. "What about Tom..." He shakes his head. "Never mind. What is going on?"

I shift out of Eli's hold. "Phil, this is Elijah, Tommy's brother. Eli, this is my friend Bree's man and the father of her baby," I add, in case he's harboring any more macho-man issues over Phil's appearance here. "He's also been a close personal friend of mine and Gigi's for the past several years. He knew Tommy."

Elijah holds out a hand. "Any friend of my brother's is a friend of mine. Sorry about the harsh words. The situation warrants it right now. I'm not taking any chances with her safety." He nods to me.

Phillip shakes Eli's hand, his face still showing signs of amazement. I know the feeling. Though now I've spent more time with Eli, I see more of the differences between the two brothers than their similarities. They literally are only similar in facial features. Everything else about Eli is a vast contradiction to his brother.

"No, man, I understand. Can someone tell me what went down? Who trashed your place and why?"

"We think it was Tony," I mention, knowing I don't have to go into too much detail. Phil was around when I met Gigi. He knows more than anyone else what I went through to put Antonio in jail. Sat with me and Gigi while the court put his ass away for ten years. Little did we know he'd be out in half that for good behavior.

Phil closes his eyes and drops his head forward. "He's out? How?"

"Good behavior," I answer flatly.

"This is good behavior? Has there been anything else?" he asks.

I clasp him on the shoulder, appreciating the worry in his stance and tone of voice. "Yeah, he sent a couple texts, but he went radio silent after Elijah warned him off almost two weeks ago. Then this. And worse, we're not going to be able to prove he did it." Of that I'm certain. Antonio is too fucking smart. Always has been.

"Let me get you out of here. Come stay with Bree and me."

"And put you, your pregnant girlfriend, and your five-year-old daughter in harm's way? *De ninguna manera. No esta pasando,*" I rattle off in Spanish, forgetting Phillip doesn't understand the language.

He furrows his brow.

"I said, no way. Not happening. *Gracias, mi amigo,* but no."

"She'll be staying with me. It's safest. I can protect her," Eli counters.

"Obviously not, if this is what happens on your watch." Phillip's tone is harsher than I would have thought him capable of.

Eli glowers. "I was with her at your wife's studio making sure she was safe when this went down. The building here is supposed to be secure. Davis and Porter are on that now."

"She's not my wife," Phil shoots back.

Eli makes a startled snort sound. "Well then maybe you should be working on nailing down your own woman instead of worrying about mine, yeah?"

No. He. Didn't. Oh *hell* no!

Phil's eyes go wide, but there's nothing I can say because I've straight swallowed my tongue and lost all ability to speak. Literally, my lips are numb, and no sound is coming out no matter how many times I open and close them.

Thank God Chase and Jack come up to our little huddle and slice through the tension surrounding us. I focus on Jack fully, ignoring both Eli and Phillip. The last thing I need right now is a pissing match, or worse, to explain myself. Mostly because I'm incapable of doing so.

And why the fuck didn't I say anything? Deny what he insinuated?

One ticket to hell, please. I'm going over the edge kicking and screaming all the way down.

"There are no fingerprints," Jack says. "The perpetrator must have been wearing gloves. We've got the spray paint can he left behind. We'll see if it was bought locally. It's a common, run-of-the-mill brand, but we may get lucky canvasing local stores that sell it in the area. Maybe somebody remembers the purchase, provided it was recent."

"That's it?" I ask, shock and fury layering my question.

"No. One of the neighbors on your floor saw the profile of a man in a painter's uniform and a hat rushing into the stairwell. Said the man looked to be of Hispanic descent with black hair that curled around his collar. That's about all he saw."

"That's Antonio. I know it."

"The police will follow up with Antonio Ramirez by paying a visit to his workplace and getting his alibi. Hopefully, he doesn't have one. Unfortunately, the neighbor couldn't identify Mr. Ramirez from a sheet of men with similar height, build, and characteristics. That means eyewitness identification is out."

I close my eyes and press my hands on the top of my dining table. "He's going to get to me. Maybe not now, maybe not next week, but he will get to me. I know him. He won't stop." The anxiety and fear rush out of my mouth as a chant.

"Over my dead body," Eli says forcibly.

Slowly I lift my head and look into the same face I have almost every day for nine months, only this time it's totally different. Still comforting, but it reminds me of what's already happened to one man I cared for.

"Be careful what you wish for, Eli. You might get it. I'm toxic. One Redding has already been killed because he fell for me. I don't want you to suffer that same fate." The single thought sends a knife to my gut. I grab around my waist, wincing. "Chase, can I stay with you and Gigi until I figure this..."

Eli's pulling me away from the group and down the hall before Chase can even summon an answer. I stumble over a few pictures and broken glass until he gets me far enough away from the group of men to speak privately.

"I know you're scared. I know you're giving up. The fear is all over your face. But I'm not going to let anything happen to you. We *will* take him down. I promise you. Give me a chance," Eli begs. His confidence and sincerity warm my heart and soul.

With my arms crossed over my chest, I shake my head. "I'm not worth the danger."

"Babe, you are." He grabs my biceps. "You were to Thomas and you sure as fuck are for me. You think I can kiss you, touch you, feel your heat, and not be affected by you? Not be all in? I'm telling you right here, right now. From the moment I met you, there was something special there. And yeah, this situation is fucked. You being my brother's girl first is fucked, but I don't care. And the way you kissed me, wrapped your arms around me, pulled me closer... You can't deny you're feeling it, too."

I swallow down the tears building, but they fall down each cheek anyway. I whisk them away as fast as I can. "This is not normal. Everyone's going to think I'm a whore! My friends, your family, your parents!"

"They love you. Told me to protect you like Thomas would."

The tears pour out when I think of Tommy's parents and

how they had taken to me, made me part of their family in such a short amount of time. "What are they going to think?" I choke and gasp, gripping Eli's shirt in one of my fists to stay standing. He curves both of his hands around my hips, keeping me upright.

"We'll talk about it later. Right now, what's important is me keeping you in my sights at all times. Can you understand I need that right now? I *need* that, Maria. Come home with me. Stay. With. Me," he whispers harshly through a tight jaw and clenched teeth.

No longer able to fight, I nod. There's nothing more I can do right now. I'm exhausted, emotionally spent, and fucked six ways from Sunday. I don't even know what to do with myself, let alone verbally battle with a man who can sway me with a simple touch of his lips to my neck.

"Okay. Me and my boys got this. You're safe with me." I fear this is a promise he will regret one day soon.

I glance up and look into his eyes. They are honest and a brilliant green. A dash of tenderness comes and goes in a flash before his tough bounty hunter mask falls into place.

"I believe you."

CHAPTER TEN

Eli is kind to me when he brings me back to his home. I go straight up to the room he's given me to use, remove my workout clothes, and pull a tank top over my head. At least Antonio hadn't opened the door for the laundry closet while he was destroying everything I own. The two duffle bags of clothes I'd brought to Eli's originally were still sitting on top of the washing machine where I'd left them before I headed out to the studio earlier today.

Once I'm dressed, I yank back the covers and plop into the middle of the cloudlike bed, pulling the comforter over my head.

What am I going to do? He'll never stop. The exhaustion takes over and I'm out.

★ ★ ★

"You have screwed around for the last time, mi reina. *Tonight's lesson is going to be a hard one,"* Antonio sneered as he took slow, calculating steps toward me.

I held up my hands and stepped backward, mimicking his steps. "What did I do, Tony? Please, tell me what I did to make you so mad!" I cried.

His eyes were black pools of hate. "You know what you did!

Não minta para mim." Don't lie to me, he said in Portuguese.

I shook my head and got down on my knees, holding my hands clasped in front of my chest, prepared to beg. He loved when I begged. Sometimes, instead of hurting me, he'd just fuck my mouth and then take me roughly. I'd much prefer a violent round in bed than any of the other "lessons" he liked to teach me based solely on some psychotic infraction he believed I committed against him.

His lips twisted into a white snarl. "You think your pretty mouth can fix this, mi reina? Fix what you did? What you told the producers of the show?"

I closed my mouth and thought hard about any conversations I'd had with them. Yes, two of the executives cornered me and offered me a position as lead for the second half of the tour because the current lead dancer had recently found out she was pregnant and needed to take a back seat to all the lifts, tumbles, and harsh hours. The two of us switching places would be an easy change. I was already her understudy.

Antonio stood right in front of me. "Falar. Speak. You have five seconds to admit your deceit. Based on your response, I will decide your lesson accordingly."

I shook my head and wrung my hands together in front of my chest.

"Five, four, three..."

"No, Tony. I don't know what you're talking about. I didn't deceive you. I would never ever do anything to hurt you."

He frowned. "They are moving you into the lead position. Yes? Two..."

"Um, yes. I was going to tell you tonight. They asked me..."
"One."

An explosion of pain burst across my face where Antonio's

fist plowed into my cheekbone and left eye. I fell back, the agony flaring instantly against the tender tissue.

"Back on your knees, woman!" he roared.

I scrambled to comply, my face throbbing. The skin around my eye was already swelling, feeling tighter by the second, filling with fire. I held up my hands again. "They asked me."

"And you agreed?" he sneered.

"Yes, I thought you'd be happy."

He punched me again, this time harder than the first, his ring cutting my cheek open. Blood sprayed out and down my cheek. I held my hand over the wound, trying to stop the flow of blood but also to prevent him from hitting that spot again.

"Feliz! You thought I'd be happy with you being touched by every man in the show? Your position is by my side in all things, mi reina! Or have you forgotten that?"

I shook my head. "No, no. I'm sorry. I'll tell them tomorrow I can't. I won't leave my spot. Please..."

He lowered himself down to a crouch, his head tipping awkwardly to the side in an unnatural pose. With his eyes a coal-black nothingness, his lips in a snarl, and his skin tight over his high cheekbones and Portuguese features, he was by far the most menacing individual I'd ever known. Not for the first time, I looked into Antonio's face and saw evil, but in that moment it was terrifying.

The man I thought I loved didn't exist in this violent shell of a human being. The man I laughed with, danced with, made love to was no longer there. In his place was el diablo. *The devil incarnate.*

Antonio breathed white-hot fire into my battered face like a dragon. Then abruptly he stood. "Stand up and close your eyes."

"Tony...please," I begged. More than anything I didn't want

to close my eyes. I would rather see what he was going to do to me, versus anticipate the lesson he deemed appropriate.

"Cale-se! Cállate! *Shut up!*" he said in Portuguese, Spanish, and English, to get his point across.

With every speck of pride and stamina I had left, I stood up. My face ached, but in light of the fear that overwhelmed every cell, it had finally gone numb. I would be in pain later, but right then, with adrenalin and my survival instincts in full force, the pain took a backseat. I could fight back, but the last time I did, I ended up in the hospital for a week.

"Whatever you wish, mi rey." My king. I used his special endearment in the hope he'd have mercy on me. I shouldn't have, though. He never did. I took one last look at Antonio standing across the room, wearing all black. His shirt sleeves were rolled up to the elbows and a couple buttons were left undone at the collar. His black hair was long and slicked back in the way I always found devastatingly sexy. Even then. With hate in his eyes, he was a wolf in sheep's clothing, the demon that mothers warn their daughters about. Only I didn't have a mother to do that. Maybe my path would have been different if I'd had.

Taking a full deep breath in and letting it out slowly, I closed my eyes and prayed.

Prayed he would go easy on me.

Prayed I would survive this night with my life.

Prayed one day I'd find a way out.

The single blow to my thighs hit like a truck running me over without so much as pressing on the brakes. The sound of bones cracking and snapping warred with the volume of my guttural, terrified, thoroughly inhuman scream. I opened my eyes, my vision swirling in a haze of pain. Antonio held a metal baseball bat in his hands. The one he just used to break both of *my legs at the thigh. His mouth was a twisted mess of rage.*

"Now you'll never dance again." The words slithered past his lips like a thousand tiny snakes.

Torturous, incomprehensible pain catapulted out from my thighs and up through my body as I lay on the floor. I was unable to move. My vision blinked in and out until, finally, I couldn't take it anymore. The lower half of my body hurt so much it stole the breath straight from my lungs.

The next thing I knew, I was being dragged by my hair across the condo. The fissures of pain from my scalp were nothing. The agony pumping through every orifice of my body had me completely immobile. Dimly, I sensed tears tracking down my cheek, pouring down my face in rivers of anguish and blood. I attempted to speak, say something, anything, beg for help, a hospital, but it only came out as a garbled mess of nonsensical whispered words. Wouldn't have mattered anyway. Antonio, the man I fell in love with, was no longer there. The demon inside him had taken over.

Eventually he got me to where he wanted and dropped my body onto the cold tile floor in our bathroom. The sound of water running was like a death knell. That was it. I knew instinctively that was the day I'd die.

Unable to kick and scream through the trauma, a sense of calm and peace filtered through me as if gossamer wings were lifting me up and outside of my body.

I felt no pain when he lifted me up and put me into the bathtub, broken and bleeding.

No pain when he pushed my head under the water.

No pain when I opened my eyes and saw his distorted face through the ripples above.

I opened my mouth to take a final breath, let it all go and be free, but instead of water, I sucked in air. Blessed air. No longer was Antonio standing over me, holding me underwater. I blinked the wet away and gasped the oxygen in. A face was now above me. Soft green eyes. Smooth tan skin, and no hair. A full mouth. A shiny gold badge.

★ ★ ★

Then the face above me changes. Morphs. The edges around his image blur. The room around me is changing from the blue tiled walls of the bathroom to bright white ones. The eyes, though, they are the same. The mouth still full and soft. The layers of hair falling into his face... His voice is loud. Authoritative.

"It's just a dream. Wake up, babe. Wake up. I'm here! It's me. Eli. I'm here."

Eli. Not Tommy, and most importantly, not Antonio.

I wrap my arms around him and cry into his neck, trying to spit out what I know is going to happen. "Eli! He's going to kill me. He almost did before. He'll do it again. He won't stop until my life leaves my body," I choke out through copious tears.

In one swift move, Eli lifts me up and out of the bed. I cling to his neck, my tears rolling down his bare chest and back.

He sets me down in the center of his huge bed. The entire room smells of his natural brand of leather and a spice I can't begin to name. I don't say anything but watch as he enters a room to the right, flicking on the light. I briefly hear water running and then shutting off before he flicks the light off and comes back to the side of the bed.

"Take these. A couple of Tylenol. It will help."

I follow his instructions without a word. Once I'm done,

he takes the glass back and sets it on the nightstand before moving around the bed and getting in. He rolls to his side, wraps an arm around my waist, and tugs me to him. He's a veritable furnace to my cold, gooseflesh-ridden skin. His heat quickly seeps into my skin and bones, and I finally relax, the dream starting to dissipate, its evil claws releasing their hold.

"You want to tell me about it?" His tone is gentler than he's used before.

I shake my head.

"You scared me, babe. The gut-wrenching scream made me think he'd gotten to you in my house. In. My. Fucking. House. And my house is secure. I have the best security possible."

I swallow and nod.

"Tell me," he urges, locking his arm over my waist more fully.

Safe. "It was the night he almost killed me. The night your brother saved me from him."

"That's how you met? You and Thomas?"

"Yeah. He saved me all those years ago, took me to a hospital, and came back months later when I was released from the hospital and brought me to the shelter where I met Gigi. Both of our men had done a number on us, and we escaped with our lives."

"I read the report. But I thought you weren't together that long." His voice is low and comforting in the still of the night.

"We weren't. I hadn't seen him after that for years until we ran into one another at the local pub where the girls and I hang out. He was there with some of his detective buddies. He asked how I was doing, if I was single, and then asked me out." I smile, remembering that night fondly.

Eli chuckles behind me. "Smart man. But I wouldn't have waited. I'd have followed up with you after the hospital and shelter."

"I didn't look like I do now. He wouldn't have seen me the same way. I was black-and-blue and broken in a million pieces when he saved me that night."

"Babe, you could be bald, forty pounds heavier, and have pink and purple polka dots all over your body, and I'd still want you."

Dios mio, he's breaking me down. "Charming," I say sarcastically, but truthfully, it was one of the nicest things a man had ever said to me.

He sucks in a long breath. "I call 'em like I see 'em."

"That is true. You definitely don't mince words."

"You know what else I'm telling the truth on?"

My heartbeat picks up, beating against my chest the same way it did when I was lost to the nightmare, or should I say memory. "What?"

"You're safe with me. Here in my arms. You're safe, Maria."

I sigh and snuggle into the pillow and the warmth against my back. "Thank you."

Eli leans over, touches his lips to my neck three times, and then tugs me even closer to his form. "Like you right here."

The edges of sleep are taking me away, along with it my ability to be snarky. "Me too," I mumble.

"Go to sleep, babe."

★ ★ ★

"You have got to be kidding me. He has a goddamned alibi?" Eli's voice is a harsh whisper as I blink awake to his angry grumble. He lifts the covers back and sits at the edge of the bed, elbows on his knees, phone to one ear, head hanging down. "Two men at the warehouse vouch they saw him. It has to be him."

Eli listens a few moments as I sit up and push my hair over my shoulder.

"She's sure, man. Unless it's a random stranger stalking her, but that would be pretty surprising and coincidental since she just got out of a stalker situation with her best friend. Yeah, Gillian Davis, used to be Callahan. Yes, *that* Davis. Uh-huh. Keep looking. I want this one, Dice. Bad. Get me something." Eli hangs up the phone abruptly.

I stare at the tan skin of his muscular back. Tommy was fit and worked out here and there, but Eli seems twice the size. Briefly, I wonder if the other half of his job is to lift weights. He'd have to spend some serious time in the gym to look like that. Not that I'm complaining. He's *perfección*.

Eli sighs and tugs at his hair. I shift my legs, getting more comfortable. He looks over his shoulder. "Didn't realize you were up. Sorry. I tried to be quiet."

Like a foghorn on the Bay. I think our versions of quiet are two different things.

"Antonio alibied out?" I pick at the fibers of his deep burgundy comforter. The rich black threads weave in and out of the quilted look.

Eli lies back, his head falling into my lap so he's looking up at me and I down at him. Without thought, I tunnel my fingers into his locks of hair. It's surprisingly thick, but then again, the better part of my year was spent with a man who shaved his head every few days.

"Yeah, but we'll get him. Catch him in a lie. I've got my

guy doing some reconnaissance on his life. Flipping over some stones. That kind of thing."

I nod. "Who's Dice?"

"One of my staff members."

"Bounty hunter?"

"One of the best." He grins up at me.

"Who's the best?"

"You're looking at him."

That makes me laugh out loud.

"Love it when you smile and laugh. You're beautiful all the time, but when you smile, smoldering."

I roll my eyes and run my fingers through his hair. "Thank you for last night. Being there for me. Not pushing too hard."

He lifts a hand up to cup my face. His body follows it until his lips are over mine. He kisses me much slower than our hasty smash-and-grab the two times we went at it yesterday before everything went to shit.

His tongue softly traces the outline of my bottom lip, requesting entry. Wanting his kiss, this connection, I open for him.

For long moments, we sit and kiss. Deep plunges of tongues tangling, lips pressing, teeth nibbling. We're learning each other, finding what the other likes best.

Eventually, we kiss for so long, only the sound of his phone ringing breaks us away from one another. I glance at the clock and realize we've been kissing for the past fifteen minutes. Just kissing. Neither of us even made a single move for more. And it was amazing. Absolutely what I needed today after everything I've been through. To connect, face-to-face, with a man I'm beyond attracted to, leery of falling for, and still ashamed to be with. I don't know what an acceptable amount of time is before you start dating again after your boyfriend is murdered, but I do not think there is ever an acceptable time to start dating a dead boyfriend's brother.

Holding my hand over my mouth, I crawl out of bed and head to the bathroom. Space. I need space right now.

I close the door and lean against the wood. *Maria, you've got a screw loose, girl. Being with Eli is wrong. Being with anyone this soon is wrong. Isn't it?*

The answers don't come. What does is the sound of Eli's angry voice and drawers slamming. I open the door and peek out the few inches while he paces the room and tosses clothing on the bed. A pair of jeans goes flying.

"Fuck! I'll get to her phone before she does. No, I don't want her to see another fucking text. Yeah!"

A shirt is catapulted out of the closet and lands on the bed. "Order her a new phone. Yes, charge it to my account. Look, Scooter, I know this is going to shock the shit out of you, but this woman? She's it."

Eli opens a drawer. "It means she's important to me. What are we, in high school?" He scowls into the phone and stops, standing ramrod still, and grips his hair. "I'm sorry. I know you got out of high school a year ago. No, that wasn't directed at you. Fuck!" he roars, and drops his pajama pants.

I'm greeted with the finest, most toned ass on the west coast. *¡Por Dios que es magnífica!* Eli stands completely nude facing the window. His golden body is that of a Viking or a mythical god back in the time of Odin and the Valkyries. It's something to behold. Until he turns around. His cock hangs down in front of him, long and thick, even at rest.

I gasp and realize my error when Eli's head launches up and his gaze meets mine. Instead of hiding himself like I would imagine, he stands up straighter, puts one hand on his hip, and lets me look my fill. The man is unashamed and comfortable in his own body in a way that makes him a hundred times sexier, which is already impossible to do. He's the epitome of greatness.

He holds the phone against his breastbone and grins before speaking softly. "You done ogling me, Spicy? Can I get dressed now?"

"I, uh...I wasn't, um..."

"Sure you weren't. Next time, it's me sitting on that bed and you standing here letting me look my fill. Got it?"

I cringe and glare.

"Yeah, nah, it's fine. Get me everything you have on Antonio's financials. I want his debit card transactions, credit cards, details on his place of business. Is it on the up-and-up financially, or are there some shady things happening? Two someones gave our boy a get-out-of-jail-free card with an alibi, or someone else he hired did the job. I want to know whatever you can find."

Again, he hangs up abruptly on whomever he's talking to and slips on his jeans, sans underwear. Damn, that's sexy as hell.

I swallow and watch him get dressed. I'm unable to look away. Like a sunset over the ocean, some things are too pretty to miss.

"Do you always bark orders and then hang up on people?"

He pulls on a dark chocolate-colored Henley. "If I'm paying them to work for me, time is money. No need to mince words, remember?"

I glare back, cock a hip, and place my hands on both. "You could be nicer. These people are choosing to work for you."

Eli doesn't respond for a few long seconds. His eyes are moving all over my body. I glance down and realize not only am I not wearing pants, I'm in the pair of deep purple satin panties that only have a string of elastic holding them up on both hips and a lavender threadbare tank top. My exorbitant bust is bursting against the fabric, my nipples erect, hot points of need after having watched the godlike man get dressed in front of me.

"*Mierda*." I puff out my lips and cover my tits with my arm.

"Oh, don't cover up those beauties on my account. I'm all about your tits, babe. They're fucking huge. As a matter of fact, I'm getting hard looking at you. You better go before I do something about it," he warns.

Not wanting to risk another snafu like yesterday, I dodge toward the door.

"Christ. Your goddamned ass is lush, too. Fucking hell!" he grunts. "You're killin' me, woman!" he yells as I lock myself away in the spare room and find something clean to wear. Jeans, a tank, and a cardigan from the laundry basket I grabbed will have to do.

As I I'm getting dressed, I hear a knock at the door. "Bring something warm and comfortable. Also, pack an overnight bag for two nights. I'm taking you away from here. You need some time to decompress. We both do."

All I hear are his footsteps, loud and clear, heading down the wooden stairs.

He's taking me away for a couple days. I don't know whether to thank my lucky stars I'm leaving the city, or start praying that I'll survive hurricane Eli and his unstoppable sexual advances.

After last night, when he held me and took care of me, and

then this morning, seeing him naked and confident in all his masculine glory, the real question I should be asking myself is...do I want to avoid his advances?

I close my eyes, take a deep breath, and pack a bag, making sure I have my sexiest underwear and my razor. Not that I'm going to use them. Because I won't be having any sex. Probably. Most definitely not.

CHAPTER ELEVEN

The open road is remarkably, blessedly quiet. Eli drives steadily down the highway, our destination unknown. At least to me. And frankly, he could take me to Timbuktu and I wouldn't care. Getting away is paramount. Anywhere would be better than the city.

Outside the car window, the California hills roll by. The landscape is dusty, brown, and dry. We didn't have much of a winter and have had below average rainfall, even for us. Still, I enjoy the varying colors and contrast from the horizon line. With the city in the rearview mirror, I can finally breathe a little easier.

"You doin' all right?" Eli breaks the stillness.

"Yeah. Glad to be getting away. The farther we get away from Antonio the better." I sigh and lean my head back on the headrest.

Eli changes lanes and taps his fingers against the leather steering wheel. "I'm not going to let him get to you." He speaks with a sincerity that pierces through to the soft, gooey side of me.

I slant my head against the seat and check out his profile. His square jaw and full head of hair complement a strong Roman nose and high cheekbones. Even from the side he's still the most handsome man I've ever known. And I thought his brother was a catch in the looks department. Which he was, but Elijah is unique, more edgy. There are enough subtle differences in the two men to really see how special both of them are in their own right. The more time I spend with Eli, the more I like him. Not just the handsome package, but his protectiveness, confidence, alpha nature, and even for the sweetness like last night when he held me tight so I'd feel safe. And I did. In his arms is the only place I feel any sense of peace. Still, Antonio is out there, and I know him better. He'll never stop.

"I know you believe that, but I know Antonio." I frown.

"But you don't know what I'm capable of, either." His tone is straightforward and direct.

"*Si.* I don't. How's about we get to know one another a little bit better?" I turn my frown upside down and decide I'm going to make an effort with this man—at the very least, get to know more about what makes Elijah Redding the man he is today. I shimmy into a more comfortable position.

He smiles and drums his fingers against the steering wheel again. "Shoot. Ask me anything."

I think about it for a couple seconds. "Okay, where have you been the past few years?"

"Working all over the nation. I'd take a job in Omaha that would lead me to New York, which would send me off to Florida. Wherever the high-profile needs were, I went. I try to keep my home base in San Francisco though."

"And you never got lonely on the road?"

He glances my way, and the look in his eye says, "Are you sure you want to know the answer to that question?"

"Babe, I had my bed warmed when I needed it. Most of

the time I was busy trying to catch criminals."

I nod. "I can see that. So let's start with something easy. Favorite food?"

"Steak."

"Shocker." I roll my eyes. "Mine's Italian."

He grins. "Like I couldn't have guessed that one."

"Are you calling me *grasa*...fat?" I sit up more completely in my seat, making sure my curves don't create a muffin top over my pants, adding to his point.

His eyes widen and he shakes his head. "No, I'm calling you Italian."

I laugh. "Oh. *Si*. I am half Italian and half Spanish."

"Got that from your body, babe. No woman has an hourglass figure, a speck of a waist, and is tall like you are with such a fiery temper without being Italian or Spanish, or in your case, both." He winks.

"Whatever."

"My turn." He purses his lips. "Do you mind if I ask about your past?"

I shrug. "Depends on what you want to know."

"I want to know why a woman who's as smart, talented, and as beautiful as you are stayed with a man who beat and tortured her every day for years?"

His words hit my heart like an avalanche on the snowy mountains of Lake Tahoe, covering my soul with an icy chill. I kick off my boots and put my socked feet up on the seat. Eli waits, focusing on the road, not forcing me along. I appreciate his patience more than I'm willing to show. Finally, I decide I have to take the plunge and get it over with.

"Honestly, Tony was the man of my dreams. He was the answer to my prayers. I wanted someone to care about me.

Antonio, he cared too much." I take a full, deep breath in and let it out slowly before continuing. "At first, the abuse started small. Yelling, accusing me of things I didn't or wouldn't do. Then, after a year, it progressed to shoving me into things, to the floor, etcetera. Each and every time he'd apologize, promise never to do it again... The usual. Then he started in on the mind games. Making me believe I'd wronged him in some horrible way."

"But you knew you didn't. Somewhere deep that fire inside had to tell you he was full of shit." Eli's tone is soft, sweet even.

I nod and frown. "*Sí*, but he made me believe I was wrong somehow. That I was the one constantly jeopardizing our relationship. He'd accuse me of not loving him enough or not as much as he loved me. When you have someone belittling you over and over... I don't know, it starts to stick. You trust the lies."

Eli scratches a hand over his chin. "I can see that."

"You can? I mean, you don't see me as *débiles* because of it?" Anxiety fills my limbs with a jittery mess of discomfort.

"Weak? Nah. Far as I can see, you made do in a touchy situation. But why didn't you leave?" He places a hand on my knee. The touch is one of compassion, not lust, and is exactly what I need to keep going.

I push a hand through my hair, letting the knots loosen and release as my fingers comb through. "My upbringing wasn't average. I grew up in the system, bounced from place to place. No family to speak of. By the time Antonio came around and we became a couple, I didn't have anyone else in my life to fall back on. Leaving him would have been leaving everything, including dance, because he was the lead dancer in the show.

In all honesty, dance was the only thing I loved more than life itself. For a long time I felt stuck, confined in a straitjacket to the decisions I'd made." I glance down and twist my fingers. "Then, well, you know what happened. After a while, things got worse and I could no longer control anything. By then, the decision was made for me. I was lucky to survive that night. Your brother came in the nick of time. You know that, right?"

Eli's jaw hardens. I can hear him grinding his teeth. "Yes. I read the report."

Wanting to change the heavy mood in the car, I flick on the radio. "What do you normally listen to?"

"Soft rock mostly. You?" His words are still harsh, but I can tell he is trying to go with the flow.

"I love all music. Maybe being a dancer has instilled the love of all types of music, but it's true. There isn't a genre I don't like."

"What about country?" One eyebrow rises.

"Even country." I smile.

"Pop?"

"Of course."

"Jazz?"

"Absolutely. Great to dance to."

"Okay." He rubs a hand against that ever-present scruff again.

A zing of arousal rips through my chest to settle heavily between my thighs. Why does the man have to be so damned sexy? I mean, of all men I could desire, why does it have to be this one? Tommy's twin brother.

"Tell me this, Spicy. What do you plan to do when you can't dance anymore? Teach?"

I tug at a lock of hair and spin it around my finger.

"Maybe. It's something I've been thinking about more and more recently. I'm pretty old for a dancer."

"Old? How did you come up with that cockamamie rationale? What are you, twenty-five?"

I smile full, teeth and all. "*Gracias.* No, I'm twenty-eight. Not only that, I've been nursing broken legs for years. They're doing well in general, but won't last. I've got maybe another year if I take it on the road. A couple, tops, if I dance locally and less often."

Eli cringes. "You tellin' me your legs hurt all the time, and you still dance on them for hours on end?"

I nod. "*Si,* but it's a pain I'm used to. Nothing I can help."

"Sure you could. You could stop dancing. Do something else. Like you were doing the other day with those students. You danced some to show them the moves, and then you walked around perfecting them. Couldn't you do that?"

I take a breath and sit sideways in my seat so I can look at him more fully. "I could."

"And a few of those sessions you did were your dance routines, right?"

"What are you getting at?"

"Could you do it for a whole show or at the very least for a single song? Like a chor—"

"Choreographer?" The word spills out of my mouth. The same one I've been thinking the last couple days.

"Yeah, that. You're good, great even. I was surprised at what you know how to do. Plus, you knew all the names of the moves, the positions of the body parts. Seems like a no-brainer to me." He glances my way and smiles.

I love Eli's smile. When he graces you with one, it is *magnifico.*

"It's definitely something I've been thinking about." I admit the truth, one I haven't told a soul—not even the girls.

He shrugs. "What's to think about? What you're doing is hurting you. You love dancing. You don't want to leave it completely, right?"

I shake my head. "*Dios mio*, no. I'd be lost without dance. I wouldn't know what to do with myself. Dance is all I've ever known. It's the only thing I'm good at."

He nods. "Okay, sounds to me like you need to figure out the best way to do what you love and have it still work for your life. If being a choreographer is the next big step, you have to make it happen."

I laugh. "You make it sound so easy."

"Babe, it is. You're a smart girl. You'll figure it out. 'Sides, I'll help you."

That time I snort-laugh and giggle. "You'll help me? You barely know me."

He smirks. "I like what I know."

"You're not helping me." I roll my eyes. Help me? For Heaven's sake, the man's known me all of three weeks. Plus, he doesn't know anything about dance.

One of Eli's eyebrows rises into his hairline. "And why not?"

"Because once this is all over and Antonio's caught, you'll be on your way to the next big score."

"And what does that have to do with the price of rice in China?"

"*El precio del arroz?* What are you talking about?"

"What does one have to do with the other? I already told you, babe. I'm in this. We're a thing. The everyday can be worked out with time."

I focus on the side of his face, sending laser beams of fire with my mind's eye. "We are *not* a thing." Unfortunately, I'm not Superman, so it doesn't work.

"Babe, we are." His tone brooks no argument.

Unfortunately for him, I've never been good at keeping my mouth shut. "How many times do I have to say it? Here, I'll say it in Spanish. *Usted y yo no somos una pareja.*"

He grins and takes the exit toward Santa Cruz, letting his silence be his response. Frustrating man! He thinks he can say we're together and boom, it's fact. One thing is for certain, he's got a lot to learn about women.

★ ★ ★

We've been in the car over an hour and a half when Eli turns onto a road called Davenport Landing.

"Where are we going?" I'm unfamiliar with the area. I've lived in the San Francisco area my entire life, but I've never been to this section of Santa Cruz.

"You'll see," he says cryptically while following a winding little road.

The sun is high above the Pacific, the water a dark, inviting blue. Reminds me of the times I've gone to the beach with my soul sisters. We'd spread out a blanket, bring wine and snacks, and spend an entire day gabbing, eating, and getting tipsy. We try to do it at least once a year. Those are the days where the things that have been bothering us are brought to light, each of us making a point to work through whatever problem the other sister is having at the time. Sister solidarity is paramount, and we take one day a year to hash it all out. It's worked for five years and counting so far.

Thinking of Gigi, Bree, and Kat, I realize I didn't tell any of them I was leaving town. Phillip is going to spread the word about the evisceration of my apartment, although as Eli was ushering me out the door, Chase promised me he'd have the place cleaned and replacement furnishings brought in. I told him not to worry about it, but Chase rarely listens to anyone once he's made a decision. Guess that's what made him a billionaire. He did what he wanted and made good use of his analytical mind and critical thinking abilities. Gigi is the only person who can cut him down at the knees.

Once we arrive at wherever Eli's taking me, I'll shoot off a quick text letting them know I am okay.

Before long, he turns into the driveway of a good-sized three-story wooden beach house. He leads me toward the single door to the house and presses the button to close the garage.

"Is this your home?"

He shakes his head. "Nope, but it belongs to a good friend of mine. He lets me stay here in exchange for checking in on the place once a month."

I nod and enter when he holds open the door. The inside is beyond my expectations. White fluffy couches with blue pinstripes greet me as I look over the open floor plan. A simple navy-colored ottoman is centered between the couches with a serving tray on top where a couple of remotes sit with several magazines perfectly fanned out. A widescreen TV is nestled in the middle of an entertainment center that runs across the entire left-hand wall. Books mixed with large conch shells and artsy pieces fill the shelves surrounding it. The kitchen is to the right, and I can already see that the stainless steel appliances are top-notch. Several hanging lamps dot above the island with an ocean-meets-earth mosaic printed across the blown glass. Everything I see is amazing, but nothing beats the floor-to-ceiling windows along the back wall.

The room comes up into a church-point steeple with dark wooden beams highlighting the view. Each of the beams comes down around a geometric presentation of the ocean beyond. The ocean in all its wonder and glory can be seen clearly as far as the eye can see. I walk over to the windows in awe of the breathtaking view.

"Spectacular, isn't it?" Eli comes up next to me, standing shoulder to shoulder. "It never gets old."

I sigh. "I can't imagine it does."

He wraps his hand around my wrist and runs his fingers down to where I'm clutching my bag. "I'll take this to our room."

Our room.

As in one. *Uno.* Singular. I close my eyes. A red devil appears on my right shoulder and a white angel on my left. Red Devil is fist pumping the air and cheering as though she's won a marathon and received a shiny new trophy. White Angel is wagging her finger and shaking her head, obviously disappointed. Then, Red Devil walks along my shoulder, throat-punches White Angel, and shoves her off my shoulder.

Decision made.

Our room.

Our bed.

Lord, have mercy on my soul.

Eli comes back and heads to the fridge. "Wine or beer?"

I scrunch up my nose. "You have food here?"

He smiles. "I called a local college kid I work with on occasion to come ahead and fill the fridge with some essentials."

"Which would be wine or beer?"

Eli pulls out a bottle of beer and a bottle of chilled white wine.

"Obviously."

"White, please. What else?"

"Some meat for grilling, veggies, sandwich and breakfast stuff."

I shrug. "As long as you're the one cooking I'm happy to be the one eating."

He laughs full and deep. The rumble tingles against the sensitive space above my tailbone like a feather tickling me seductively.

"Don't worry, Spicy. I got you."

I nibble on my lip and watch while his muscular arms shift and move, working the wine cork like a professional. The black lines of tattoos running down both arms add to the intensity and fierceness that seem to be such an integral part of his personality. One I'm becoming far more attached to than I'd like to admit.

"But you'll be the one doing the dishes if I'm the one cooking. Deal?" He hands me a glass of white wine, and I take a sip. The crisp, fruity flavors of the Pinot Grigio rush over my taste buds in a flurry of citrus tingles.

"Mmm. *Muy bien. Gracias. Si,* I'll do the dishes. No *problemo!*"

"How's about we kick off our shoes and take these on the beach? I'd like to show you something." He extends his arm toward the wall of windows.

I follow Eli through the living room, past the stunning porch complete with teak patio furniture, a fire pit, a stone hot tub, and a calming waterfall. The thought of soaking my sore muscles and body has me drooling, but I didn't bring a swimsuit.

Eli waits at the gate as I look longingly at the hot tub.

"You coming or are you going to take a soak in the tub? Because if that's what you want to do, feel free to strip right here. I'll protect you." He grins wickedly and waggles his brows.

"*Cállate!* I didn't bring a swimsuit so I won't be going in." I lift my chin and push past him where he holds the gate open. There's a small path of stone stairs that leads right to the beach. As in, the sand of the beach covers the last of the steps.

When we hit the bottom, we both kick off our boots. He tucks his socks into his shoes and then wiggles his toes in the sand. There's something so cute and boyish about the movement, I giggle.

He frowns. "What so funny?"

I grin. "You and your feet."

This time he scowls. "What's wrong with my feet?"

"Nothing." I snicker behind my hand.

"Then why are you laughing?" He lifts one up. "They're too big? You know what they say about big feet?" He tries to go for the old standby joke.

"Don't bother. I've already seen your equipment. Remember?" I pucker my lips and hold back a grin.

He leers. "Then you know I'm packing some big shoes."

That does it. I can't stop the full belly laugh. I actually laugh so hard I almost spill my wine. He grabs it and holds it up until I get my guffaws under control.

"Ahhhh. I needed that. Thank you."

"Glad I could be the comic relief, but I wasn't kidding about my equipment." He gestures in the general vicinity of his manhood.

"You realize not only did I see you naked today, I had sex with your brother. I already knew what to expect."

His grin turns flat at the mention of Tommy. "Don't remind me."

For some reason, him saying that pisses me off. It's as if I'm the only one who can see how screwed up his pursual of me is. "Why not?"

He tightens his jaw. "Because I don't want to think about you with him, okay?"

"And you know why that is?" My voice rises as my frustration starts to heat up my temper.

He leads me down the beach. Regardless, I'm not going to let this go. It needs to be said. So I do the only thing I can—I storm after him, ranting all the way down the beach. "I've had sex with your brother. Many times! So many times I can't even remember half of them. Do you understand that?"

He stops when he gets closer to the water, and the sand is a slick slope where the waves are crashing softly. Finally, he turns to me, and I'm shocked by what I see. His face is a mask of white-hot anger. Eyes squinting, nostrils flared, even his chin looks like rock-hard stone.

"Don't you think I know that? It destroys me he had you first. That he knew what you look like, soft and sweet in the morning. He knew how you like to be loved. What the tight heat of your cunt feels like. And I don't. It fucking kills me you gave it to him, and no matter what I do or say from here on out, I'll always wonder if you're comparing me to my brother and finding me lacking!

"And you know what the worst part is, Maria?" My name is acid on his tongue. "I. Still. Want. You. I want to kiss you so hard you forget every kiss he ever gave you. I want to take your body to a place he never could. I want to own your goddamned soul and have you own mine. So you see, I do know what you had with my brother. That will *never* change. I can only manage the here and now and find a way to make you mine in whatever way he couldn't."

He takes a few angry steps toward me, sand spraying the area around me. It takes everything I have not to back up when he curls a hand around my chin, forcing me to look into his green eyes.

"And I'm going to do everything in my power to do it."

"Eli..." I gasp as his lips slant over mine.

CHAPTER TWELVE

The kiss is feral. He plunders my mouth with his tongue in wild, hedonistic abandon. Both of us drop our drinks to the sand below without a care, preferring to hold on to one another.

Mi culo.

Mi cintura.

Mis muslos.

His hands are all over me. He moves them up my back until both hands are threaded through my hair, holding me in place, while he devours my mouth. His ardent tongue searches for mine, and I comply with equal passion. He tastes of minty beer and man. A mind-melting concoction.

The wall between us is gone. Obliterated by his honesty. I can no longer deny this man what he wants. What I want. What we both *need*. Each other.

Eli kisses me so hard, and for so long, my lips are swollen and bruised when he pulls away on a mighty breath. His chest rises with every inhalation. "You can't stop this," he murmurs, his lips a succulent snarl of desire.

I shake my head and firm my jaw, ready to take whatever he can give me and more. "No. I can't."

"We are fire and ice, baby. Both run scalding hot when stimulated. I want to make you mine. Make you forget him, and everything and everyone that came before. This heat between us, it's all-consuming."

I close my eyes and lean my forehead against his, praying I'm making the right decision. "Burn me," I whisper against his lips. "Set me on fire." I press my mouth against his and nibble on the plump bottom lip. "I want to forget. Today, just make me forget."

The second after my words slip past my lips, he's on me. With a strength I've not experienced before, he lifts me up by my ass. I separate my legs on instinct and wrap them around his waist.

With powerful footsteps, he tromps through the sand, up the stone stairs, past the patio, and into the house. The breeze from the overhead fans tingles against my fiery-hot skin, but my focus is on the man carrying me away, taking me to the place of no return.

I lick a line up his neck from his clavicle to a spot I've found is sensitive for him behind his ear. One that makes him shudder. He tastes of salt and the sea, a delicious appetizer for what I'm dying to wrap my lips around.

I've always been a blow job kind of girl. I love cock. I love sucking cock. It's not the act that turns me on—it's the power I have when I hold that firm muscle in my hand, or better yet, within the heat of my mouth. The way a man loses his focus, his control. Such a turn-on. I can't wait to make Eli purr for me. I grin and sink my teeth into the meat of his shoulder, imagining it was another spot on his body.

"Aw, fuck," he says before tossing me onto a fluffy cloud. I bounce a few times before he cinches both ankles, slides his strong hands up my calves, thighs, and to my waist, where he unbuttons my jeans and drags them down my legs and off.

I mewl when he lays a firm kiss on the space below my belly button.

I shouldn't want this, but Lord have mercy...I do.

Eli stands and rips his shirt over his head, gifting me with a view of his golden chest. He's much larger than Tommy was. Bigger by many pounds of rock-hard muscle. The black tribal tats swirl down his arms like ribbons wrapping my present up in a pretty package. All I can think about is tracing each of those lines with my tongue, digging my teeth into one of them, and memorizing his taste.

"I've been waiting to see that look in your eye, Spicy. That feral sexual creature hiding under the surface. You can unleash her with me. I can take anything you've got and give it back in spades, baby."

A heightened awareness comes over me. My skin feels prickly, ready to burst into flame, my mouth waters, and I'm grinding my teeth in response to the musky male scent in the room. I sit up on my knees and pull my shirt over my head. I'm clad only in a red satin bra and tiny matching G-string that ties at each hip.

Eli's jaw tightens, and his hands move into fists as a predatory gleam turns his eyes a dark forest green. His nostrils flare as if he's scenting the room the same way an animal would.

"I can smell you, babe. How's about you remove that sorry excuse for a pair of underwear and show me how hot you are for me?"

"You first, *Cazador*." I smirk and wink.

He grins salaciously while unbuttoning his jeans and slowly pulling down his zipper. His thick cock comes into view. I've never been so happy a man has gone commando in my life. The sight of his straining erection makes me dizzy with desire.

"You look hungry." His voice is low, a rumbling timbre that causes more wetness to flow down south.

I smack my chops. "I could eat."

He chuckles and inhales loudly. It's the only sound I hear in the room besides the low warble of the fan spinning above the bed. With a curl to his lips and a sexy pout, he fists his massive cock.

I moan at the sight, not able to hold back. He's completely hair-free. He's the first man I've ever seen completely smooth. With no hair nestled at the base, his length looks *enorme*. Huge. I want to lick a circle around the base and nip at the skin there until he jerks his hips with need.

"Now you. Show me," he snarls, barely holding back.

With a flick of my fingers I've got both bows at my hips untied and the scrap of satin falls between my legs to the bed below, showing him the small landing strip of hair I keep down *there*. Moisture is building at the apex of my sex, drops of arousal coating my slit as he looks his fill.

"The bra. I've dreamed of that fucking rack for weeks. Present it to me." His words come out almost angry, as if the sheer fact he's had to wait to get to this moment has been a hardship, a torturous experience for him.

I unhook the back of my bra and shrug out of the fabric, tossing it over my shoulder to the floor beyond.

My nipples tighten into eraser-sized nubs of need under his greedy gaze. Eli swallows and stares intently. His eyes seem to caress my skin with every new bit he discovers. For long minutes, I stay perfectly still, the only movement the raging beat of my heart, my chest shifting up and down with each ragged breath, and the effervescent tingle at the core of me.

"You're my dream come to life. I wanted you before I even

knew you. And tonight, I'm going to have you. Over and over again until you beg me to stop."

His cock seems to grow in front of my eyes, and I want nothing more than to wrap my lips around it and suck to my heart's content. But he's faster than me. He lifts a knee to the bed and prowls forward. One hand wraps around my hip and the other around my back as he catapults me to the bed. When I'm prone, he hovers over me, his lips barely touching mine.

"Do you have any idea what you do to a man?"

I shake my head. "Tell me," I whisper against his mouth.

He wraps one of his large hands around my neck in a lover's caress. "From your neck down to each perfect tit." He lifts one and plumps it for good measure, letting his thumb caress the hardened peak. "This body... Jesus Christ, Maria. You're a goddamned vision of the perfect woman. Do you not see what every man sees?"

His words are blunt and forceful. Words I've never heard before under these circumstances. Elijah speaks his mind and nothing but the truth at all times. It's something I appreciate more than flattery. He's honest. Men in my past haven't always been forthcoming. Antonio specifically. That man spent years making me feel less than. Tommy, on the other hand, gave nine months of putting me on a pedestal. And here's Elijah, spitting his desire with a giant erection and hands that tug and pull as if he can't control his need to touch me.

Me. The busted-up, broken girl from the wrong side of the tracks with no real home and a family of friends I've chosen to call my own. I'm nobody special, but in his eyes, I feel like a goddess.

"I'm going to adore you the way you should be adored, and then I'm going to fuck the hell out of you until you pass out."

His words incite the lust within me a hundred times over.

"Please..." I plead, not sure how to make my need any clearer.

Eli's head dips down and he takes a nipple into his mouth. I clasp my hands around his head, letting my fingers slip through the silky layers. It feels so damn good to have his mouth wrapped around my tip. I moan and lift my hips, searching for something on him to rub against. My head spins, a veritable vortex of arousal and need, as he works me into a frenzy.

"More," I groan.

And he responds. *Dios mio,* does he respond. Those lips of his wrap around one tightened peak, and his teeth clamp down until the sparks fly. I cry out with the pleasure and pain ripping through my chest.

"Fuck yes!" I hiss as he nibbles and pricks the sensitive tissue.

Before long, he moves to the other breast and gives it the same blessed torture. Eli is methodical and thorough with each breast. He squeezes each globe, tugs on one tip and then the other until both are white-hot burning points of want. I lift my hips, searching, until Eli finally, blessedly, settles between my open thighs. He rests his hands on either side of my head and kisses me, long, hard, and with intent. His breath comes fast against my neck as he slides down, kissing my ear, my chest, and all around my abdomen until he's nestled between my thighs.

He holds my thighs apart with a firm press of each hand. "Keep your legs open. I want to see all of you," he says breathily, hovering over my sex.

Eli's face is a mask of carnal desire. He presses his nose

right against my slit and inhales. The air around my wet center shifts and flows until a primal grunt passes his lips. He rubs his nose and his lips in a featherlight caress all over my pussy as though coating himself in my essence. It's the hottest thing I've ever seen. I swallow and grip my knees, opening myself farther. His gaze, filled with an unashamed craving, flicks up to mine.

"Good girl," he murmurs against my flesh.

Those two simple words make me preen for him. It's not something I ever imagined I'd want or need from a man, but with Elijah, I want his approval.

Eli takes his thumbs and separates the lips of my sex. He hasn't even touched me with his tongue, and I'm so aroused I fear I'll come at the tiniest touch. With his fingers he flowers open my lower lips. His mouth is only a scant few inches away from my slit. I know I'm insanely wet, not having been this turned on in years.

With nimble thumbs, Eli presses one thumb against my clit and the other against the forbidden rosette I haven't allowed any man to touch since Antonio. I keen loudly, those two points of pressure forcing me to tip my head back in uncontrolled glee. His mouth covers my sex, and my entire body convulses at the blissful sensation.

Eli's tongue dips into my heat and swirls and flutters, reaching deep inside. An orgasm I hadn't prepared for bursts through me. He holds me open, locks his shoulders against my thighs for extra leverage, and eats me like he's starved for it. I clasp both of my hands around his head, fingers threaded into his hair, and ride his face, forcing him to give me more pressure where I want it most. He does, spinning one thumb around my clit and pressing the other deep into my ass. The dual penetration makes me cry out.

"*Si, si, si! Justo ahi.* Right there. *Dios mio!*" I scream as another orgasm builds, threatening to cut me in half with the power behind it.

Eli doesn't stop. Instead, he lifts his weight onto his knees so he's crouched over my pussy, giving him more power to manipulate me into yet another bone-melting experience. It's so much, I try to close my legs against his tireless ministrations, my clit pulsing and throbbing with every twirl of his thumb.

"Don't you dare move! You hold your legs open. I want more of this sweet cunt!" he says through clenched teeth.

"Baby, too much," I gasp.

He lifts his face and his eyes are so dark I no longer see color. "Never enough." He licks his lips graphically. "Need more. So good," he pants, his words coming out staccato and primal like a caveman, before he dips his head once more.

I lock my hands in his hair and hold on for dear life. Right before I go off again, he removes his dexterous thumbs, and I whimper, sighing in relief, but he still doesn't stop. This time he takes it slower, bathing me with long licks of his tongue against every centimeter, dipping inside for slippery kisses.

The man is a god at oral.

Lazily, he drags his tongue around the tight knot of nerves, and I am arching, my abdomen coming off the bed. Splinters of ecstasy ripple through my entire body, my nerve endings on fire, and I realize the man hasn't even fucked me yet. I don't know if I'll be able to handle it when he does.

A softer, gentler orgasm flows through me when Eli alternates between long, slow sucks and a bathing rub down of his tongue against my clit. He licks me through my release until I'm a boneless heap.

Eli lifts my body up the bed so my head is firmly planted

on the pillows. He grabs a couple king-size ones, lifts my hips up, and sets my ass on them, tilting my pelvis up so it's at a better incline. "Now I'm going to make you mine."

"Didn't you just do that?" I mumble in awe.

He grins wickedly, centers his cock right at my entrance, and then stops. He frowns and bites down on his lip. The veins in his forearms stand out, a fine sheen of sweat mists his skin, making the erect disks of his nipples look like tasty butterscotch candies.

I lick my lips and focus on those two sugary spots.

"You on the pill?" he asks, almost angry, his hands shaking against my hips.

I blink a few times in my sated haze, trying to figure out what he asked. Pill? Oh, birth control. "*Si*, of course."

"Good, because the only way I can fully make you mine is to flood your pussy with all of me."

"But uh..." I start to tell him he needs to wear a condom but lose my mind instead. "Go bare. Just do it now!"

He lines up his cock, grips my hips, and slams home.

"*Santo inferno!*" I scream as he slides back out and rams home again.

A cross between an animalistic howl and a groan rips from Eli's lungs, his hands keeping me locked to him.

His dick is long, thick, and so deep in this position I think he may be touching my ribs internally. "*Tan profunda.* So deep," I reiterate in English, shaking my head from left to right, not knowing what to do with the rush of pleasure flowing through me. I've got my eyes closed tight, allowing myself to feel every thick inch, my walls expanding to accommodate his girth, the wet steel of his pelvis grinding against my clit with every jab.

"So goddamned good. I knew it would be. I knew you'd be

the best I ever had. Your body is perfect to fuck."

I open my eyes and watch as he takes me, on his knees, his hands gripping my hips possessively. His gaze alternates between the bouncing of my breasts with each thrust to the area where we're joined. A salacious grin is plastered across his mouth while sweat beads on his forehead. Before long, he moves his hands and opens my lower lips wider. He leans over me and sucks on a nipple while he thrusts home.

Deep. Immersed. Taken.

His cock is reaching places inside me that I didn't know existed. Eli picks up the pace, pounding that velvet steel into me as though he's branding me. My body jolts up the bed with each powerful plunge. I lift my arms and flatten my hands against the headboard so I'm providing resistance against each mighty thrust.

"That's it, Spicy. Unleash her," he rumbles on a moan.

At his goading, I lose it. I wrap my legs around his waist, tilt my hips up even more, and power into each of his brutal thrusts, fucking myself while he fucks me in return. It's everything I want and more—savage, dirty, unexplainable.

"God, yes! Fuck! Give it to me, Maria. Give it to me like you've never given it to anyone before."

On those words of encouragement, I unwrap my legs, catapult off his cock, and turn the tables, pushing him on his back. His erection is coated in my arousal and the sight makes me feral, proud, and insane with lust. Before he knows what happens, I'm on top of him, slamming down over his cock, letting him pierce so deep we both cry out in agonized delight.

He grabs me around the hips, fingers digging in viciously while I wrap both hands around the top of the headboard and bob up and down like an out of control and demented carousel ride. He lifts his massive thighs, forcing our bodies an extra inch closer and presenting a new angle where his cock grates along that hidden patch inside, the one no man has ever reached.

"There you go. That's it. I've got you right where I want you. Now fuck your man," he roars, his lips set in a determined snarl.

Mindless, I take his direction, power into my calves and arms, and pound my hips up and down, taking him to the tippy top and then ramming home.

The sounds coming out of our mouths are violent, passionate, all-consuming.

"I'm so close." I sigh, placing my hands on his chest and rocking my clit at the same time he's pounding me down over him.

He shifts up the bed so his back is now against the headboard and we're face-to-face.

"Get there. Give me all you got," he encourages.

I close my eyes and focus on the heat building between my thighs, the tingles running up and down my spine, and the hair standing on edge all over my body. Everything becomes tight, strained, my focus solely on the space where he's taking me, so high I should fear the fall. But I don't. He'll save me. He's promised he would.

One of his arms locks around my back, grounding me, his hand floating into my hair so we're nose to nose. "Look at me." He groans, his lips barely touching mine with each jerk.

I open my eyes and whimper at the intensity in his gaze, lust so clearly filling his every feature. "I want to see your eyes and kiss your mouth while we come together this first time. You'll never forget who you now belong to."

"Eli..." I whisper, not sure how to commit to a man three

weeks after losing another.

He continues to fuck me, our lips touching, our gazes searing one another with the powerful truth living just beyond this moment.

Both of our bodies start quaking, falling out of perfect sync as our combined orgasms take us over the edge. He holds me so tight I know I'll have bruises all over, and I don't care. These marks will be the proof of a night of passion and intimacy I don't want to soon forget. I expect he, too, will have some of his own war wounds. Eli presses his lips firmly against mine, his breath powering out of his mouth and nose as we kiss. His gaze turns glassy, as I imagine my own does, and then it hits, and it's enormous, gigantic...explosive.

I lock my limbs around his. He grips me excruciatingly tight as our bodies mold into one combustible device, shattering in one another's arms.

I tip my head back and cry out to the heavens. Eli plants his face against my outstretched neck and offers a battle-cry-type howl as the heat of his release scalds me from the inside out. My pussy locks down around him, milking him for every last drop.

Eventually our hips stop moving, and the viselike clamp Eli has on me loosens. His lips trail up my neck and over my shoulders in wet paths and sweet presses against my heated skin. With the tips of his fingers, he caresses my arms, down the moist skin of my back, and along my thighs, hips, and waist. I let him, catching my breath as I'm slumped over his body.

"Like you salty and sweet like this, babe."

I hum and nuzzle into his neck, enjoying the musky scent of sex filtering through the air in the room. The passionate smell is such a calming aphrodisiac, I could sleep for a thousand years and be happy.

For at least twenty minutes I lie across him, boneless, allowing myself to come down from the three orgasms he gave me. I'm spent physically and emotionally.

Eli must understand I need some time because he doesn't push, doesn't ask to talk about what just happened, and more importantly, doesn't joke about it. My emotions and feelings are as raw as an exposed nerve ending. One touch will bring me to my knees in total and complete self-deprecation.

"You thirsty?" Eli eventually asks against my hairline.

I nod, preferring the silence.

"Let me clean you up and get us something to eat and drink. Yeah?"

Again I nod. I'd pretty much agree to anything right now.

He lifts me up off his body and gently places me back on the bed. He pulls the sheet over me and I snuggle into it. Right now, I don't know what to think or how to feel. I just had sex with my dead boyfriend's brother, and it was the best sexual experience of my life. I've never been that open and free. Eli encourages the sexual demon in me to come out and play. It's definitely a side I suspected was there, and I'm curiously interested to experience again.

Eli comes back into the room naked, unashamed of his body—not that he should be. He pulls the sheet back and wipes the mess between my thighs. "Don't want you to have to sleep in the wet spot. I hear girls hate that." He winks.

"I wouldn't know," I mumble.

He tosses the cloth into the hamper near the closet and turns around with his hands on his hips. "Surely a sexual creature like you has experienced a little blowout in the bedroom." He smirks.

I yawn and shake my head. "No. This was my first time without a condom."

Eli frowns and rubs at his scruffy chin. The sound alone reminds me of how good that scruff feels against the tender skin of my inner thigh. My clit throbs and tingles as if it also remembers. I cross my legs, staving off the ridiculous desire that spears into my groin. Jesus, the man had me repeatedly, and I'm already thinking about more.

Apparently, I'm not the only one with those thoughts, because right before my eyes, Eli's sated cock swells and hardens, the bulbous crown stretching into full size.

"You mean to tell me I'm the only man who has taken you bare?" His voice is low, a sexy rumble that speaks of more intense rounds of mind-numbing sex, and soon.

I nod and watch as he licks his lips.

"Antonio?" he asks softly.

I groan and push a hand through the tangles in my knotted hair. "Was obsessed with not getting me pregnant. He didn't want to ruin his career by having a child to watch over. Plus, he liked to say he was protecting his cock from whatever man I was fucking when he wasn't around. As if he was ever not around."

Eli paces from one side of the bed around to the other. He interlaces his fingers behind his neck. His cock bobbing with every step is amusing, so I watch while he wraps his head around this new information.

"Thomas?"

I sit up and tuck the sheet under my arms so it stays in place. "No. I insisted with him."

He furrows his brow. "Why? You were with him for nine months. That's a long time to earn someone's trust."

My hair falls into my face and I play with my fingers in my lap. "I don't know. It's a very personal thing."

He stops at the edge of the bed. "And yet, you let me take you bare."

I glance away, not wanting him to dig into my soul. "Can you let it go?"

He prowls along the bed until I lean back flat on my back with him hovering over me. He tugs the sheet in a flourish until I'm exposed to him in all my naked glory. He locks a knee on either side of my hips and plants one hand by my head, the other he uses to caress my face.

"This changes everything." His words are a benediction.

I giggle and bite at his finger tracing my lips, wanting to play it off as no big deal. "It changes nothing." I smile and bat my eyelashes.

"Oh, I beg to differ. You trusting me like that, giving me your body completely, in a way no man has ever had. Babe, I'm honored."

Just when I think he's going to hunt and peck at me until I spill out all my secrets, he surprises me by taking the fun and flirty route.

"And now I'm going to show you just how much."

"By taking me again?" I lift one brow into a questioning point.

His corresponding smile is so huge I can't help but match it. "Absolutely. I think that trust has earned you another handful of orgasms."

I think about it, arousal coating my sex already. I lift my hands, tunnel them into his dark hair, and bring his mouth close to mine. "You know, I think you're right."

He chuckles. "Greedy girl."

CHAPTER THIRTEEN

Trying to be quiet, I mix up the eggs and pour them into the pan the way Gigi taught me. They start to bubble instantly. Okay, seems to be going good. With a fork, I turn over the bacon. Hmm, not quite done on that side, but when Gigi does it, she flips it a bunch of times. I gaze warily at the eggs doing their thing, willing them to be nice to me, and move to the coffeepot.

I pour the coffee grounds all the way to the top and peer into the little basket. Should be good. I slap it back into place and pour the water into the back. The burner sizzles and starts pouring coffee out before I can put the glass back in place.

"*Mierda, mierda!*" I whisper, shoving the glass carafe thingy under the trickle of scalding hot coffee.

I shove a paper towel under the coffeepot burner to sop up the spill so it doesn't keep burning. Works like a charm. I do a little shaking-my-ass dance and search for the coffee cups.

"Score!" I fist pump.

A set of manly arms encircles me from behind. I grip the mug handles in a firm hold and squeak-scream until I look down and see the tribal tats I spent a lot of time admiring last night. I set the glasses down on the counter and lean back into his warmth.

"What are you doing, Spicy?" Eli rumbles into my ear and

then kisses his way down my neck.

His hands find the hem of his T-shirt that I threw on. He cups both cheeks of my bare *culo*, groaning his pleasure into my neck.

"Mmm, like that, babe. Like you naked and wearing my shirt. But what are you doing?"

I grin and lock my arms around his much bigger ones, leaning into his comfortable weight. "Making you breakfast, *Cazador*," I say proudly.

He turns me around in a flash, slips his hands firmly on my *culo*, and hikes me against his half-naked body. He's wearing a pair of those maddeningly sexy plaid pajama pants. No woman on this earth would think plaid pj's were sexy, but on this man...I want to drop to my knees and remove them to get at what's hidden beneath. Especially now that I know exactly what's waiting for me.

I lock my arms around his neck and lean my forehead against his. "I wanted to do something nice, you know, after *everything*." I nip his earlobe.

He grins and rubs his nose against mine. "After everything, meaning the exceptional fucking including the eleven orgasms I gave you last night."

"Eleven? I remember ten." I pout trying to think back.

"Trust me, babe. There were eleven."

I shrug. "If you say so." I lean forward and slant my lips over his.

Eli does not wait to thrust his tongue inside and immediately explore every crevice. Thank God we both brushed our teeth. He tastes of mint and man, just the way I like him. Though I can't say I don't appreciate his flavor when his tongue is coated in me either. Together, we taste like sex and sin, my absolute favorite.

"So you're making breakfast, huh?" He sniffs the air. "Is that what I smell?" He frowns and moves to the stove.

He turns down the heat on both items and picks up the fork. He turns over a piece of bacon and I'm shocked to see the other side is burnt to a crisp. The entire piece looks like a shriveled husk. Huh. I thought I followed Gigi's directions to a T.

Eli glances over his shoulder at me and then handles the spatula, lifting up the eggs. Again, the entire bottom is pitch black.

"*Que demonios. Yo hice todo bien.*" I pout and cross my arms.

His shoulders and back flutter up and down as he turns off both burners completely. "Babe, you have to watch the eggs and bacon as they cook," he says without a hint of accusation. Thank goodness he was kind in his reply or he'd be missing a limb.

"But look." I point to the eggs. "The top is still yellow and runny. Why is that?"

Eli pulls me close, wrapping his arms around my waist and flattening me against his chest. "I'll teach you how to cook eggs and bacon. It will be okay."

I frown. "Gigi already taught me. She's showed me like a hundred times," I mutter, and try to remember what she did that made them so perfect all the years we lived together.

"Well, when you've put them on the pan, you have to constantly push the eggs around so they get fluffy and the bottom doesn't burn."

I close my eyes and smack my forehead. "*Mierda!* Shit. That's right. She does do that. And the bacon? What's the special trick to that?" I ask, genuinely wanting to know.

The corner of Eli's mouth lifts up. "You have to flip it all the time. Let it rest for maybe thirty seconds and then flip it again."

"What? For each piece? That's insane. It would take forever!" I shake my head. This whole cooking business is far too involved. "You know, I was watching it closely, but then I made coffee." I pull out of his embrace and lean against the opposite counter and cross my arms.

His expression is one of horror. "Babe, please tell me you didn't make coffee." He holds his hands out as if he's placating a child.

I scowl. "I did and it's perfect. See?" I dip my chin toward the coffee pot. I can see the brown liquid is filled to the exact right point. "Have a cup."

He shakes his head. "Nuh-uh. You first." He chuckles, and I want to smack that cute laughter from his sexy face.

"Fine!" I stomp over to the pot and pour my cup to the top with coffee. "Cream, please?"

Eli pulls the milk out of the fridge and hands it to me.

"*Gracias.*" I pour the milk in and am startled to see all these black things popping up to the surface. "What the..." I gasp, not exactly sure what I'm seeing.

Eli glances over my shoulder and then starts laughing. Hard. His laughter goes on and on until he's leaning over at the waist and gripping at his stomach. "You are too damn much, babe." He smacks his knees. "Damn! I haven't laughed that hard in ages."

I tap my foot. "You finished embarrassing me?" I turn, ready to leave his laughing ass. "See if I ever do anything nice for you again, big meanie!" Before I even get a foot out of the kitchen I'm swept up in his arms and lifted to sit on the countertop near the coffeepot. He widens my legs and inserts himself between them. Not wanting to give in, I keep my gaze focused out the window where the ocean waves are smacking the surface of the beach in bursts of white and navy blue.

"I'm sorry. Spicy, I'm sorry. Look at me." His head follows mine where I'm stretching it as far to the left as I can.

I firm my lips into a flat line and shake my head.

He grips my chin with his thumb and forefinger and drags my face to his. He kisses me several times in soft pecks against my lips, until finally I can't stand it and kiss him back. Eli takes his time sucking on my bottom and then top lip, licking them and coaxing me into kissing him madly. When I sigh and lock my legs around his waist and my arms around his neck, wanting more, he pulls back.

"I'm sorry I hurt your feelings. You were doing something nice for me, and I appreciate the thought. But how's about I do the cooking from here on out in this relationship? You're a shit cook, babe. It's just the way it is." He kisses my chin, my nose, and then my lips. "Deal?"

"Will you at least tell me how I screwed up the coffee? I was so sure I got it right." I puff out my bottom lip.

He sucks it into his mouth and then pulls back. With a flick of his wrist he removes the basket thingy I put the coffee in. "No filter. Without the filter, you're drinking coffee grounds."

I slump against his wide chest. "I forgot that part. Maybe I'll make a note. I should be able to make coffee for myself."

"Why, when you've got your man to do it for you?" He winks.

"Cute. But you're not going to be around all the time now, are you?" I put words to something we've nowhere near gotten close to discussing. We barely took the next step physically to whatever it is we're doing. I don't know if it's even going anywhere or whether or not I want it to.

I want it to. Don't I? I shouldn't. Fuck. I'm so confused.

Eli must see the unspoken freak-out session on my face because his response his perfect. "Babe, we've had one sensational night together. Stop fretting. Let's enjoy it for now. We have a long time to figure all of this out."

My mind works a hundred miles a minute, spitting out an argument. "But it won't matter because once you've gotten Antonio out of the picture, you'll be off to your next big hunt, right, *Cazador*?" I remind him about his position as a bounty hunter.

He sighs and tugs my center directly against his warm waist. Instantly, my lower half pays attention, and a bolt of lust zips down to land right at my clit. It throbs and aches, readying for the next round of smokin' hot sex with the world's most sinful man. Only right now, said man is looking at me as if I'd spoken in tongues.

Eli threads a hand through my hair, the other wrapping around my hips so he can grind his now-rigid erection against my pussy.

"Babe, you think if I have a hot piece like you warming my bed, burning my breakfast, looking like a sex goddess in my T-shirts, I'm going to want to leave all that often? No way. Not when I've got this to sink my dick in." He thrusts his hips against my crotch. "Or this succulent mouth to quarrel with and kiss." He covers my lips in a bruising, wet tangle of tongues before pulling back with an audible *plop*. "I've got plenty of men on my team to take most of the burden. Men who want more responsibility. Single men. Me, I'm thirty-one. I'd be much happier at home if I had you clipping my wings."

I close my eyes and shiver, his words sinking deep into the hidden recesses of my soul. How can I feel so much for Eli so fast? Why is this happening now, and not a year from now when it would be more acceptable?

"Eli, I don't know what to say," I whisper and pull him into a hug.

"Don't say anything." He runs his big paws up and down my back in a soothing, rhythmic gesture that lulls me into submission. "Right now, all you have to do is live in the moment. Enjoy what we're building on."

I swallow down the fear and nod. "Okay."

"With that in mind, I'm gonna enjoy this sweet cunt of mine for breakfast, and then I'm going to fuck you in the shower, and then I'll take you out to eat. Yeah? You with me?"

"You do not hold back." I push my hair behind me.

Eli grips me to him so that I lock my legs around him where he can lift me into his arms. "No, babe, I hold on."

★ ★ ★

"Jesus Christ, yes, just like that." Eli's head falls back against the tile as I swallow his long cock down my throat.

After he shattered my mind with his mouth, I decided to shower him with my own sexual tricks. One being how much I love sucking dick.

"I love your *polla, Cazador*. So thick, long, and mmm..." I allow my words to get cut off by him shoving his cock deep. I take it all the way back to my throat and hum around the fat head.

"Maria, babe, your mouth. Can't get enough. Shit." He

groans and fists one hand in my hair while he starts to thrust.

I love this part. When they start to lose all control and act like primal cavemen focused solely on coming.

I pull back to encourage him. "Fuck my face. Hard. You know you want to. I can take it," I say, using my sex-laced rumble before going back to working him over.

"Perfect." *Thrust.* "Fucking." *Thrust.* "Woman." *Thrust.* "And." *Thrust.* "All." *Thrust.* "Mine."

Eli's body starts to tremble. The hand not maneuvering my face is locked in a tight fist. I pull back, forcing him to let go of my hair.

"What are you doing? Get back on my cock." His words forceful, need controlling every syllable.

I grip his length in one hand and jack it a few times. "Trust me to make you feel everything, *Cazador.* Let me play." I'm in full seductress mode, planning to rock his world.

"God, your hands are almost as good as your mouth."

I grin. "Oh yeah. What about these?" I push his knees out farther apart where he's sitting on the bench seat in the shower. After soaping up my boobs, I press both of them around his slippery cock.

His eyes glaze over and hit that dark forest green that makes my pussy weep. Knowing I'm taking this hulk of man down to his knees, to a carnal place that only sees me, is overwhelming with its beauty and power. Eli thrusts his hips up and down so his length pops through my breasts, playing a sexy game of peekaboo with his luscious cock.

Once the soap washes away under the shower spray, I tip my head down and lick the crown every time it appears.

He hisses and groans through a few more strokes. Once he gets close to coming and the head looks like an angry top ready to explode, I push him back at the pelvis, wrap my lips around his length, and take him down my throat.

"Holy shit, fuck!" His entire body tightens and convulses.

I don't stop sucking and swallowing until I taste the first burst of saltiness hit my tongue.

"Babe, babe, babe," he chants mindlessly.

I squeeze the root of his penis with one hand and fondle his balls with the other while I slip my mouth off for long enough to say the words I know he wants to hear before he lets go.

"Give me all you got. I'll swallow it all," I say around a grin and take him in again.

"Perfect woman. Damn you. Damn you." He thrusts up at the same time I suck him down. He cries out. "Ahhhh, yesssss!" As spurt after spurt of his slick release slides down my throat, I swallow furiously and lick at the sensitive underside near the crown before swirling my tongue and lips around the tip as he slowly softens.

Before I even have a chance to stand, he's pulled me up, lifted a leg until my foot rests on his thigh, and his tongue is piercing my slit. "Sweet *madre*!" I call out and brace both hands against the tile walls. He tongues me deep, the angle providing easy access. Without warning he plunges two fingers in and locks his mouth around my clit.

His fingers delve deep, finding that spot he'd found before and manipulating it until I'm shaking and coming against his lips.

"That's right. Give me that sweet cream. Never get enough." He moans and licks deep, spreading me open like a flower with his thumbs so he can get his entire mouth around me.

The shower water has turned cold, battering against my back as I convulse, holding his head between my thighs and riding his face like I'll never get another chance. Though I know I will. Now that I've gotten a taste of him, felt his passion, I'm powerless to stop this train of devastation. All I can hope is we don't destroy one another or anyone else in the process.

Once he's brought me off another two times to his one, which seems wildly unfair, he lifts me up, wraps me in a towel, and sets me on the vanity. He turns off the water and grabs a towel of his own.

"You're going to fuck me stupid." I'm trying to get my faculties back and failing.

He grins wickedly. "You'll get used to it. I'm a healthy man who likes to fuck...a lot."

"Doesn't every man?" My words drip with sarcasm.

He comes over to me and wedges himself between my thighs. He removes his towel, proving his insane virility.

"*Dios mio.* You're hard again?" I ask as he undoes my towel. I'm in such shock I don't realize he's opening my thighs and centering himself against my core.

I blink, and he's inside me. My swollen walls throb and clamp at the invasion, but I still want him. I think I always will. He's such a perfect match to the sexual creature I've only ever let out with him.

He grips my ass and hauls me against him, plummeting deep in my tight channel. I moan and drop my head back against the mirror. He controls my lower half with precision and speed, ramping me up to a thousand in only a few well-placed strokes.

"Never doubt how much I want you, Maria. *Never,*" he says through clenched teeth. His jaw is firm, his eyes laser-focused on mine as he speaks. "I'll always be ready to fuck you. I'm addicted to this sweet cunt. The taste, the feel of your viselike hold, and the way it sends me through the goddamned roof when you come." He groans and power-dives into me in hard, punishing jabs that hit all the right places. "I'll never, ever, pass up an opportunity to accept what you've given me."

My mind is a gooey ball of mush as he grinds into me, crushing my clit with exact accuracy on every thrust. He knows how to make me a mindless heap and uses it to his advantage. Every nerve is tingling, my pores are singing, and I'm lost to sexual nirvana. Nothing can hurt me here—only happiness, pleasure, and unending joy lives in this place.

"Love me, Eli. Show me what your love looks like," I murmur while a euphoric light smooths over my body, taking me away.

* * *

I come to with Eli breathing heavily between my breasts and my entire body locked around his. My head is pounding and my legs are jelly. I run my fingers through the wet strands of his hair.

"Okay, so this time, fucking you made *me* stupid." He laughs against my breasts.

"Yeah, well, I blacked out." I sigh and straighten my legs, letting them fall to the sides of us.

He lifts his head enough so I can see his appreciative, sexy grin before he licks and kisses each nipple. On cue, they both pucker up for more attention.

Jesus, I'm a sex-starved ho.

He swirls his tongue around one tip. "I'll play with you

later," he promises the one before licking and sucking the second. "You, too."

I snicker and push at him. "*Suficiente, Cazador.* Enough. I'm closing up shop. No more. I need food, ibuprofen, coffee, and some time away from your *polla.*"

He pouts and backs up and looks down at his dick. "Don't worry, man. She didn't mean it," he offers to his cock.

I shake my head and slip off the counter and head back into the shower. Eli turns to come in. I place a hand on his chest. "You remember what happened the last time we tried to shower together a half hour ago?"

He bites down on his bottom lip, his eyes twinkling with mirth. "I'll never forget."

"Exactly. Use the other bathroom, please, and we'll meet in the middle."

"What? You don't trust me not to jump you?" He grins and glances down my naked body and back up. Again, his dick starts to harden.

I shake my head. "No. I don't trust me."

He chuckles and backs away with his hands up. "Fine, fine. How's pizza sound?"

I close the shower door and get under the spray. "For breakfast?"

"Babe, it's almost noon now. We've been fucking all morning."

"*Mierda.* Time flies when you're on your back." I sigh, sated.

"Or the chair, or against the sliding glass door, or the balcony, or the shower, or the vanity..." he says, reminding me of all the places he took me last night and this morning.

"*Cállate!*" I groan and drop my head. I wait a few moments

while Eli leaves the bathroom, and then I hear the water start to run in the other room. Shame builds in my heart and spreads out through my veins as the realization of what I've done truly hits. Tears fill my eyes and fall down, hidden within the sheet of water rushing over me.

How am I ever going to look at myself in the mirror again?

I spent an entire evening and half a day having filthy, dirty, wild, uninhibited sex with Elijah Redding. The brother of the man who gave his life to protect my best friend and me from a murdering stalker. I'm definitely going to hell. The sobs release, and I cover my mouth.

The little devil on my shoulder sends a thought barreling through my head. *Then again, if I'm already going, why not go out with just-fucked hair and a dozen orgasms?*

Good Lord, I'm so messed up.

Yep, definitely going to hell.

CHAPTER FOURTEEN

The shower did little to calm my beating heart or the bucketload of shame that suddenly towers over last night and this morning's experiences with Eli. I'm certain he'd disagree with every single doubt that riddled my mind, because Eli isn't the type of man to make decisions willy-nilly. Actually, for the past weeks he's been consistent and transparent in his desire to be with me. Completely and unapologetically. He'd even gone so far as to suggest there would be more than just the physical aspect to a relationship with me. Not that I dare to believe or even agree with him.

I wish I could turn off my mind and live in the moment. Only, I know life is compiled of single individual moments that shape and change who a person is and how they walk through life.

Flash. Antonio beating me, breaking my legs, and trying to drown me until the light goes out.

Flash. Locking hands with Gillian in the woman's shelter, both of us battered and bruised, cementing what would become a lifelong friendship.

Flash. Meeting Kathleen in my first show in the San Francisco Dance Company.

Flash. Taking Bree's first yoga class, connecting with her and with my body in a new way through her words.

Flash. Seeing the lifeless body of a woman I thought was my soul sister, and the sheer relief when I found out it wasn't.

Flash. Learning of Gillian being kidnapped on her wedding day, thinking I'd lost her forever.

Flash. Hearing of Tommy's death.

Flash. Eli moving over my body, inside me, the bliss of the orgasm that poured through every vein in white-hot, euphoric blasts as I lost myself to him.

My cell phone buzzing like crazy in my purse breaks me out of my wayward thoughts. I don't remember having one since Eli took my other phone. Guess he replaced it. This one has a bright red case that's totally my style but not something I bought myself. I glance down at the display and am surprised to see my soul sister's name appear as I'd typed it in my other phone. Sneaky *Cazador.* I wonder what Antonio texted before Eli switched out my phone.

The phone blares again, and I see...

Yoga Hottie

I click the accept button and put it to my ear. "*Hola, preggo*," I say with fake enthusiasm.

"*Hola* my big white pregnant ass!" Bree's tone is vehement. "How dare you make us worry? Make me lose what little precious sleep your giant niece I'm carrying around deems to give me. No call, no text, radio silence."

"Bree—"

"Oh, hell no. I've got this baby using my bladder as a punching bag, and a five-year-old flying around the house as though the world is made up of rainbows and unicorns. My best friend's house gets broken into, and she's whisked away by some dude and disappears with no word. Do you know how hard it is to sleep when you have a watermelon sitting on your gut and worry in your soul? Do you?" she screeches.

I pull the phone away from my ear as Eli enters the bedroom. "You okay?" he asks.

"I'm fine. Thank you. Just need a minute."

"A minute! You're going to give me a minute! Have you not been paying attention, Ria? I'm losing my mind over here! Ouch!" She moans in pain.

"Bree? Bree, are you okay? What happened, *chica*?" Worry rushes over me, my protectiveness over my soul sisters, the only family I have, coming straight to the surface, lightning fast.

"Your niece decided punching wasn't fun anymore and took up kick-boxing against my ribs!" She bites through the connection. "God, I hate being pregnant!" she groans.

I fall back on the bed in a heap and wave off Eli, who has been standing guard, waiting patiently for me to give the all clear signal.

"I'm sorry, *chica*. Really, I didn't mean to stress you out."

She groans. "No, I'm sorry. I shouldn't give you a load of shit when you're already dealing with so much. This baby makes the demon bitch in me come out. Forgive me?" she asks in her normal sweet tone.

There's my girl. "Of course. And I'm fine." I sigh heavily, the weight of my current problem like a ton of bricks on my chest.

"You don't sound fine. Gigi says Chase is not only having your place cleaned, but they're also salvaging everything and moving you into a new apartment across the street."

Great. Another move. Just when I was getting used to having my own place. I push the shorter layers of my hair to the side and off my forehead. "He didn't need to do that."

"Seeing as his wife lost it when she saw what happened to your pad..."

I sit up straight as a board. "How the hell did she see it?"

"Girl, you know Gigi does what she wants when she wants to do it." She laughs. "Apparently, Chase was on the phone discussing something with Jack and Austin, and she slipped out of the house. Took her spare key and walked herself right over to your apartment."

"*Dios mio.* If she saw how bad it was..." She is going to lose it. One thing none of us handles well is a threat to a sister.

"Yeah, let's just say Gigi demanded you move right into their house, but Chase told her you would never agree to it. So they came to an understanding, which was to move you to a new apartment altogether and hire better security."

A twinge of pain prods at my temples. I rub my thumb and forefinger into the new ache. "*Mierda.* Glad I wasn't there to witness that showdown."

Bree giggles. "Never mess with a preggo intent on protecting her family. We can be brutal. Remember, Ria, Gigi only has us, too."

I don't have to remember. My entire life is wrapped up in my three soul sisters. "I know." My voice trails off, and I blow out a long breath.

"What else is going on?" Bree's hint of encouragement is all I need to offload my current dilemma.

I glance at the doorway, making sure he's not listening in. "I slept with Elijah last night."

A dead silence greets my admission.

"Bree? *Chica?*"

"Uh, I'm here. Just...a little taken aback. Who's Elijah?"

I frown. "Phil didn't tell you?"

"No. He told me you were being protected by a bounty hunter."

I suck in a huge breath and let it out again. "Yeah, that's true. But he, uh, is more than that."

"Okay. So, you relieved some sexual frustration. You've always been our resident nympho. I'm not surprised you had sex with a hot bounty hunter. Feel free to share all the sexy details. My libido is insane right now. Poor Phil can barely keep up. I want him day and night."

I groan and flop back on the bed.

"Was it any good?"

"So good. Ugh, the best I've had."

"No way? Hard to believe. You've had a lot of sex." She doesn't sound convinced.

"Are you calling me a *puta*?"

She laughs again, and the mere sound sends butterflies of joy to my heart. "Not exactly. I'd say...experienced?"

"And you aren't?" I shoot back.

"Touché! But, we're not talking about me. We're talking about you and your freak-nasty self."

"Freak-nasty!" I laugh, feeling so good I want to hold on to this moment forever.

"Ah, there's that happiness I like to hear. Now can you get to the part about why you're upset about sleeping with him? Is it Tommy?"

Tommy. It always comes back to Tommy.

"*Si,*" I admit softly.

"Oh, babe, you feel like you betrayed him, huh?"

Jesucristo, she hits the nail on the head and hammers it home right away.

"You can't think like that. Tommy would want you to live your life. You weren't celibate before him. I mean, am I a little surprised you had sex so soon? Maybe. But didn't you say it had been a while before he died?"

"A month."

"Fuck me running! A month. Were you guys having problems? I'm big, fat, and pregnant, and Phil and I still fuck like rabbits!"

"Ugggh, it's complicated. He was busy with work. I was doing rehearsals late every night. Then Gigi. Then the fire."

"Uh-huh, okay. I guess I understand, but that doesn't sound like you. Not that it matters, but honey, he's been gone for—what—a few weeks now? Add a month on top of that and you've been celibate for longer than I've ever known you to be."

I *am* the resident sex fiend in the group. Before all this, I owned my sexuality and never felt guilty for my choices.

"There's more you're not telling me about this dude, isn't there? I can feel it in my heart."

Bree has a weird sixth sense about her friends. I blame it on her yoga training and practice. That Eastern stuff gets you super close to your inner self and those around you.

I close my eyes. "Maybe."

"If you don't let it out, it's going to eat you alive. If you can't tell one of your best friends, who can you tell?"

"Elijah is Tommy's twin brother." I swallow and wait for the fire and brimstone to rain down from the sky, through the phone, in a sudden shaking of the earth, but nothing happens. "Bree?"

I wait. And wait.

"Bree! Are you there?"

"I'm here," she says in a strained tone. "I'm just trying to wrap my mind around..." *Giggle.*

Oh no. She is not...

A huge bout of laughter fills the phone and hurts my ear. "Oh my God, Maria, I'm going to pee my pants. Only you. Only you would hook up with your boyfriend's twin brother." She guffaws loud and long. "I mean, do they look exactly the same?"

"Kind of. I mean, they are identical."

"Identical!" she screams, and her laughter takes her to the piggy-snort place where she starts coughing.

"This. Is. Not. Funny." My voice is strained, ready to go off.

"Oh yes it is! Think about it, Ria. Only you could bang the identical brother"—she is breathing heavily—"this is made-for-TV movie shit. Seriously, I can't even."

"You are not helping."

Eventually her laughter subsides. "I know, I know. But, honey, it's really wild."

"Now that's the truth. But I don't know what to do."

Finally she calms down, her voice softening to the tone she uses when she speaks to her yoga clientele. "Honey, do you like this Elijah?"

More flashes of last night filter through my mind. Him kissing me, taking me to new heights, our long chats, the shower, sleeping wrapped in his arms. The safety I feel when I'm with him.

"Yeah."

"Then what's the problem?"

"You don't think it's weird or wrong?" I need to hear what she thinks.

"A little weird, definitely not wrong. But honey, Tommy's

gone, and by the sounds of it, there was already a bit of strain happening between you two."

"Maybe *un poco*." Again, I blow out a long breath, not knowing what to do. "I just feel like I'm shaming him and his memory."

"Oh no, Ria. Not even close. When we lose someone close to us, we grieve in our own way, but we have to move on. We have to live."

She has a point, but I'm not sure I'm not just hanging on to any thread of hope that will make this ache in my chest go away. "But do most do it so soon?"

"Do you miss Tommy?"

"Every day," I say instantly.

"Do you wish he was still here?"

"*Si*. So much."

"Will you honor his memory by living life to the fullest, accepting the sacrifice he made for you and Gigi?"

"*Dios mio*, of course. *Si!*"

"Then you've got your answer. Live your life to the best of your ability. Remember him and his sacrifice. Who you choose to lie down with at night, or who you let into your day-to-day life from here on out has absolutely nothing to do with honoring Tommy. That's private and personal between you and him."

When did she become so deep? Bree has always been the universal lover of all things in our group. She can bring a profound light to any darkness plaguing a person.

Honor his sacrifice. Now that I can do.

"*Gracias. Te amo mi amiga*."

"I love you, too. And hey, if you can find some joy in all this chaos, I say, live it up!"

This time I laugh. "Live it up. I'll try."

"Call soon. I need my sleep."

"Take care of you, the girls, and Phil, okay? I'll be in touch. *Besos.*"

"*Besos.*"

★ ★ ★

We sit down on a concrete ledge with two huge slices of pizza on a pair of flimsy plates. My mouth waters at the fresh tomatoes, black olives, and cheese.

"Pizza My Heart is the best around," Eli says proudly, and then eats half a slice in one go. Jeez, he can eat.

I take a giant bite and let the Romano cheese tease my tongue with its sharp flavor. I close my eyes while finishing my first bite. He is *not wrong*. "This pizza rocks!" I take a tomato off the top and plop it into my mouth.

"I love the way you eat, as if every meal is the best you've ever had." He smiles, his eyes a brilliant green with the sun bounding off them.

Once I've swallowed, I nod. "Growing up, food was scarce. As an adult, I enjoy every meal to the fullest. I guess it's because back then I didn't know when I'd have another."

Eli scowls. "Was your upbringing that bad?"

I shrug. "Lots of people have it bad. I try not to focus on the past. Living in the past means you miss out on the present. Every day is a gift, right? I think between the two of us, we've recently learned that the hard way."

He frowns. "Yeah, that's the truth."

For some reason, I choose to tell him more, share more than I usually share with a man. "I grew up in foster care in

Oakland after my drug addict parents both overdosed on some bad heroin. Sharing is caring, right?" I smile, but it falls flat when Eli's own smile falls.

"Anyway, I bounced around a bit in foster care after my grandmother died before being put into a girls' home. The other girls were mean, thieves, and didn't like anyone who hadn't been there as long as them. So I stayed away mostly, danced at the free centers the city put on. Made my way to the top of the dancers. Then, when I turned eighteen, I no longer had a home. Lived on the streets for a few weeks until I scored the audition that changed my life."

"In more ways than one," he remarks flatly.

I take another bite, chew, and then wash it away with a long drink of water. "There's good and evil to all things. Yin and yang. My friend Bree taught me that."

"Bree's the one you were talking to on the phone earlier?"

I nod. "Yeah, she's with Phil, my friend you met last night. Hugely pregnant and *muy mal humor* about it. Grumpy," I add, even though he seems to understand everything I say in Spanish.

"You were on the phone with her a long time. Before that, in the shower... Uh, I heard you crying in there. It took everything in me to give you the space you needed." His nostrils flare, and he looks down.

My shoulders fall as if they have a mind of their own. "This situation." I gesture between the two of us. "It's strange. I mean, I was just in a relationship with your brother."

"True. And?" He encourages me to continue talking. Apparently he wants to hash this out now.

I take a quick breath and find the energy within me to let it out. Eli covers my hand with his, a comforting gesture that instantly fills me with strength and a sense of love and compassion.

"You can always be honest with me. As a matter of fact, I demand it. No lies or half-truths between us."

I swallow and nod. "Last night was beyond amazing, *fantástico*, better than I would have thought possible. I was open and free with you in a way I didn't know I could be with a man. It was..."

"Refreshing, mind-bending, erotic, and addicting."

"*Si*, all of that." I smile. "But..."

"But you're worried about what people will think?" His tone is low, his gaze filled with understanding.

I shrug. "Sometimes it's that. Other times, it's Tommy."

"Tommy's dead," Eli says with finality.

Tears prick against my eyes. "Yes, but he was the man I was going to be with, maybe forever," I whisper.

Eli shakes his head. "No. I can't believe that. Not after what we had last night, this morning."

"That's physical. Just sex."

His eyes narrow into burning points of anger. "Don't lie to me. You felt the shift between us. What we have together between the sheets and out is far more than just sex." He stands up, crumbles his plate in half, and tosses it in the garbage can near us.

"Eli, please don't be mad. I'm trying to be honest." I set my unfinished meal to the side and look out over the beach and ocean beyond. The waves crash in angry slaps against the sand, mimicking the raging storm brewing in my head.

My side warms as he sits next to me on the bench, facing the opposite direction so we're facing each other. I close my eyes, relishing his presence—his real-life presence. One of his hands curls around the nape of my neck. He grips the roots of my hair and turns my head to face him.

"I'll never be mad when you're honest with me. Frustrated, irritated, uncertain, yeah. But never angry. You are entitled to how you feel, but Spicy, it's my job to obliterate those feelings and show you reality."

"Which is?" I'm no longer sure what's up and down.

"Thomas was never going to be your forever, babe. At some point down the road, we would have met and the sparks would fly. No matter when in time I laid my eyes on this face, this body, heard you speak to me with your sharp tongue and your cute bursts of Spanish mixed in with English, would I have ever not moved heaven and earth to make you mine?"

My heart beats hard in my chest, and the truth in his green eyes makes my stomach flutter. The need to kiss him and seal this moment is all-consuming. From the tips of my tingling fingers to the prick of pain at the roots of my hair where he hasn't let me go, I'm connected to this man.

"Babe, it was only a matter of time before our souls met, and that would be it."

"It?" I whisper, moving my head closer to his, licking my lips, preparing for his kiss.

"Life."

I close my eyes and rub my lips against his. He returns my soft kiss with one of his own. "And why life?" I ask against the moisture of his beautiful mouth.

"Because if we're not together, we're not truly living. We're just going through the motions."

"I give you life?" I gasp and pull back the couple inches he'll allow until our gazes meet.

"Look at me." Eli's words are fierce, territorial, his clutch on my hair tight and unyielding.

"I am." I set my hand against his cheek.

"Do you see it?"

"See what?"

"Our lives reflecting back at you. Yours, mine, the family we'll make. It's inevitable." His words pierce my heart and burrow straight into my soul.

I caress his face and focus on his strong brow, the small creases at the corners of his eyes, the straight nose, the strong, proud chin and his smooth, kissable lips. There's a tiny scar on the bottom one that's hidden when he smiles. I learn forward and kiss the flaw, knowing the tiny imperfection makes this man more perfect. Special. Mine.

Tears fill my eyes as I lock my gaze with his. How can this be happening? Falling hard and fast for a man I barely know, but feel like I've known my entire life?

Eli holds me close, flattens his chest to mine, and forces me to focus on him. Only him. As though I could tear my eyes away.

"It was always going to be me, Maria. Tommy brought us together, but it was me you were meant for."

On shaky breath, I see the truth swarming around our little huddle as if the entire beach slips away, and visions of the two of us slam against the recesses of my mind. Visions of Eli and me tumbling in bed together, eating dinner, seeing movies, hanging out with friends, getting married, having a child, growing old together. A whole lifetime of...living.

"I see it, Eli. Life. My life with you...and *Dios mio*, it's beautiful." My words are a prayer against his lips.

He grins and kisses me as if the world could end any moment. Every swipe of his tongue is a pledge. Every growl, a promise. And each gasp, a commitment—one I would spend the rest of my life cherishing. Whatever else comes, we'll figure out, together.

CHAPTER FIFTEEN

Elijah walked with me hand-in-hand through Capitola. The sun kissed our skin, and the worries about Antonio, our relationship, and everything in between fell away while we lived in the moment. Every second, just letting ourselves be present.

He took me to dinner at a somewhat fancy place called Shadowbrook in Santa Cruz. We were totally underdressed in jeans, but Eli didn't care. He pulled out my chair, ordered a fancy bottle of wine, and we drank and ate forty-dollar steaks until we had our fill. When we were done, he hustled me to the beach house where we stripped our clothes, shed our misgivings, and fucked on the sand as the waves tickled our naked skin.

Sure, we got sand in places no one would ever want to have sand, but after we showered, we hit the hot tub where he gave me the best shoulder massage known to man.

It was the best day of my life. Every chance he got, he kissed me, showed his affection, and for the first time in years, I allowed the public displays. I was proud to be on his arm, and he felt the same about me.

After the intense discussion we'd had earlier in the day, it was as though we'd come to an understanding. We were going to be together—whatever that means. We'd allow it to grow and change as we did. Of course, there is still the issue of his parents, but he promised me he'd handle it, even though I offered to go with him to their house to explain. He said it was on him, especially since he'd been outside of the normal family day-to-day.

I asked him why he'd kept his distance, and instead of answering, he distracted me with his body and his hard cock. I'm a sucker for a pretty, ready, and willing dick, but I planned to go back to the question, and soon. If this—whatever it is— was going to work between us, we would have to open the closet doors and let all the skeletons blow in the breeze.

Which brings me to now, us heading back to San Francisco. Apparently, his IT kid, Scooter, who I found out had graduated from high school this past June, has some information for us. Plus, Gigi has texted me a million times. Until she can see me live in the flesh, she's not going to stop.

"You never told me what the last text said." I split the comfortable silence and imply what I've been wondering since the new phone showed up.

Eli frowns and rubs at his chin. "Does it matter? It wasn't pretty. That's all you need to know."

I cringe. "*Cazador*, I need to be kept in the loop. Remember, no secrets. That's your rule, in fact."

He locks his jaw, and a tiny muscle in his unshaven cheek tics. Reminds me of Chase. He always has that muscle tic. Maybe it's Gigi that brings it to life? I'll have to compare notes with my girl.

Eli inhales loudly and exhales out his mouth. "The text said, *'Mi reina, I will get you. I will pull you under and you'll never see the light again.'* Happy?" Eli adds roughly, the tone tinged with disgust.

I push back the flashback of being held underwater that wants so badly to rush to the surface. Instead, I grip Eli's hand and breathe through it. Without thinking, I make him promise me something I should never, ever make him promise.

"Promise me you won't let him get me," I say, the fear reflected in every word.

He lifts my hand to his lips and kisses each finger and then the center of my palm. "I promise. You are mine now. Not his queen. You're my fucking woman. Period." Disgust laces each syllable. "I take care of what's mine."

I nod, unbuckle my seat belt, and scooch against his side, needing the close proximity to his warmth and bulk. I pull his arm up and hold it between my breasts, his fingers at my lips.

"Thank you." I kiss each of his fingers and set my chin on his knuckles, praying nothing will happen to this man because of me. Not another man I care so deeply about.

"For what?"

"It would take all day to list the reasons I'm thankful right now."

Eli moves his arm out of my grip, places it around my shoulders, and kisses my temple. "Rest, babe. We'll be home before you know it."

Home.

I don't have a home anymore. Did I ever really? The only time I felt at peace was when I lived with Gillian. We were two peas in a pod. For years, that relationship was all I had. Now, I've got all three girls and their extended families through Chase and Phillip. And, of course, the Reddings. I still have no idea how Eli and Tommy's mother and father are going to take this shift. I close my eyes and force myself to repeat the Lord's

Prayer over and over until I fall asleep against Eli's side.

"This too shall pass, mi niña hermosa."

The phrase is the first thing I can remember of my childhood that didn't give me nightmares. My mother whispering those words against my head as she ran her fingers through my hair is something I hear when I need comforting.

This too shall pass...

★ ★ ★

When we enter Eli's San Francisco home, I'm bum-rushed by a speeding redhead.

"Oh my God, Ria! I was so worried." Gigi catapults into my arms and sobs dramatically into my neck.

I hold my girl tightly. *"Cara bonita,* I'm fine. I am fine!" I repeat until her sobbing subsides.

Chase is standing behind us, a soft smile on his lips.

"Sorry, Maria. She wouldn't wait until you guys were home. A Mr. Scooter let us in with approval from the big guy there." Chase tips his chin to Eli behind me.

Gigi eventually stops crying. "You scared the hell out of me. Your apartment..." She holds up a hand to her chest. "Those words." Her lips compress into a line. A determined look comes over her face, and she stiffens her spine. "Between Chase and Elijah, there is no way we're letting Antonio get anywhere near you."

I smile, more for her benefit, but appreciate with my whole heart the fervor and grit with which she is speaking.

In order to make a point of how our relationship has progressed since I've been gone, I plaster myself to Eli's side and wrap an arm around his waist. "Eli's got me. Right,

Cazador?" I glance up, beaming.

In front of my best friend and her husband, he dips his head down and takes my lips in a short but telling kiss.

"Oh! Well, yeah...huh...okay then," Gigi stammers.

"Mr. Redding, I understand your colleague upstairs has some information he wants to share with us." Chase gestures to the second floor, and then turns to Jack and Austin. "Austin, please stay close to the women."

"Yes, sir," he says, his southern drawl prevalent in every vowel.

As Eli heads toward the stairs, I grip his wrist. "No secrets. Whatever Scooter has to say can be said in front of me."

"Spicy..." He attempts to placate me.

He definitely has some things to learn about me, but I've got years to ingrain the nuances of my temper.

"I'm guessing you don't want me to show you my spicy temper right now, then?" I bat my eyes rapidly, showing I'm not in the mood for this macho *mierda*.

Eli's gaze sears mine with intention and passion. He clenches his jaw and grinds his teeth from side to side. I know he doesn't like it, but he also knows I'm right. I wait patiently for him to come to the only conclusion that will not get him a kick to the shin and a cold bed tonight.

He licks his lips and grins before wrapping an arm around my shoulders. "She's right. The best way to keep her safe is to keep her vigilant. Come on, ladies."

As we're walking up the stairs I nudge his side. "You're so getting laid tonight," I whisper, so only he can hear.

"Like there was ever a doubt. You want my cock just as much as I want to stick it in you."

I pretend to be thinking about it while we make our way

up. "*Cierto.*" True, I admit under my breath.

He chuckles softly and leads us into the Batcave command center.

A pimply-faced kid with messy curly hair and a pair of Clark Kent-style glasses turns around as though he's a god in the high-back chair made to fit Elijah's two-hundred-and-forty-pound bulk. This kid is at best a buck forty sopping wet. He grins when he sees the crowd of people. Then his lips flatten when he looks at the imposing stances of Austin, Jack, and Chase, all of whom are wearing black suits.

"What's up with the men in black?" He hooks a thumb toward the men but looks to Eli.

I bite my lip so hard a drop of blood hits my tongue.

Do not laugh. Do not laugh. These people are here to help you.

"Friends of ours."

Scooter crosses his spindly arms. "I need more info than that, Red. I'm not going down for your new girlfriend."

Eli glowers at his young employee before turning around. He points to Chase first. "Billionaire Chase Davis, husband to Maria's best friend Gillian."

Gigi waves. "Nice to meet you, uh, Scooter."

Then he points to Jack. "Jack Porter, ex-military, bodyguard to Mr. Davis. Austin Campbell, ex-military, bodyguard to Mrs. Davis."

"Why do you two need a bodyguard apiece? To guard all your billions?" The kid's attempt at humor falls flat in a room filled with testosterone-driven alpha males.

By this point, Eli's lost it. He roars, "Get to the goddamned information, Scooter!"

The kid fumbles, pushes his glasses up his nose, and spins

around to face the wall of monitors. "Okay, so I've been looking into Antonio's alibi. Since you seem certain it's him, I've been trying to find a way to prove he was, in fact, there."

He points to monitor number one. "I've tapped into the street cams from the Department of Transportation. There you see the guy in a uniform wearing a hat."

I squint to get a closer look, but it definitely looks like Antonio with a bit more bulk than a dancer's body usually has and a tad longer hair.

"He enters the building from the side stairwell. Someone lets him in. All I can see is an arm holding the door open. That means the security team or someone who works in that building is helping our suspect," Scooter adds.

I glance over at Chase. His lips go into a flat line, and that jaw tic thing pops up. His nostrils flare as he inhales loudly, his eyes focused on the monitor. Gillian grasps Chase's hand, giving her own form of silent support. "I want the traitor found. I promise the tenants in my building a safe and secure environment, and they pay for the extra security. Jack..."

"I'll handle it after this meeting," he says with absolutely zero emotion. I wonder if he even has a heart.

"But that's not all." Scooter's voice is chipper, as if he's recently eaten a king-size bag of M&M's and washed it down with a Red Bull. His fingers hit the keyboard, flying across so fast I can barely see them moving. "Check monitors two, three, and four."

Eli furrows his brow and steps closer. "What am I looking at?"

Scooter points to the grainy images in black and white. It looks like a warehouse with boxes and pallets. Every so often, a pallet truck zips by carrying a load.

"I've tapped into the cameras we installed at Antonio's workplace and cross-checked the time and day of the burglary with when his two coworkers claim he was at work. As you can see in these images, from multiple angles, he wasn't there."

"Wait, you said the cameras we installed?" I ask. A zap of worry prickles against the tiny hairs on the back of my neck.

Eli doesn't take his eyes off the images. "When I went to visit him that first time, I had another member of my team install video bugs. They don't pick up sound, but I wanted to keep an eye on him."

"Well then, this proves their alibis were fake! All we have to do is take this to the police and they'll put him back in the slammer for breaking his parole. Right?" I can't suppress my excitement. I almost want to do a jig, or at the very least, a congratulatory booty shake, but the silence surrounding me cuts off any joy I'm feeling.

None of the men say a word.

"Uh, guys, this is what we needed."

Eli shakes his head and drops it down. "Babe, these videos are not legal. Even if they were the company's cameras, we still would have hacked them illegally. These videos will not hold up, plus they'll get me and my guys in trouble for placing them without permission."

Sadness engulfs me. "This sucks! So basically we've got nothing again."

I turn on my toe and fly out of the room, down the stairs to the kitchen. Gigi follows me, and I'm sure right behind her is Austin.

Gillian is hot on my heels when I make it to the kitchen.

"Honey, they're trying really hard. And this does prove his alibi is toast. But we need more to tie him to the break-in.

Regardless, Chase will make a call to the San Francisco police and give them a heads up that he knows Antonio's coworkers were lying about the alibi. He'll have some detective interview the guys again and see if they can break them. Maybe separate them and play them against one another. There's hope. Okay?"

Even after all the shit she's been through, she's ever the optimist.

I pop the top on a cold beer and chug it back before slamming the can on the tile counter. "I'm so tired of everything being screwed up! We just got over months of the Danny hell, and now Antonio. Kat's not even clear to go home yet from the hospital, and I can't even get in my own car to go visit her. We're still living our lives in the dark, under the shadow of fear. I'm so tired of it!" My voice cracks and shakes.

Gigi plops herself onto a stool and places her head in her hand. "I know. I'm sorry. We had some years there where we felt super solid, and things were normal. That's not exactly the case as of late."

"*Si*, what happened to those days? I miss them." I crinkle my nose and wish we were back to a simpler time.

"Then again, without all the strife, I wouldn't have met Chase, Bree might have never gone for Phil, and you wouldn't have met Tommy or Eli."

"If we go on that train of thought, you would've never been kidnapped, all those people would still be alive, and Kat wouldn't have been burned."

"Oh, Ria, things are simply not that black and white. Danny would have come after me no matter what. I'm thankful I had Chase to help get me through, and as much as we have lost, there's so much more that we've gained." She rubs her abdomen where her two unborn children rest. "Our family is getting bigger. Bree and I are going to have three more children for all of us to love, and they need their auntie to teach them to dance, how to speak Spanish, and how to be the most amazing woman in the world."

I lean my arms on the counter and try to even out my breathing due to the sheer anger rippling through my chest. She's right, though. Our family is growing. "You're right, *cara bonita,* you always are. *Gracias.* Sometimes I think I need to see the light."

Gigi slips off her stool, comes over to me, and places a delicate white hand on my shoulder. "I'll always be there to offer you a light and to lift you up when you're down, the same way we always have for one another. We're sisters by choice, not by blood. That bond is special and can never be broken by the ups and downs life brings our way. Remember that when you feel lost."

I turn around and wrap my arms around her. "*Dios mio, te quiero.*"

"I love you more. Now, let's start brainstorming ways to get this cockroach out from hiding behind the fridge so we can squash him like the disgusting bug he is."

★ ★ ★

Eli shuts the door and comes back with the Chinese food he ordered and two long, white business envelopes.

"What are those?" I ask, gesturing to the envelopes.

"Don't know." He sits down and places the food on the table and glances at the envelopes. "A courier from the law firm handling my brother's estate dropped these off at the same time I was paying the delivery guy."

Mention of Tommy in any way, shape, or form causes me to break out in a cold sweat.

He hands me an envelope. "One has your name on it and one has mine."

I swallow and hold it up into the light. As he stated, the front has my name in Tommy's uneven scrawl.

"I thought you said you already spoke to the attorney?"

He nods. "Yeah, regarding his will. As you know, he didn't have much, being so young, but for what he had, he listed me as the beneficiary. There was nothing else that said I should give this or that to specific people."

"Tommy was married to the job, that's for sure," I admit. Now that I'm genuinely thinking about it, we hadn't spent a lot of time together. He'd be on the job for days on end, and I wouldn't even see him. I've seen Eli more in the past three weeks than the nine months I spent as Tommy's girlfriend.

"The guy dropping these off said they'd been instructed to deliver them a few weeks after his burial. Why, I don't know. I guess there's only one way to find out."

"You gonna open yours?" There's no hiding the trepidation currently running rampant through my system.

I tip my head toward his. "You first."

He takes a deep breath, rips open the envelope, and leans back into the couch. I watch his face as he reads. His eyes fill with unshed tears. His chest lifts up and down in a labored pattern. His beautiful lips that were smiling a moment ago are flat and white with unchecked emotion.

I scramble up and sit next to him on the couch. "*Cazador*," I say softly, using the nickname he seems to enjoy the most, probably because it's special to him and him alone. I sure as hell love that he calls me Spicy.

His arm jerks when I touch him. His skin is misted with sweat and burning hot to the touch. Whatever he's reading is hitting him hard.

"Eli..."

"Fuck. Fuck me." He rubs his face. "Thomas, why the fuck did you have to be so good? Man, I want to hate you for this." He tosses the letter on the table and ruffles a hand through his hair. He leans forward, holding his head in his hands, elbows to his knees. His body shakes with tremors.

"Christ." He stands up abruptly. "I gotta take a shower!" he says in an earth-shattering, gutted tone.

"Do you want me to come, I..."

He shakes his head. "No, no, babe. Sorry. I need to be alone." These are the last words I hear before he storms up the stairs.

I slump back into the couch, holding my unopened letter, but it's not the one I want to read. Not yet. I glance at the half-folded letter lying on the table. I can barely see the introduction of "EJ" at the top.

I shake my foot a hundred times like I'm powered by the Energizer Bunny. I glance back and forth at that letter and the stairs. If he didn't want me to see it, he wouldn't have so casually left it there for me to read. Right? I mean, he would have taken it with him.

The desire to open the letter is eating me alive one inch of flesh at a time. Slowly, biting away my resistance with every second, I can't control the need to see what Tommy's last words to his brother were. My heart is pounding so hard in my chest and sounds so loud in my ears, I may go deaf.

I close my eyes, tighten my hands into fists, and then open them to glare at the letter, willing it to magically disappear. It's too late. I scramble for the letter, take one last parting glance at the empty staircase, and unfold it flat.

"*Lo siento*, Eli. I'm sorry," I whisper.

★ ★ ★

EJ -

If you're getting this letter, it means one of the pieces of shit I was going after turned the tables and took me out. Hopefully I got the bastard going down. Then again, I could have been taken out by a car crash. Whatever the situation, there are words between us that haven't been said, and dammit, they should have been.

I don't blame you for that night. Being put in the same circumstance, I don't know if I could have made another choice, either. Right or wrong, I'm sorry it put a rift between us. Sorry for not backing you the way a brother should, the way a twin should. I was shocked and angry at what went down. Older and wiser, I know we both handled it wrong. Not only did that night end a life, it ended our brotherhood.

Too many years of not having my brother taught me a valuable lesson.

Family is everything.

I wish we could have fixed our relationship before it came to this. Just know that I wanted to. I really missed you, EJ.

Unlike years ago when you won Shelly Ann fair and square, though it busted my balls something good she picked you over me, I'm still going to do something I never thought I'd do...

Maria De La Torre is my girlfriend. She's beautiful, man. Inside and out. But the woman has a fire I can't contain. Lord knows I tried. As much as I wanted to think she'd stick it out with me, I know she was with me because I saved her from a bad situation, and she thinks I'm safe. She's been dealt a shit hand. No woman deserves to suffer what she has, but my girl, Maria, she's a survivor.

I want you to take care of her. Hell man, if you could find a way to love her like I do, I'll be able to rest in peace. There is no man on the planet I would trust with the woman of my dreams but you.

I'm giving you my blessing, bro. And if I know you, and you know I do, we have the same taste in women, always have... She's going to blow your mind. Please find her. Maybe she can love you the way she couldn't love me.

On our blood vow as brothers, you owe me this last request.

Hold on to her. Keep her safe. She's feisty, but if you can get her to love you the way she loves her friends, you'll be a better man than me. And in my eyes, you have always been the better man. Give her the world. She deserves it.

All that I have, I leave to you. Be happy, bro.

~Thomas

CHAPTER SIXTEEN

Last night, I slept alone. First time in the past three days. I tossed and turned all night, half expecting Eli to come to me. Obviously the letter shredded him. How could it not? It tore a hole in my heart so huge I'm not sure anything manmade could ever repair the wound. Still, I wanted to be there for him, so when it was time to go to bed, I took off my pants and sweater and slept in a tank and panties, hoping he'd eventually join me.

I heard him downstairs, playing music softly. As much as I wanted to go down and comfort him, he needed his time. Hell, I needed it too. Due to that letter, I now have so many unanswered questions.

I don't blame you for that night.

What happened between them, and why hasn't Eli shared it with me? I've made myself available for him to open up to, but he always changes the subject. I told him everything that happened with Antonio on the worst night of my entire life, yet he still holds this back? Why?

Not only did that night end a life, it ended our brotherhood.

I can't imagine anything so horrible that Thomas, my Tommy, would turn his back on his own flesh and blood. He was so committed to his family, even more so than to me. He doted on his *madre y padre*. Something devastating had to have happened. It made me wonder if it had anything to do with Eli leaving the force. At one time, he admitted to having been a cop, working with his brother, but he left it a few years ago and became a bounty hunter.

Unlike years ago when you won Shelly Ann fair and square.

Who the hell is Shelly Ann, and why is she so important she was brought up in the last words a brother had to say to his twin? From the sound of the letter, she was a woman they were both after. One that Eli ended up with. But where is she now? Was she part of the rift the night that Eli won't talk about?

The irony is not lost on me. Here I am, sleeping with the twin brother. Though Eli didn't win me per se, he definitely broke me down bit by bit and won me over. That's when the stuff Tommy said about me rolls around like a ping-pong machine of destruction in my mind.

I want you to take care of her.

Tommy's last request, the words he'd left behind for the one man he could trust, was to keep me safe. I close my eyes and let the tears fall. There's no use in trying to avoid or hide them. It would be a disgrace to Tommy.

His last words, and the emphasis with which he made his requests known, bring me to my knees by the side of the bed.

Love her like I do, and I'll be able to rest in peace.

There is no man on the planet I would trust with the woman of my dreams but you.

Maybe she can love you the way she couldn't love me.

I'm giving you my blessing.

I break down and sob into the fluffy white comforter of the guest room, hoping it muffles the sound. Tears pour down my cheeks in rivers of sadness and grief.

"Why you, Tommy? Why did it have to be you to go after

Danny?" I cry out, and my body heaves and lurches with each painful memory, wishing I could take it all back.

"I cared about you. And I did love you in my own way. You have to know that." I focus on the ceiling, hoping Tommy is watching, listening to my plight.

"You were everything I should have wanted in a man. Everything I needed at the time. Thank you for being that for me. Making me feel cared for." I sniff and pick at the blanket. "I'm sorry I never told you I loved you. Maybe our relationship wasn't the rainbows and flowers type, but we mutually enjoyed one another. Made each other happy. Right?"

I drop my shoulders and head to the mattress. "I'm sorry I couldn't give you all of me. I'm sorry we didn't have a love that spans lifetimes. I wish I could go back and feel that way now. Feel everything you felt for me. I would try. For you, I would try.

"God, what am I saying? I'm lying even in my prayers. That just makes me a hypocrite." I groan and wipe my nose on a crumpled-up tissue I've been holding in my hand like a talisman.

I take a few breaths, trying to figure out how to say what I need to say to him. "The truth is, I wouldn't have wanted you to stay with me forever. I would have wanted you to find a woman who lost her breath every time you looked at her. A woman who wanted the two point five kids and the white picket fence you dreamed of. I was never going to be that girl.

"Thank you, Tommy, for saving me all those years ago. I'm not sure I ever fully thanked you for that. If it hadn't been for you, I wouldn't be here. And if it hadn't been for you, neither would my soul sister, Gigi. Bree tells me to honor your sacrifice and I will find a way to do that. I swear it."

"You're doing it now, Spicy," Eli's voice booms from the doorway.

I glance up with what I know is a heavily tear-streaked face. He's doing the usual Eli doorjamb lean, wearing a pair of jeans and a T-shirt that stretches tightly over his broad chest. His hair is a mess of layers poking this way and that, as though he's been running his hands through it a million times. His eyes are downcast, sad, showing the same grief likely reflected in my own.

"How do you figure that?"

"By living your life. You read the letter. He wanted the best for you, always."

More tears build behind the dam getting ready to trickle over. "I never told him I loved him," I admit on a rushed whisper.

Eli tilts his head and focuses his mossy gaze on me. "Why?"

"Because I didn't love him the same way he loved me. And I would never lie to him. I cared for him. Loved him definitely, but not the knife-to-the-heart, wind-siphoned-from-the-lungs, would-do-anything-for-him kind that a couple needs in order to last. The love I believe lasts forever."

"Do you think he felt that way about you?"

I lick my lips, stand up, and then sit on the bed. "I think he believed he did. But it wasn't real. Not like it is with y—" I turn my head quickly and push my hair out of my eyes, wiping at the tears. "Um, I mean..."

"No lies," he states firmly. "Finish what you were going to say." Eli strides into the room, stands in front of me and gets on his knees so I'm forced to look directly into his eyes. "Finish."

"I can't. It's not right. It's too soon." My voice splinters with every breath.

He shakes his head viciously. "Maria, by God, woman, take a fucking chance. For once in your life, take a chance on someone." He pounds his fist into his chest. "Take a chance on me."

I swallow and try to speak, but my panic, dread, and despair are leading me toward the cowardly route.

Eli cups my cheeks and lifts my face with his thumbs. "Finish. It wasn't real. Not like it is with..."

I look into Eli's eyes, and all I see is rapture, understanding, and hope. He's letting me see it all. Opening the doors and windows to his soul and inviting me in to stay.

"I want to," I whisper, my heart aching, my body trembling. "I want to so badly."

"Then do it. Don't hold back. Take a chance on me, babe. Please." He kisses my lips briefly, enough to prove he's there with me. Right here, in this moment, ready to fall if I'll just take the leap with him.

"Will you fall with me?" I whisper so low, I'm not sure if he can hear them.

Then Eli leans his forehead against mine. "Maria, I fell for you the moment I laid eyes on you. So the answer is no, babe, I won't fall with you, because I've already tumbled over that cliff. But it had to be that way, because if I didn't fall first, I wouldn't be there to catch you."

"I love you, Eli." I gasp the words as if they are a surprise to me, too. "I don't know how it happened so fast. I'm scared out of my mind, still freaked out by everything that's happened, but you, me, we're real. So real it hurts." I rub my hand over my chest to staunch the pounding pressure there.

"I love you too, Spicy. Too fuckin' much, I'll tell you right now. You damn near kill me with your beauty. Your mouth is a sin I never tire of." He looks over my curves. "This body breaks me down to the basest instincts. And your heart? Fuck it. Let's just say it. I own that heart, and I always will." His gaze pierces straight through me with an honesty I'll never forget years from now when I relive this moment.

"Never giving it back. No matter what you try to do to sabotage this, your heart is mine."

I pull away from our tiny little huddle. "Me sabotage it? If anyone is going to do the screwing up, it's you!" I shoot back.

He grins with a wicked intent I know far too well.

"Damn right it's me that will be doing the screwing!" he says while lifting me by the waist and pushing me on my back. He settles his large body between my legs. "And I'm going to prove it to you, too."

"Not if I say no, you're not!" I puff out a breath, pushing my hair out of my face again.

"Babe, you're not going to say no." He grins, his hard shaft in the perfect spot between my legs.

I moan and wrap my legs around his waist urging the friction. "I could."

"You can't. You're unable to resist my charm."

I scoff. "Unable to resist. I totally could if I wanted to."

Eli chuckles and plants a line of kisses down my neck. He lifts my thigh higher so he can press in delicious circles exactly where I want him.

"You were saying something about resisting?" He lifts up my tank and my braless breasts bounce free.

His lips encircle one nipple while his talented tongue laves at the tightening peak.

"I could resist. If I wanted to," I say as I grip his head and arch into the luscious kiss.

He bites down on the tip hard enough to send a bolt of arousal between my thighs. I jerk my hips up into him, moaning with desire.

"No lies." He sucks hard at one tip before releasing it. The nipple shimmers with wetness, an erotic sight that causes shivers down my spine in waves of ecstasy.

"You're the one who started it!" I press against his thigh with my toes, urging him into a faster pace against my center.

He stops everything he's doing. "Woman. Can you shut it while I make love to you?" He lifts his considerable bulk to a kneeling position, unbuttons his pants, and lowers the zipper. His hard cock comes into view, a drop of precum already moistening the head. He strokes his dick a few times directly over my chest. My mouth waters, and I open my mouth in invitation.

"Babe, if you can't be quiet, I'm going to have to put something in that fiery mouth of yours to keep you busy."

"Oh, *Cazador*, please do. Teach me a lesson." I lick my lips and bite down on the bottom one, waiting for his next move.

He shakes his head. "Spicy as fuck, but I love her."

Then my man proceeds to teach me his "lessons" until, eventually, I shut up and let him love me. All night long.

★ ★ ★

Once again, a week has passed, and we've heard nothing from Antonio. Patient *bastardo*. He's always had the patience of a saint. Too bad he doesn't have the spiritual good nature in him, too. All in all, the entire thing is making me cranky. Beyond cranky, if I'm honest. Eli says I'm downright disagreeable. Not that he has anything to complain about. He has me exactly where he wants me. In his bed, day and night. Then again, I'm not exactly capable of coming up with any problems in that deal. Eli is a master in the sack—a giving and generous lover all the way up until he's ready to get his, and then he's greedy and gluttonous. I can't complain about that, either. I love giving as much as receiving when it comes to sex. We're well paired in the physical sense. We can't seem to get enough of one another.

The only problem is I want to re-enter my life. Teach my clients. Dance on stage, perhaps. Visit Kat when I feel like it. She's supposed to be going home today, and I've had to make Batman promise to take me in the next couple days. Heaven forbid I go on my own. He says he's not taking any chances with my safety. And as much as I'm learning to love him for it, it's also making me have a violent need to take a broom to his giant television screen. Why? Because it's all I've seen day after day. Night after night. The walls of his home.

Well, I've had it. Just as I grab my phone and start to plot an escape plan, Eli bundles down the stairs.

"Uh hey, I've got to ask you about something important. Can you sit down?" Eli points to the couch.

I walk over and sit down. "What? *Por favor, dime que has encontrado algo?*"

He sits down on the table across from me instead of next to me. After a few weeks with him, this does not bode well for the conversation he wants to have. I've quickly picked up on his body language. If he's about to tell me something that will piss me off, he stands a good ten feet away. I've been known to toss cell phones, remote controls, throw pillows—that type of thing. Obviously with good reason. Then, if he wants to go over the case, he'll sit by my side and face me with a leg up, or request that I meet him in the Batcave command center.

This response—the sitting in front of me so he can hold my hands—means he needs to break something to me, and he wants to be close. Close enough to hold my hands and look into my eyes to gauge the reaction to whatever it is he's going to impart.

"No, we haven't found anything. Your ex is still playing the choirboy card." He grasps my hands. "I need to go to Thomas's house. Start going through his things, determine what to keep and donate. My parents have been hounding me to go there. They want to meet us there today."

I swallow the giant rock scratching its way down my throat. "Us?"

He nods. "Yeah, babe. I told them about us. Also shared part of the letter where Thomas told me to take care of you. Apparently, they got one too. In that letter, he mentions that they should wrap you in their love."

I grip his hands so tight my knuckles turn white. "What if they think I'm a slut or a bad person? I mean, barely a month ago we buried their son, my ex-boyfriend, and now I'm already with you. If it sounds bad to me, how's it going to sound to them?"

Eli caresses the side of my face with his hand. "We won't know until we face it, now will we? Day to day. One thing at a time. We cannot control what other people think or do. We can only control how we react to them and whether or not we're going to let it control us. I, for one, am prepared to fight for us. Are you?"

I close my eyes and nod. "Yeah, it's just so hard with them. They took me in and made me part of their family. And now..."

"Now what? Nothing for them has changed. You're still

the woman standing by one of their sons. A future daughter-in-law. Just because it's me and not Thomas makes no difference in the grand scheme of things."

"Daughter-in-law, *Dios mio,* no." I push back, but Eli keeps ahold.

"Relax, Spicy. You're like a stick of dynamite ready to go off at any moment. Chill. I'm not talking marriage at the moment. And we're not going to fret over seeing my parents. It's going to be fine."

I nod. "If you say so."

"I do say so. Is there any other reason I should be worried about you going to Thomas's?"

Mierda. I got caught up in the fact his parents were going to be there, I forgot we'd be entering Tommy's home. Without him in it. A place he would never return to again. And I have stuff there. Some clothes, toiletries. Not much by any stretch, but enough to show a woman had been there somewhat regularly.

"No. Let's go." I lock hands with Eli and follow him out to the truck.

★ ★ ★

The second I place a single foot on the concrete step of Tommy's home the door swings open and a woman in her early fifties rushes out. Before I can even say a word, Marion Redding's arms and her floral scent embrace me.

"Maria, my dear, thank goodness you came." She hugs me tight, rocking me from side to side.

I hold her with the same energy. This woman has been a rock for me since the moment I started dating Tommy. She opened her arms and her home many times for us in the early months of our relationship. Not having had my mother, I've always enjoyed and looked forward to her company. Since losing Tommy, I hadn't realized how much I appreciated her presence in my life until this moment.

"Dear, you've lost weight. And you were already so thin." She tsks the way a real mother would, worrying over her child.

I chuckle. "You say the sweetest things, Mama Redding."

"Ask my boy. I only ever speak the truth."

When she finally lets me go, I have to wipe the few tears that made their way out. Yes, I totally missed her.

"And what about your Papa Redding? Come here, beautiful." Jeremy Redding tugs me into his arms for a quick bear hug and a kiss to the temple. "How you holding up?"

"Like a cat. I always land on my feet."

He grins. "Damn straight."

Marion smacks her husband's arm. "Come on in. I've got a lasagna heating in the oven. We have a lot to discuss." Her words are direct but not unkind.

"That we do," Eli says, wrapping an arm around my shoulders.

Both of his parents clock the move and respond the exact opposite of the way I expect. Marion smiles and takes a deep breath, looking up into the open sky. Jeremy winks at me and then opens the door. That's it. The only one feeling strange and out of place is me. These people have accepted this shift between Eli and me without a hateful word or any variety of accusations they could have thrown. I would have gladly accepted any lashings for any pain the decisions I've made have caused to their hearts, but it doesn't seem to be a problem.

I don't get it, but I'm not about to bring it up right now.

Eli leads me into the house. A house I've been to more times in the last year than I have fingers and toes. It still smells of gun oil and Tommy's wintery shaving cream. A pang of guilt and grief hits me like a linebacker, and I take a step back, the air in my lungs restricting painfully. Eli holds me from behind, both hands a comforting weight on my shoulders. He leans toward my neck.

"You going to be okay? You don't have to do this with us. I can call Davis or one of my guys to pick you up."

I shake my head instantly. "No. I need to do this. It's all part of the process. If I don't, I'll grieve him forever. As it is, I'll have a living, breathing reminder in you." I hold up my hand, gesturing to his beautiful face.

Marion comes over to me and tags my waist. "How about we start with the bedroom? You can box up anything of yours and anything you'd like to keep," she says while leading me down the hall. It's a trip I've taken a bunch of times, only usually thrown over Tommy's shoulders or alone, waiting for him to come home from one of his cases. Typically, those nights I'd find out I'd slept alone, and we'd cross paths while I was heading out to rehearsal and he was finally heading to bed.

When we get to the room, it's exactly as I remember it, even though it's been close to two months since I've been here. My things are only in a few places, so I grab one of the medium-sized open boxes on the bed and go to the closet. There's a handful of my things hanging which I pull off, fold, and toss into the box.

"Maria dear, can I ask you a question?" Marion's voice shakes, and I tighten my hands into fists, digging my nails into the sensitive skin, prepping myself for the emotional devastation this woman can so easily bring down on me.

"I'd be surprised if you didn't," I say, gathering my underthings from the single drawer Tommy allotted me and tossing them into the box.

I watch through the dresser mirror as she paces from one side of the bed to the other, a hand at her neck, just like Eli. He must have picked up that trait from her. "Well, it's... You know, this thing between you and Elijah..."

Swallowing down my guilt, I turn around. "Mama Redding... Marion...look, Eli and I didn't expect for this to happen. I certainly never in a million years would have willingly fallen for Tommy's brother, but I couldn't stop it, either, nor do I want to, and I..."

"Then you're not with him out of respect for Thomas's last wishes?" Her question comes out in a rush of emotion.

I cringe and blink a few times. "What are you talking about?"

"Thomas's letter to us clearly stated his wish was for you to meet Elijah. He made it crystal clear he wanted Jeremy and I to play matchmaker."

I roll my eyes. "*Jesucristo*, Tommy. Always trying to make everyone happy." I plop down on the bed and rub at my forehead. "No, my hand to God, I'm not with Eli because of Tommy's dying wishes."

Marion smiles so huge at the same time tears fall from her eyes. "Then we don't lose you, too. And because of you, we get our son back." She pulls me into her arms for another warm embrace.

This time I cry with her. "I'm sorry, so sorry about Tommy. I never wanted anything like that to ever happen, and I was so worried you'd think I was some kind of street walker because of how close Eli and I have become since Tommy's death." The words are rushing out of my mouth so fast I can't even keep up.

Marion cups my cheeks. "You poor, poor dear. We don't get to choose who we love. Timing doesn't matter if the person is your soul mate. I've seen you with Thomas, and I knew you weren't meant for him. He might have thought otherwise, which is unfortunate. Now, Elijah... That boy of mine is a wild card. Lives life burning through every second as though his hair is on fire." She chuckles. "My Thomas never kept a head of hair. Too much fuss. Well, life is fussy and you, my dear, are also a wild card."

"So you're not mad that I'm with Eli now...after everything?"

She takes my hand into hers. "No, dear. It means my odds of keeping you in my family have doubled, and I'd bet on those odds."

I close my eyes against the tears brought on by the joy of having this woman, this *family*, this set of men in my life. It's beyond overwhelming. "I cared for Tommy. I did. You know I did."

Marion pulls her head back and pats my cheek. "Yes, dear. I know you did. But you love my Elijah. I can see it in your eyes every time I mention his name. It means you met the wrong man first. I'm just glad we don't lose you, too. Plus, with Elijah with you, I'm bound to see my son more often. And now that we've lost Thomas, it's more important than ever we all stick together."

"I couldn't agree more," I whisper and hug her again. "*Gracias*, Mama Redding. Thank you for being you."

CHAPTER SEVENTEEN

My second glass of wine goes down the hatch in a flash of scrumptious cherry and plum flavors. I lick my lips, allowing the swirling notes of my favorite wine to tease and taunt my taste buds before I set the glass down on the nightstand. "I'm sorry you can't have any vino, *gatito*." I puff out my bottom lip and pat Kathleen's ankle where she's recuperating in her bed.

In the next few months, she'll complete the healing process from the last grafting surgeries and then go in for more. Apparently, it's going to be a series of surgeries to smooth out the burned flesh on her right arm, side, and neck. Even now, she has bandages up her neck to her ear and down under her nightgown where I can't see.

"You're the only one drinking, you lush puppy!" Bree says snidely. Pregnancy has not made my petite soul sister happy.

Gillian rubs her tiny bump. "I don't mind. I'm so happy nothing can get me down. The doctors said I'm officially in my second trimester and both babies are perfect in size, the heartbeats are strong, and I'm healthy. I finally feel as if I have something to look forward to."

Kat smiles wide and leans her head back against the pillow. We can tell she's tired, but she's putting up a valiant effort to enjoy this evening. It's been a while since the four of us were together outside a hospital.

"How are you doing, Kat? Really. You've been listening to me bitch about my pregnancy and Gigi gloat about how great hers is, but you haven't said anything about you and how you're holding up," Bree asks.

Kat pushes herself up to a better seated position. The three of us are gathered around her, eating pizza, and I'm drinking wine in her bed. The soft acoustic music playing in the background sets a comfortable mood.

"I'm okay. It hurts, sometimes the nerves tingle in the middle of the night, and then it's as if the entire arm is on fire again." She shakes her head, letting her blond curls fall in front of her face. "Honestly, I'm frickin' done with dealing with doctors and future speculations about my prognosis. I need some time to wrap my head around not being able to do what I've always done and how that's going to affect me long-term, you know?"

I nod, but Gigi jumps right into the fray.

"According to my husband, you're set financially for the next few years while you get back into fighting shape. There's no rush."

Kat groans. "Honey, I cannot let Chase pay my way for the next few years while I sit around and mope."

Gigi put her hand on Kat's knee. "You'll be doing me a favor. Chase feels as though we are responsible for all of this. Danny hurt us in so many ways, Chase is making it his life mission to put everything back in order. He's a fixer. That's what he does. He will not rest until each and every one of you"—Gigi points a finger at me, and then Bree, and finally Kat—"is back to living happy, healthy, comfortable lives. You'd be doing me an enormous favor if you just roll with it."

"It's too much, Gigi. I could never repay him, and I'm not a mooch." Her tone is direct and lacking any subtlety.

"Do you think I'm a *vagara*?" I ask.

Her eyebrows rise so high into her hairline they almost disappear. "No, of course not."

"Chase has been paying for my apartment for almost a year now. Since everything went down with Danny, and Gillian moved in to the penthouse. I keep saving up the money, thinking eventually he'll let me pay, but it hasn't happened yet," I admit, a frustration in my tone I can't deny.

That's when Bree jumps in. "And I don't pay rent on my studio space in Davis Industries. I make twenty times the amount I was making when I had the other studio due to Chase paying for the staff in his company to have comped classes as part of their regular health benefits. Plus, we no longer have to pay for daycare for Anabelle, nor will we pay anything for this little one since Chase put in a daycare." Bree rubs her belly adoringly.

Gillian stands up and paces the room. Her long red ponytail bounces along with each step. "Look, ladies, my husband takes care of what he feels is his. You are now his family. That is a serious position to be in." She stops and turns to all of us with both hands on her hips. "So many want to take advantage and hurt my husband because of his wealth and the business deals he makes. You three and your extended families are what he lives for. I really need for all of you to accept it and move on. To him, it's like handing you a couple of quarters for a stamp. It's a drop in the bucket of his billions. Money might be cause for a disagreement for you, but to him, money is a means to an end. He wants it only to be able to take care of what he loves. Being us. Can you understand?"

Bree rubs her giant belly. "I'm all for it. Phillip and I have never been happier, and having extra is allowing us to plan for the girls' colleges, and we're even considering buying a bigger place outside of the city. Chase suggested something with a gate."

Gillian laughs. "Of course he did. Don't let him go house shopping with you! You'll end up with some gargantuan thing with a security guard sitting in a box at the gate. I'm not kidding. He'd wrap all of you up in Bubble Wrap and tissue paper if he thought it would make you safer."

Kat sighs. "Why is that? I mean, I get that he sees us as part of his extended family, but it's a little extreme."

Gigi nods. "Yeah, but he knows you're all I have and the loss of any one of you would be devastating. In order to ensure I have what he feels keeps me happy, he wants to keep each one of you safe. If I let him, all of you would still have a dedicated bodyguard."

I groan. "*Dios,* no. Eli would be all over that in a hot minute."

All three women stop speaking and all eyes come to me. Kat breaks the silence first.

"Care to elaborate on this Eli fella? I'm unfamiliar with him outside of the fact Gigi and Bree told me he's Tommy's twin brother. Start at the beginning because I've been out of the loop." She purses her lips.

"Not on purpose! It's just with Antonio back in the mix, everything's been going to *infierno en una cesta de mano.*"

Kat squints and her lips flatten. "Antonio is back? When?" She lifts a shaky hand to her chest.

I push my hair off my shoulder. "Right after the funeral. He got out of jail early, has been sending threatening texts, and broke into my apartment and trashed it. I've been staying with Eli ever since."

For the next few minutes, I update them on all the news we've received to date, including the fact we know his alibi is bogus but can't prove it because it will get Eli and his men in trouble with the law.

"So where is he now?" Bree asks.

I shrug. "Don't know. The guys took my old phone so I wouldn't get any more scary texts."

Gillian puts a finger to her mouth, tapping her nail against her lip. "But from what you told me about him, he's persistent. Will a massive hulk of a man like Elijah scare him off for good?" Her question is filled with alarm.

"No. I don't think so. He's biding his time. I don't know him anymore, but what I do know of him is not good. The man tried to kill me. He blames me for putting him in jail and ruining his career. Those two things together make him volatile. And if he's been stewing about this in jail for the past five years, he probably loathes the ground I walk on. There's no telling what he's capable of."

It feels so good to admit all the things that are frightening me about this situation. With Eli, I don't want him to think I'm not strong. I've already proved I'm a crybaby with as many times as I've broken down the past month. I want him to see me as strong. I need him to.

All three women look horrified, their faces masks of dread and anxiety. "Girls, it's going to be okay. Eli wouldn't let anything get to me. He's promised me." I smile, thinking about our private conversation when he committed to doing just that.

Gigi tips her head to the side and stares at me. I glance at her and then at Bree and Kat, who are sharing equally pensive looks on their faces.

"¿Qué? ¿Qué es?"

All three of them continue to stare silently. It's as if they are digging into my psyche for information through super-BFF telepathy.

Finally, Gigi breaks the stare down first. "Holy shit! You're in love with him."

"Huh? Um..." I try scratching my nails along my scalp and looking away.

"You are! You're batshit crazy in love with Eli, Tommy's twin brother. No fucking way!"

"Gillian..." I whisper.

"Gillian? I'm Gillian now. You can't fool me, sister. I know you better than I know myself half the time. Oh my God! You so are," she gasps.

Her emerald gaze hits my grieving one. Before my eyes, hers soften and she comes over to me and takes my hand. "You can tell us. We're not going to judge you. We're the only women in the entire world who will always love you more than you love yourself. Time to be free of this burden and admit the truth."

"I...I..."

"Go ahead, Ria. It's okay. We're here for you." Bree puts a hand to my shoulder, and her warmth seeps straight through to my bones. A calming sense of solidarity enters my mind.

Kat reaches out a shaking, tentative hand, putting her good one on my knee. "It's okay. We're your best friends, and here for you always. Don't ever forget that."

I bite my bottom lip and glance at each woman. Gigi's fiery red hair is pulled back in a ponytail, her green eyes pools of love and understanding. Bree has a hand on me and another around her giant baby bump, always protecting her unborn daughter. Those eyes of hers are a bright startling blue, the color of a perfectly clear sky in spring, and right now they are open and receiving. And my *gatita*. My Kathleen, her caramel-colored eyes looking too big on her sallow face, her golden curls filled with less life than usual, but she's healing and happy to be home. Right now, that's all we can ask for.

These women are everything to me. The sun, moon, stars—hell, the galaxy above. Without them, I'll never be me. They deserve the truth, and I need to put on my *niña grande bragas* and spit it out once and for all.

"*Cara bonita*, you're right. I don't know how or when it happened, but somehow along the way I've fallen for Elijah. It's so *estúpido,* right? I mean, we barely know each other, but it's so much more than anything I've ever felt for another human being. When I'm with him, I feel at peace. As long as I have his arms around me, I'll be happy forever. Isn't that *loco*?"

None of the girls say a word. The collective silence is deafening.

"Girls?" I choke out.

Gillian pulls me into her arms in a brutal hug. One so strong she might even leave fingerprint-sized bruises on my back. "You deserve to feel that way. I can only share my experience, but with everyone before Chase it was good, great even. I thought I was happy. Being with Chase has taught me there's a whole level of completeness I didn't have before I met him. If Eli makes you feel whole, there is nothing you can do but give in to it. It's meant to be."

Bree and Gillian trade places. Bree sits next to me and grabs my hand. "Before Phillip, I was with a lot of men. I enjoyed the relationships I had. Some were long, some short, some for the fun of it. But the moment we were together physically, I knew it would be him for the rest of my life. I didn't want anyone else. He ruins me for any other man just by being him. My perfect other half."

I kiss her cheek, place my hands on both sides of the bump, and kiss the top.

"Let me get in there," Kat complains from behind Bree.

Bree giggles her pretty laugh and stands, hugging Gillian.

"Come here. I can't move over there." She pats the side next to her on the bed.

I move up toward her side and sit facing her. She holds my hand in hers. The other lays lifelessly propped up on a pillow, her fingers, what I can see of them peeking out of the bandages, are a mess of burned tissue. Regret and sadness undulate through my veins. I wish more than anything I could have gotten to her sooner.

"Maria, let me ask you this. Has Elijah told you he loves you?" Kat asks with absolute sincerity. A feeling deep in my gut tells me this question means something huge to her.

I close my eyes and remember the exact moment he told me. "*Si.*"

Her eyes fill with unshed tears. "And do you believe him?"

I nod. "*Si. Con todo mi corazón.*" With my whole heart, I confirm.

"Are you in love with him?"

I swallow and nod. "*Si.* Yes, so much. It doesn't make sense, but I am," I whisper, holding her hand up to my lips where I kiss her fingers, self-consciously needing that physical connection to my best friend.

"Then, honey, you have nothing to worry about. You fell in love. He loves you back. Live your life. Enjoy it. There's nothing more important than true love."

"But Tommy..." I whisper around the plum-sized ball of guilt stuck in my throat.

Bree chokes on a cough.

Kat gasps.

Gillian's eyes widen and her hand goes to her throat.

Kat speaks first. "It's unfortunate Tommy had to leave this earth the way he did, and we will all miss him and appreciate his sacrifice. But you and each woman in here know he was not your forever mate. Honey, you may have cared for him, but all of us could see you enjoyed the safety that came with being a cop's girlfriend. After what you've been through in the past, it makes a great deal of sense, and at the time, that's what you wanted, so the three of us supported your decision. But I don't think anyone here is surprised you fell in love with someone other than Tommy. Ladies?"

I look up at Bree and then Gigi, who are both shaking their heads.

"So you're not upset?" I ask the three of them.

"Goodness, no!"

"Heck no!"

"No way!"

All of them answer at the same time. An anchor-sized weight floats off my shoulders with their admission.

"I'm still trying to wrap my mind around it, but having the support from the three of you means more to me than anything. I can't tell you how much. *Te amo, damas.*"

"Love you more," Gigi says.

"Right back atcha, babe," Bree adds.

"Always," Kat finishes.

When the Creator above decided my path would contain years of hardship, struggle, and surviving against all odds, at least He graced me with three gifts—Gillian, Bree, and Kathleen. I'll always be thankful to the big guy above for them. And as long as I have them in my life, I can make it through anything.

★ ★ ★

"That was so great!" Gigi locks her arm with mine as we walk out of the elevator. The small lobby in Kat's building is empty of residents.

"It was. I'm so glad Kathleen is home and Chase has a nurse coming regularly. Especially since she won't allow any of us to stay with her. Stubborn *la mocoso*," I mumble, calling her a brat.

Gigi laughs. "I remember that one!"

"Probably because I used it on you plenty of times over the years." I smile wide and open the door to the street for Gigi to precede me out of Kat's building.

The sun has set, but it's still light out. Strangely, Gillian's bodyguard and car are not waiting at the curb. Usually, Jack greets us outside the elevator. I should have noticed he wasn't there right away. "Where's the limo and Jack?" I'm standing under the awning to the building, looking up and down the street. The wind blows my hair off my neck, chilling my face with its crispness.

Gillian frowns. "Shoot, I forgot to tell him we were ready." She glances left and then right. "Oh, no problem. The limo's parked a block down. We'll meet him."

The hairs on the back of my neck stand up. "Maybe we should go back inside and call." I look around at the buildings, the busy street, and the sidewalks. People are milling about, getting into taxis, going into different buildings, ducking into stores. It seems fine, but still, something at the back of my mind is sending a soft buzzing to the surface. Not quite alarm bells, but I've definitely got the heebie-jeebies.

"Oh please. I can see Jack leaning on the front of the car now." She points down the block and tugs my arm. I have no choice but to follow her.

A sizzling prickle hits my spine, and I glance around, walking briskly. I hold my purse close to my side and put an arm around Gillian's waist to keep her moving. Glancing left and right, I'm trying to focus on the details of the people around us.

Woman and man getting into a taxi.

Homeless man sitting on the sidewalk shaking a can of change.

Two people standing at the ATMs across the street.

Cars going by at normal, regular speeds.

The crosswalk signals beeping to cross on our side.

We're getting closer to the car, but it's still more than half a block down, and a nauseous spike digs into my gut. This is not good. Wrong. Bad. Danger.

From the distance, Jack glances up. His form gets taller before my eyes, and I pick up my pace, wanting to run at full speed, but I hold back the urge.

Maria, relax. You're being irrational. Calm, chica.

"Ria, I can't keep up with those long dancer's legs. Slow down," Gigi complains and yanks me to the side. I start to stumble and then catch us. "Oh no. Jack has seen us, and he's storming our way. Wait a minute... What's in his hand?" Gillian frowns and squints.

I focus my gaze on what Jack has in his right hand as he

starts to run toward us. It's a gun. What the fuck is going on? *A gun?*

"Down! Get down!" Jack roars, pointing his gun right at us.

Just as I'm about to glance over my shoulder, both Gigi and I are hit by something hard—a man, careening into us. The two of us plow forward, tumbling face first toward the concrete as a shot goes off. A searing pain rips through my back by my shoulder as I fall, my hands and knees hitting first.

Gillian screams, and that's the last thing I hear before I black out.

★ ★ ★

"Wake up, Maria. Now! Wake the fuck up!" Jack is roaring, shaking my body and slapping my face a little too hard for my liking.

I shake my head and grab for my left shoulder. Blood is seeping down my back. Razor blades of agony tear through me as I come to. "Gillian!"

"She's fine, in the limo already. Come on, now!" He lifts me up by my good arm and tosses me over his shoulder like a towel. He sets out at a dead run toward the car. He opens the back door and throws me inside like a sack of potatoes. Then he slams the door and is gone.

"Maria. Oh my God. I thought you'd been shot. I'm so glad you're okay!" Gigi cries, tears slicing down her cheeks. Her hair is a mess with fly-aways poking out, and her silk blouse is matted with dirt and what looks like sprays of blood. Her knees are bleeding, and her hands look like they've gotten a heaping dose of road rash. As I was going down, I tried to break her fall, but the pain piercing my shoulder made me turn and land on the right side.

"I'm fine, I'm fine." I hug her close. Her body is shaking. "I wasn't shot."

"You're bleeding. Why are you bleeding?" She grabs at my shoulder and turns me around so she can see my back. "You've been cut. It's pretty deep." She grabs for the bar towel and puts pressure on the wound.

"Ahhh *joderme!*" I yell, not able to control the excruciating burning pain blistering down my arm from the wound.

Gigi presses a button above us, and the privacy window goes down.

Jack's no-nonsense voice is barking responses into a cell phone. "Yes, sir, I'm bringing them to St. Mary's Medical Center now. It's the closest one. No, she seems banged up but fine. Mrs. Davis, are you bleeding?"

"Um, a little bit. On my knees." She glances down and then looks at her hands.

"Between your legs?" His question and the way his voice dips is by far the meanest I've heard him speak to date.

I want to tell him to fuck off but realize who's probably asking. What a total clusterfuck.

Her face turns pensive for a moment. "I don't think so. I don't feel pain in my abdomen. Just my knees and my hands," she says. "But Maria has a huge laceration on her shoulder. She needs medical attention immediately."

I blink back the tweety birds spinning around my vision. Gillian hands me a bottle of water. When I try to open it, it's as if I'm shredding the tissue of my shoulder open like grating cheese. The blackness threatens to swallow me up when we reach the hospital.

The door to the limo bursts open and Eli is there. Beautiful, huge, with sexy tats and a kissable... Wait. No, an angry scowl on his handsome face.

"Do you ever take orders? I told you not to get into any trouble and to have fun with your friends, Spicy, not get knifed in the back and almost kidnapped in broad daylight."

"Knifed?"

"Yeah, babe. Porter says the guy with the hoodie and sunglasses behind you ladies was holding a knife. He thinks he got him in the arm, but he couldn't run after him and leave you and Gillian. What were you thinking leaving that building alone? I could spank the living shit out of you. But first we need to get you stitched up... Then all bets are off." He holds the towel to my wound and picks me up in a cradle hold from the limo at the receiving dock of the hospital.

I hear a screech of tires and glance over my shoulder. I hold on to Eli, and he shelters me with his bulk. Chase bails from his gunmetal-gray Aston Martin, the door left open and the car still running. "Gillian!" he roars, storming to the limo.

She jumps out of the car, her arms up in the air. "Chase, baby, I'm fine."

His eyes do what looks like an assessment of her entire body. His gaze locks on her bloody knees and torn up palms. Then he lifts her up into his arms and kisses her hard. I roll my eyes back to Eli. "Now that's how you greet your woman. Not threaten to spank her."

"She's not the one who has a maniac after her."

I close my eyes. I'm getting so tired my eyes are closing on their own as if disconnected from my brain. "True. Can you just kiss me anyway?" I mumble, and then I feel the delicious press of his mouth to mine. For a second, I touch my tongue to his lips to appreciate his manly taste.

"Yum. *Te amo, Cazador.*" The pain takes its toll, and everything goes black once again.

CHAPTER EIGHTEEN

Murmuring voices bring me back from the fog of sleep. Without opening my eyes, I assess my body, moving fingers and toes. I shift around, and a dagger of pain rips through my left shoulder, spindles down my arm and out my fingers. I clench my fist and a warm, familiar hand surrounds it. Eli.

"You done faking, Spicy?" I blink my eyes at Eli's familiar rumble, the fogginess and heaviness slowing my eyelids.

I smack my chops and grimace at the cotton mouth. He hands me a pink cup, and I suck down the heavenly water. It's cold, refreshing, and exactly what I need.

"Gracias."

"Doc says the cut is clean and the wound didn't go deep enough to harm anything important. Mostly a surface wound. Still, you need to take it easy with the arm. You got twenty stitches though." His mouth tightens into a thin, white line. "You got knifed, babe. What were you thinking?"

I take a breath, close my eyes, and open them, to be seared straight through my heart by his worried green ones.

"It was dumb. I knew we should have called the car. Gillian forgot, and we could see Jack just up the block. We didn't..." I sigh and shake my head. "We didn't think it was a big deal, but I knew. I felt the lick of evil at my heels with each step. I should have listened to my gut. Next time, I will."

He brings my hand up to kiss it. "There won't be a next time. You're going to be under lock and key until we figure this out."

"*Cazador*, you can't make me a prisoner."

"The fuck I can't, if it keeps you safe."

I grip his hand and bring it to my chest. "I love you, but that won't work with me. I have to live. The second I let Antonio take that away, he wins."

Eli lowers his head to his chest. His shoulders seem to drop down in defeat. "I wasn't there. He could have had you. Killed you right on the street."

I put my hand into the long, dark layers of his hair. "But he didn't. I'm still here, fighting and surviving like usual. Only this time, I've got you in my corner."

"Damn straight." He brings my hand to his chest. "I don't like this. Him attacking in daylight, right on the street? And how did he know where to go?"

I shrug and then wince as the pain shocks me. I hiss, unable to contain it.

"Easy girl, easy," Eli coos, rubbing my scalp in a soothing pattern until the pain subsides.

"Maybe he, uh..." I cringe, trying to manage the pain now throbbing down my arm. "Maybe he knows where Kat lives?"

"Definitely possible. If he's watched you, he'll know you visited her in the hospital."

"Hospital? Did anyone matching his description get admitted to any of the local hospitals for a gunshot wound?"

He shakes his head. "Not yet. The San Francisco PD is on it. Chase updated the chief. Says he's sending a couple units to Antonio's place to check in on him."

He won't be there. I know him too well. If Antonio wants to be found, he will be. Until then, he's in the wind.

"There was enough blood at the scene of the attack to determine he was indeed shot, but we can't be sure how much damage or where. Jack thinks he got the arm holding the knife, which is why your wound wasn't fatal. He was aiming for the side your heart is on."

"And Jack didn't see where he went, or if he got into a car?"

Eli shakes his head. "No. His orders are to protect Gillian at all cost. He had her in the limo before he could even assess whether or not you were alive." Eli's face hardens into a mask of anger. "Fucker."

I pat his arm. "Hey, he's just doing his job."

"Yeah, but you were the one attacked and the person of interest. He should have moved you first."

"And deal with Chase's outrage? You don't know him well. He seems like a rich businessman with too much money, but his wife and those babies she's carrying are his entire world. He would risk it all for them. I'm not unhappy Jack did his job. I would want her safe above all others, too. She's more important."

He scoffs. "Not to me she's not!" he grates between clenched teeth.

"And that is why you're *mi hombre*." I grin and his anger seems to visibly dissipate. "When can I get out of here?"

"Doc says you'll be released in a few hours. Now that you're all sewn up, and he can check to make sure you don't have a concussion from the fall..."

"Which I don't. I'd know if I hit my head. What about Gigi?"

He shrugs. "Don't know."

"Are you fucking kidding me? You get up and go find out where my best friend is and whether or not her and the twins are okay. And do not come back here until you do!" I push at his muscled chest with my good hand and then start mumbling my irritation. "*Dios mío. No puedo creer que este hombre. Un dolor en el culo.*"

He stands up abruptly and holds his hands up in surrender. "Fine, fine. I'll go check on your girl, but you"—he points at me—"are a pain in my ass, too! Damn woman." He starts to walk out. "Spicy as fuck. Damn, now I want to fuck you," he grumbles.

I grab the tissue box close to the bed and toss it at him. "Go!"

★ ★ ★

A few days later, I'm squeezing the tension ball the doctor gave me to work the muscle around my wound so it doesn't get too tight. Gillian and her babies are fine, although Chase is worse for wear. He doesn't seem to be planning on letting his wife out of his sight anytime in the near future. Gillian blames herself I got hurt, so she's putting up with his protectiveness as well as calling me three times a day to make sure I'm okay. It's positively annoying, but since I can't dance and can't leave the house due to a Hulk-sized bounty hunter, at least her calls break up the monotony.

"I've got to get out of this house," I groan into the phone.

"I know. I'm sorry," she says for the millionth time.

Ignoring her apology, I push forward. "He has to let me out this weekend since it's Bree's baby shower."

"True! And it's going to be so fun. We're going to have it at our rooftop garden. We'll be painting onesies she can keep that are special, letting off balloons as wishes for the baby's future, and playing a few games."

"Will there be any liquor at this party?" I ask.

She groans. "Ria, you will be festive. You will enjoy this shindig and play along. I know the crafty girlie stuff is not your gig, but this is for your soul sister. And she's got all these Buddha Zen things planned. Plus, it's a co-ed party."

"Co-ed? When did that happen?"

"When my husband decided he was going to rain on every parade I have. And since Phillip is so chill, he thought it would be fun to hang out with the guys while the women do their thing. Most of the time, they'll be in our game and media room. Technically, Chase promised me space, but he's not good at the space thing right now. I swear, that man is attached to my hip and his hand is constantly hovering over our children. It's as if he's got some type of mighty force field attached to his hand. It's annoying as hell."

I laugh hard for the first time in a long time. I can imagine the crap Chase is putting my girl through.

"This is not funny. He's driving me crazy." A muffled groan combined with the sound of her hand coming down on a hard surface pierces my ear through the phone.

I cringe, pulling the phone away momentarily. "Oh, I don't doubt it. Eli won't let me so much as ride in the car right now, so getting to come to your house will be a treat." I pick at a hangnail, thinking about how much I'd love to get out and get a manicure and pedicure.

When I'm about to ask Gigi if she thinks we should do a spa day once this is all over, Eli bounds down the stairs like a herd of buffalo.

"Hey, *cara bonita*, gotta go. Talk later?"

"Sure. Be well."

"I will. I'm healing just fine. Call you later. *Besos*."

"*Besos*."

Eli has a huge smile on his face when he enters the room. "I've got news!"

I sit up straight. "*Excelente. ¿Qué es?*"

"We've got proof Antonio attacked you."

I'm certain my eyes look like giant saucers. "Really? How?"

He grins. "The San Francisco PD were able to score some security footage off a camera on Kat's building and a bank across the street. Between the two of them, it's not only clear it's Antonio, but it also shows the entire attack. He watched from around the building for you two to leave. Once he could ascertain you were walking alone, he made his move. Only Jack prevented it."

"So did you see him get shot?" I ask with glee.

"Yep. Though it's a surface wound. A couple of units found the slug down the block wedged into the side of a trash can. Since they didn't see it right away, they thought he might have the bullet still in him, but the footage clearly shows he was grazed by the bullet."

"Damnit!"

"Yeah, but this is good, babe. However, there's bad news, too."

"Which is?"

He sits across from me at the table and grabs my hands.

Not good. Sitting in front of me, close to me. All bad signs.

"Police went to his known residence. Place was cleaned

out. There's nothing left."

"And his job? Parole officer?"

He shakes his head and frowns. "Parole officer hasn't seen him in two weeks. And his boss said he hasn't shown up for work the last few days."

"Just as I thought. He's in the wind."

Eli curls his fingers around my waist and lifts me up, turns himself around, and puts me back into his lap, facing him.

"We'll get him. It's only a matter of time."

I close my eyes and lean my forehead against his. "It's already been a couple months. I can't keep doing this. Living in fear. Not able to go home."

Eli tightens his hands around my waist and then curves them down and under my butt where he grabs copious handfuls of cheek. "Spicy, you're never going home."

I cringe and jerk my head back. My shoulder smarts, and I wince in pain. "What? Why?"

"Babe, you're already home. This is where your home is now. Not some cold fucking apartment."

"Eli, this is not my home." I speak softly, trying to be sensitive.

"Babe." He says it as if the single word answers any questions I may have.

"Don't 'babe' me! I don't live here. I'm just staying here."

"Babe, you do live here."

I literally growl like an animal and bare my teeth.

"Are all the clothes you own hanging in my closet, put away in my drawers?" he continues, unconcerned with my obvious agitation.

His statement hits me like golf club to the *cabeza*. "*Si*, but that's because you said you didn't want them in suitcases on the floor."

He nods. "Exactly. And is all your girlie shit on the vanity? Your smelly, expensive shampoo and conditioner in my shower?" He wraps a hand around my ponytail and tugs my neck back where he inhales and rubs his nose along the skin.

A river of shivers washes down my spine and settles between my thighs. "*Si.*"

He places hot, openmouthed kisses all over my neck before shoving down the top of my tank top and unclasping the front of my bra so my breasts spill out, hiked up to maximum viewing with my shirt rolled up underneath their powerful weight.

Eli cups both breasts and tweaks both nipples like he's plucking strings on a guitar. Every tug sends a bolt of desire through me. I moan, enjoying every ounce of his attention.

"Your toothbrush sitting next to mine in the holder, babe?" he asks before wrapping his mouth around one erect tip.

I grip his hair and rub my hips against his hardening erection. "Fuck yes," I say, more to keep him focused on my tits instead of his line of questioning.

"Where do you sleep?" he asks, before palming one breast and worrying the other one with lips, tongue, and teeth.

"*Dios mio*, yes." I grip his head and force him to take more of me into his mouth, ignoring his question all together.

"Stand up." His tone is demanding, and I'm so filled with lust I comply instantly by scrambling off his thighs.

He unbuttons my shorts and pushes them and my underwear down at one time. I lift my tank and bra over my head.

Eli stares at me fully naked, his gaze running up and

down every inch of me. But his hand is busy opening his pants, lowering his zipper, and freeing just his cock from the confines of his jeans. The second it comes into view I want to wrap my lips around it. Bad.

"You want this in your mouth, Spicy?"

I nod, licking my lips.

"Greedy girl. Too bad." He strokes it, teasing me. A drop of precum pearls at the top, taunting me.

"*Por favor,*" I beg. "I'll make you feel so good."

"You always do. That's why you're my woman. But I have a point to make so come here." He grips my hips and wraps his lips around my clit in a snap. He flattens his tongue and laves at the tight bundle of nerves until I'm shaking. "Knee up." His voice is a command, and I lift my leg up on the couch, opening myself to him.

"Who owns this cunt?" he demands, before opening me with both thumbs and licking deep.

His mouth feels so damned good. I grip his hair and jerk my hips against his face. "You do."

He licks me hard, alternating between fucking me with his tongue and sucking my clit. "And where do I lick this cunt of mine?"

Pleasure sizzles from my core up my body until I'm bowing closer, trying to get more pressure from his mouth. "Here," I gasp, as the first fluttering of an orgasm ripples through me.

"That's right. Come on my face, babe. Right here, in *our* living room while I suck you dry." He bites down hard enough on my clit that my entire body goes ramrod straight and tremors of pleasure splinter out from my pussy up through my chest, out my arms, and down my legs. I start to shake, but he holds me to him, sucking and licking my slit as though he's been denied my cunt for weeks when it was only yesterday we sucked one another off in the shower.

Once the orgasm subsides, he hauls my body over him. My pussy slips and slides over his cock, wetting him with my release.

"Get on my dick, babe," he says, licking a line up my neck.

I sit up and maneuver his massive erection right at my center. Before I can work him in nice and easy, he grips my hips and slams me onto his length. He bottoms out as I cry out, the pleasure mixed with the most beautiful pain.

"Who fucks this perfect pussy so good you can't stop coming?" he asks almost angrily as he lifts me up and down, on and off his cock. He loves to pull me to the absolute tip and take me deep in this position. Every thrust feels like he's farther in than the last. When our bodies come together, he maneuvers his hands between us. I tip my hips and lean back, knowing exactly what he wants. He licks both thumbs and stretches my lower lips out farther so my pussy sucks in that last half inch of his cock.

I'm split apart, pierced and hung up on his cock, completely unable to move or do anything other than take what my man gives me. It's humbling and mind-bending every time he does this. But Eli always wants more.

"You, *Cazador*. You do." I answer his question.

"Need to be deeper. To see you," he bellows, lost to his own need.

Eli holds my legs wide so the angle is such he's gifted with a graphic display of his fat cock powering in and out of me. It's raw, dirty, and the most erotic thing to watch. I can get off with him embedded to the hilt, deep enough there's no way to tell where I begin and he ends. He doesn't even have to move.

The intimate stretch of my walls to their maximum makes my pussy clench and spasm naturally around his girth.

The experience is heavenly, an out-of-body full connection with a human being that changes me, each and every time.

The root of his penis is so thick, the lips of my sex burn and tingle each time he takes me to the end. "Where do I fuck you, Maria?" he asks randomly while building up my next earth-shattering orgasm.

"Here, babe. Here."

He curls his hand over my good shoulder, and the other around my hip, tugging me on and off his cock. His thighs are like a ramp that he uses in a teeter-totter motion to catapult me up and down and into each thrust.

Stars pop and colors swirl past my vision. My pussy clamps down on his cock so hard, he roars out his passion. Then his thumb hits my clit, and I'm gone, blasting into orbit on a massive orgasm. He fucks me through it until he locks me down, rooted deep. He lifts me up so my body is smashed against his chest and his mouth is over mine. He stops kissing me long enough to shoot long washes of his release into me.

"You. Are. Home." He clenches his jaw, closes his eyes, and finishes coming hotly inside me.

I use my internal muscles to prolong his pleasure, tightening and loosening them against his cock until he's spent.

His upper body falls back to the couch, and I follow him, flattening myself against his bulk. I kiss him for a long time, my tongue licking deep, swirling with his, until I feel his dick hardening inside me again.

"Gonna fuck you until you know where you live." He kisses me hard and with so much intent, I find myself rocking my hips, helping his cock recover so round two can commence immediately.

"I know where I live."

"Do you?" He stirs his hips and reaches up for my tits. He pinches both tips, and I can't help moaning into his mouth.

"Wherever your cock is, is where I want to be." I grip his hair as he nuzzles his way down to my breasts.

He chuckles and takes a nipple into his mouth, working it into a frenzy again.

"I see how you are. You only want me for my cock."

"And your mouth. And your hands." I kiss his neck, nibbling my way up his scruff. "And your ass." I roll my hands down and dip into the back of his jeans to get some cheek. Then I work my way up until I get to his mouth again. "Where do you sleep, *Cazador*?" I ask the question he asked me earlier, the one I purposely avoided.

He sucks my top lip in and then my bottom one before pulling back and looking me in the eyes. "Where you lay that beautiful head is where I'm going to be. Always." His words are a vow that hugs my heart and breaks down any reservations I have about committing to this man.

"I sleep where you sleep. So I guess you're right. I do live here." I love his corresponding smile.

"Babe." He says the single word again as if that's all that needs to be said. And truthfully, there's a lot more behind that one word than I like to give credit for.

"Oh, shut up and fuck me."

"Spicy as fuck. Pussy is greedy as hell. I'm so screwed."

His dick is thick and long inside me. "I'll show you screwed." I lift up to my knees and take him deep in one thrust.

"Jesus!" he hollers, tipping his head back in ecstasy.

"Like I said, shut up and fuck me."

Instead of continuing to spar with me, he grips my hip and my good shoulder and hauls me onto my back. He expertly lifts my thigh high, presses it up and into my armpit, and then proceeds to jackhammer into me.

"*Dios mio*, I so live here." I wrap both legs around his waist and hold on for dear life.

CHAPTER NINETEEN

"Maria, get over here and paint your niece a onesie!" Bree harrumphs, a fist on her hip and a cute scowl on her pretty face.

The coral dress she's wearing hugs her expanded waistline and bust perfectly. A deep plunging V-neck gives Bree the opportunity to show off her new boobs. She claims it's the only thing good about being pregnant—having breasts two sizes bigger than normal. I've always had a chest bigger than all of them put together, so I'm scared to see what mine will look like swollen in pregnancy. I shudder and traipse over to the table they have set up. A long line of tiny newborn onesies is laid out.

"You realize if I do this, your baby is going to be wearing an abstract, Picasso-inspired mess," I say truthfully.

Her eyes are indigo pools and deeply focused when she replies, "I don't care. I want Dannica to have something special from each of her aunties."

"Oh, but she will, I'm going to teach her to dance. It's the gift that keeps on giving." I attempt to pacify the preggo-monster and her insane mood swings.

Now a second fist on a hip is added to the first. She looks like a pregnant superhero, and I hold back the laughter, knowing it will get me into serious trouble.

Bree points to the onesie in front of me. "Sit. Paint. Now.

No bitching," she says through her teeth.

"*Bien, bien. Mantenga sus bragas.* Keep your panties on, woman!" I roll my eyes and sit down in the chair.

"I would if I were wearing them." Bree winks and then smiles wide. Her smile is so beautiful it reminds me of the clouds parting and the sun coming out for the first time on an otherwise overcast day. "You paint. I'm going to go check on Kat."

I turn and look over my shoulder. Kat is set up in a chaise longue. She's wearing a big sun hat and smiling. Thank God she's on the mend. Glancing around, I look for Carson. He's standing off to the side, a beer dangling between his fingers and his focus one hundred percent on Kathleen. Whatever's going on between them is not good. I make a note to talk to her in private again. Tell her to stop pushing Carson away. Poor guy looks so lonely and sad.

"Hey, Spicy, what's the matter?" Eli sits down next to me. "Who are you looking at?"

I tip my chin toward Carson. "That's Carson Davis."

"Yeah, Chase's cousin. Seems like a nice guy."

I nod. "He is. The best. Only, he's Kat's man, and since the fire and her treatments, she's been steadily pushing him away."

Eli sips his beer and then dips his head down. "You planning on getting involved in other people's drama?" he asks with a conspiratorial note.

I frown. "She's my best friend, and I can see her making the biggest mistake of her life. It's my job to help her see the light."

Eli smacks his knee and laughs. "No, babe, it isn't. It's your job to be there for her when she makes those mistakes. Trust me. Don't get involved."

"You know, you've known me all of five seconds and you think you can make decisions for me about my soul sisters? You better back off, *Cazador*." My tone brooks no argument.

He laughs again, puts his arm around me, and brings his forehead to mine. "Fine. If you want to get all up in your friend's business, that's on you. I'm telling you, though, couples need to work out their problems together."

"Sure, but women need to go over every possible scenario with the people they trust. I'm a trusted confidant." I sit up straighter.

"I'm sure you are. Just don't let their problems get you down. Today's a good day. You're finally out of the house, which I know has been hard on your free spirit. So try to enjoy it, okay?"

I wrap my arms around his neck and kiss him. He tastes of beer and lime. "Mmm, you taste good."

"Want me to get you a beer?"

"*Por favor. Gracias.* Then come back and paint a tiny baby outfit with me?" I bat my eyelashes and pout.

He doesn't take the bait. "Yes to the beer, no to the painting. You're on your own."

I scrunch up my nose and scowl but set about painting a silly onesie so the *super preggo* doesn't yell at me again. At some point, a beer appears in front of me with a lime wedged into the top, but the man who brought it disappears. Stealthy *bastardo*.

I shake my head and continue making what started out to be an ocean but has turned into what I'm now converting into a night sky complete with fat, puffy, star-like bursts of yellow and orange.

"What is that?" Gigi asks while looking over my shoulder.

"Can't you tell?"

"Uh...no. Are you painting the whole thing to make it look like overalls?" she guesses.

I look at the painted cloth and turn it this way and that. "Huh. I hadn't started it that way, but your idea does make more sense. I'll adjust."

She giggles and takes a seat next to me. "So, I was wondering, what do you think about Kat and Carson?"

See, it isn't just me. I glance around, looking for Eli, but he's off chatting up Chase. Bree is sitting on the chaise next to Kat, making her laugh.

"I don't see good things in their future, unfortunately," I say.

"Which is total bull. She loves him. He loves her. It shouldn't be this hard."

"No, it shouldn't. But there is no perfect book on love to give us all the right answers. He may love her, but if he doesn't say it, she's not hearing it. His actions in this case are not speaking louder than the words she wants to hear."

"Does Eli tell you he loves you often?"

I grin. "Mostly when we're fucking."

She chokes on her water. "Cute. Very cute."

"I'm serious." I adjust my voice to a deep timbre. "Maria, I love fucking you. I love touching you. I love sticking my—"

Gillian holds up both hands, her face a bright red. "Enough! I get it."

I laugh and continue to paint. "Honestly, he does tell me all the time. So I can imagine why it hurts *gatito* so much that he's not using the words."

"If it were me, I'd need to hear it. Chase only says the words to me, but I will confess a little secret. He says it constantly.

Whispers it in my ear when he passes me in a crowded room. Tells me first thing in the morning when we wake. When we go to sleep. It's as if he's afraid I won't know how much I mean to him unless he tells me often. I think he's making up for not doing so with his mom. Even though she was a mean bitch to me, he loved her a great deal, and her loss is weighing on him."

"I'm sorry it's been so hard. But with the babies it's getting better, right?"

She looks at me sideways. "From the happiness perspective, yes. From the overprotective side of my husband, no. He's worse than a helicopter mom. I fear both of our children are going to each have bodyguards standing in the corner while they're in preschool."

"You don't think he'll homeschool them with private teachers?" I grin.

She widens her eyes and she puts a hand to her belly. "Oh goodness, no. He would so do that. Don't ever say that out loud, it will put ideas into his head. Jeez Louise. Hopefully things simmer down once we get Antonio out of the picture, and we can all go back to our normal lives."

I shake my head. "I'm not even sure what normal is anymore. I've pretty much moved in with Eli. He'll have it no other way, and frankly, I don't want to be anywhere else. Can you tell Chase I won't be needing the new furniture and apartment?"

Gillian's lips twitch. "Of course. That will work perfectly because he's already planning to move Kathleen closer. He doesn't like that I have to go across town to a shadier neighborhood to visit her."

"*Una pieza de trabajo.*" I laugh.

"Yep, you said it, sister. He's definitely a piece of work. But

I love him, and he means well. I'll have him break it to Kat. He has a way of getting whatever he wants." She smirks.

I put my hand on her stomach. "Well, he's got you and these *criaturas* to worry about. Don't give him too much trouble."

★ ★ ★

Phillip hands me a glass full of champagne from the bar in Chase's private limo. "Might as well enjoy the ride if he's forcing us to ride protected." He chuckles.

I lean into Eli's side in the back of the limo and take a sip. "Can't complain." I grin.

Phil laughs and grabs Bree's hand. "Great party, sweetheart. And you were worried we would need a ton more stuff. Between Gillian and the girls, your yoga friends and staff, and my family, we are filled to the brim with baby paraphernalia for Dannica."

"Dannica. I heard you say that before, Bree. Is that her name?" I ask.

She smiles so big. "We picked it last week. What do you think? The name means morning star. She's going to brighten our days and our nights with love and light."

"*Es perfecto. Me encanta.*"

Phil kisses the side of Bree's face. "See, even Maria thinks it's perfect. Just. Like. You." He kisses her nose and places a hand over his daughter.

She rubs her giant bump. "It is. And in a little over a month we'll be saying hello to our morning star. I can't wait."

"And shortly after, we'll be saying our vows," Phillip tosses in nonchalantly.

I sigh, nuzzling against Eli's side, getting more comfortable until it dawns on me what Phil revealed. "Wait, what? *¿Te vas a casar?*"

"English, Maria. I don't know that one." Bree frowns.

"You're getting married?" I repeat.

Bree nods and brings her hands up to her chest with excitement. "Yep, and you're the first to know!"

"Why didn't you tell us at the shower? And where is your ring?" I glance at her left hand where there is no ring to be seen.

She slumps down and pouts. "It doesn't fit. I'm too swollen."

"Girl, you are beautiful, glowing, and engaged! Felicitations. The girls are going to be so bent I found out first." I dance in my seat, wiggling around like a badass.

Phillip fills us all a new glass of champagne. Eli's glass looks like a shot glass in his giant paw.

"To my fiancée, the mother of my child. You, our daughter, and Anabelle are everything to me. I can't wait to expand my family. Thank you for making me the happiest man in the world." He leans over and kisses Bree.

"I'll drink to that." Eli lifts his glass and sucks down the liquid in one go.

"What the hell!" I follow his lead and down it all.

Just as I hold out my glass for more, a set of blinding lights cuts across my vision, coming through the side of the limo windows behind where Bree and Phillip are sitting.

I hold up my hand up to block the glare, attempting to figure out what I'm seeing when I realize the bright lights are getting closer and closer, until they're almost on top of us. "No! No! No! Get down!" I yell, but it's too late.

The sound of metal hitting metal screeches through my mind. Glass shatters, and Bree and Phillip are thrown across the limo as it skids. The tires squeal and everyone screams. My body slams into Eli's. My right side is cushioned by his at the same time his head makes contact with the glass window. It breaks and crackles, leaving a bloody circle as we bounce around.

Everything happens so fast, but it seems like slow motion. The limo teeters back and forth until it slams into a concrete building, coming to a full stop. My arms and hands are cut from the broken glass, and my right side is throbbing. I blink away the blackness, willing myself not to pass out. In front of me, Bree is on her side on the limo floor. She's bleeding from her nose, ear, and—oh my God, no!

"Bree!" I scream, but she doesn't move. Blood is pooling between her legs, coating the entire bottom of her coral dress in sickly large washes of crimson.

"The baby...the baby." I try to scramble toward her. "Phillip!" I yell, pushing over to his side. "Phil!"

He moans and blinks. "Please, Phil. Wake up. We need help!" I smack at his face. He's also bleeding from his forehead, a big gash coating my fingers as I hold his head.

"Eli, help me. We have to help Bree and the baby!" I call out, but there's no answer. I turn around to see he's slumped against the crushed side of the car. His head touching the broken window. I make it to his side. "Babe." I grab his head and turn it to the side. He's bleeding profusely, and glass is sticking out of his head. "No, no. *Cazador!* Please wake up."

I pet his forehead and scream. "Help! Somebody help me!"

That's when the limo door opens and the cool night air

rushes inside. The glare of lights blinds me, but I can see a lone figure standing there.

"It's okay, ma'am. We've got you," a woman's voice says.

The flash of the medical symbol hits my psyche like a healing balm over burnt skin. A paramedic. Thank God.

"Please help my friends. She's pregnant and bleeding. They're unconscious."

"Get out of the vehicle, ma'am, so we can get to your friends."

"Okay yeah." I kiss Eli's temple. "Help is here. Please stay with me. Help is here."

A hand appears through the door, and I grab on to it. My vision blurring and wavering with every move. I stumble out of the vehicle and into a set of large arms. I'm plastered against a man's chest. I lift my head and blink away the dizziness with all my might to stare directly into the coal-black eyes of the devil.

Antonio.

"I warned you, *mi reina*. I own you." His demon voice filters through my mind, and I go numb. No longer can I feel the pain in my head, or my side. Not even my fingers twitch.

"*No, no. Por favor. No es Dios.*"

"No one can help you now. Not even God," he bellows with an evil sneer.

"Come on, brother. Time to go before the police get here. Put her in the rig," says a woman's voice I don't recognize.

"Come, *mi reina*. Time for you to pay up for your transgressions. I think the light leaving your eyes forever will do," he says in a tone laced with hate.

"Night night, bitch," says the unfamiliar woman as a needle is stuck into my neck. And I'm out.

★ ★ ★

I come to, my ankles and feet bound together. My arms are stretched back behind me and tethered to the rope around my ankles. Uncontrollable agony ripples down every nerve as my head pounds. My mouth is as dry as the desert. The putrid scent of raw fish is in the air. A squawking sound and ocean waves filter through the banging in my head. I'm by the Bay, somewhere sea gulls frequent. A warehouse, a dock. I don't feel any movement beneath me so I couldn't be on a boat.

The pain lancing through my healing arm and a new pain in my collarbone has the blackness threatening once again.

Slowly, I breathe in through my nose and out through my mouth. If I'm going to get out of this alive, I need to be awake, cataloguing my surroundings to find a way to escape. Turning on my side, I wince as a new bout of burning pain shreds through my shoulder. I breathe through it, thinking about Eli, and Bree, and Phillip. They need me.

The accident.

I close my eyes and try to remember what happened when I came to. Eli's head was smashed against the window. It looked pretty bad, but he had a strong pulse. Phillip did wake up and then passed out again when I reached him, so he's probably going to be okay. Bree, God, Bree. The tears pour down my cheeks. I held her motionless body, the copious amount of blood between her legs staining her dress...

God, please don't take Bree or her baby. Not because of me, or because of my past. Please don't. Let them live. Spare them. Take me. Do whatever you must to me. Just save them.

"Save them. Take me," I whisper, eyes closed tight, hoping God heeds my prayer.

"Oh, I plan to take you, and there will be no saving of your soul." Antonio bites the words at my ear.

I shiver and move my head back as best I can, and then cry out as more pain rips through my clavicle and shoulder.

Antonio stands above me, his arms crossed over his chest. "You have been a bad, bad girl, haven't you, Maria. And starting today, you will pay long and hard for what you did to me."

"To you! And what about me, Tony?" I sneer. "That night, you were going to kill me. For what? For cheating on you? I never cheated."

He grimaces, and his eyes get blacker right before me. "You let men touch what was mine. All the time. I wasn't enough for you. You had to go and take on all those other dancers. The body you gave to me, promised was all mine, you gave to them, repeatedly. Do you not think you should suffer for that?"

"Let me go, Tony. Everything that happened is in the past. Just let it go. Disappear."

He scoffs and leans close to my face, spittle hitting me as he grips my hair at the roots and pulls my neck back. Something digging into my skin near my neck causes me to shriek in pain.

"You do not scare me. Your new boyfriend and that rich bitch friend of yours will never find you. And even if they do, all they'll find are the pieces I've left behind." He slams my head down onto the concrete, and I see flashing lights.

"Tony, *por favor. Mi rey*...we can still be good together." I try for reverse psychology. I now know he's too demented and twisted to let me go. He'll never reason with me. My only chance now is to give myself more time. Hopefully, someone will have seen the accident and followed him.

"Your king? Is that what you call that bounty hunter

boyfriend of yours, too?" His words slither like snakes leaping from his mouth. Then he shakes his head. "I will not fall for your deceit. Your time is up, and I want blood. But first, I need to reintroduce you to a well-known friend of yours."

He grips my head and forces me to look across the room. A tall, exotic-looking woman with black hair and dark eyes is standing by an old claw-foot tub. She flicks on the water at full blast and grins evilly.

No amount of courage or strength can stop the shaking that comes over me at the sight of the bathtub. He's going to torture me. The same reason I can't even step foot into a bathtub to this very day is because of all the torture I've suffered by his hand.

"Tony, no..." I plead.

"Si, *mi reina*. My queen. Your bathtub awaits." He lifts me by my armpits and brings his head close to my ear. His citrus-and-clove scent has me nauseous, my mouth watering, readying to vomit. "The temperature is perfect and all for you. I do it all for you."

CHAPTER TWENTY

The water is ice cold when Antonio drops me in the tub. Water sloshes out, hitting the concrete floor. My head is barely above the water. I can't move my arms, and my hands are crushed under my weight. I wiggle as much as possible, but my ankles are tied together so tight the rope cuts into the skin. Water floods into my mouth, and I maneuver best I can to keep my head above the overflowing tub.

The dark-haired woman laughs maniacally. "Look at you. Dirty, wet *cadela*. You think you're so hot now. How does it feel to be stranded? Threatened. No one to help you. Just like you did to my *irmão*." She intermingles Portuguese into her words.

"Your brother?" I gasp and suck in a bit of water. I use my toes to push against the edge of the tub to hold my head up. Water still splashes into my mouth, but I can breathe through my nose for the most part.

Her coal-black eyes become hollow puddles of disgust, the same way her brother's do. "*Sim, meu único irmão.*" My only brother, she confirms. "And you took him away for five long years. There is nothing you can do to repay that. Even your pitiful life isn't enough." She flicks my nose and then pushes me underwater.

I shake my head back and forth, trying to break loose.

My lungs burn as I hold my breath for as long as possible. Just when I'm about to suck in a breath of water, she rips my head up by my hair. My scalp stings at the violent hold.

"You think one go is enough? Oh dear, you have the hounds of hell to take you under before we give you the relief of death. Right, Antonio?" She sneers and pushes my head back against the cast iron tub, smacking the giant egg I already have from the car wreck and the slam against the concrete. I'm on the edge of consciousness, the room spinning like a twister around me.

Smack, smack, smack.

"No, no, no." Antonio tsks. "We want you awake for every moment of this," he mocks.

When I get a handle on my vision, his lips turn up in a sinister smile and he forces my head back underwater.

Over and over, they half-drown me until my lungs are burning white-hot fire, pain lancing through every limb. I can no longer feel my feet or hands as the ropes have cut off all circulation.

The sound of Tony and his sister's laughter rings in my ears like sirens as they push me under again. This time, I can no longer fight it. I hold my breath for as long as humanly possible and close my eyes. Visions fill my mind, taking with them the fear of death. Beautiful moments in time that comfort and soothe in my time of need. This. This is what people see when they say their life flashes before their eyes.

★ ★ ★

My mother's soft, dark hair, just like mine. Silky soft as I ran a brush through it when I was four years old.

My dance teacher applauding me during my final audition when I got into the elite dance company.

The defining moment of dance when I was chosen to perform a rendition of Martha Graham's famous piece, Heretic, *where I was the white dancer against the sea of dancers all in black.*

Tommy saving me all those years ago.

Gillian and I living in the city together, getting our first apartment.

Kathleen winning an award for best costume design.

Phillip introducing me to Anabelle for the first time.

All four of us girls getting the Trinity tattoo, solidifying that our past, present, and future would always be intertwined.

Bree telling us girls she was pregnant.

Chase holding Gillian and them announcing their marriage and pregnancy.

Elijah telling me he loves me.

Elijah making love to me.

Elijah promising to keep me safe...

★ ★ ★

I'm weightless, floating, everything around me soft and serene. Voices singing. Music playing. The light is so bright. I walk toward it and then stop. I look down at my hands. They are blessedly free, as are my ankles. All around me is pitch black except for the warm light ahead.

Yes, that's where I need to go.

"Come back." I hear the whispered words and shake my head, taking another step toward the light.

"Come back to me." I hear it again a little louder.

My chest hurts. I look down, and it's sunken in and lifting up. Water spills out my mouth forcefully, splashing down onto my bare feet. The darkness slowly creeps up my legs, starting with my feet, and then my ankles...

No! I look at the light and reach for it. My fingertips just barely touch the warmth. So peaceful.

"Maria! I love you. Don't leave me!" I hear the plea loud. It's all around me, filtering through my mind, my heart, and my soul. It's Elijah. His voice. He's calling to me.

I glance behind and see shadows. It's scary, and the light is so warm, so welcoming.

"Babe, please. Please. Breathe!" he cries out.

My chest feels like it's cracking, splintering in half. More water spills from my lips. I glance once more to the light, and it's smaller, only the size of a window and getting smaller by the second.

"Breathe! Breathe, goddamnit!" Eli's voice is everywhere. All around me, holding me close.

More water comes out of my mouth and nose. My chest burns, the pressure too much. I cough. And cough. Water and vomit pouring out of my mouth.

"That's it, beautiful. Good job. Get that shit out," Eli's voice is demanding, forceful.

Eli's strong hands massage and rub my back as I cough and hack.

"Good, babe. You're okay," Eli says as he turns me around and holds me in his lap.

I blink several times, my eyes feeling too heavy, my entire body scalding hot but also blistering cold. My teeth chatter, and he rubs my head, my face. "You're going to be okay." He kisses my forehead, and his warmth seeps into my body, forcing away the chill.

Tears fall down the sides of my face in hot tracks of despair. I move my arm, lifting it to his face. "You were there," I say, my voice so scratchy.

But he heard me. Of course he heard me. "I was where, babe?"

"When it all was ending. I held on to you. Our love. It made it bearable," I whisper.

Tears fill his eyes and two fall down his cheeks. "I promised to keep you safe. I didn't do it."

I pet his face. "Oh, but you did. You saved me."

He swallows and then kisses my lips softly. "You're my life now."

"And you're mine."

★ ★ ★

The lighting is low as I wake in the hospital. Gillian is sleeping against my hand, her red hair flowing over the white sheets, looking like glossy copper ribbons. Her mouth is puffing cute little noises with each breath.

I put my hand into her hair, running my fingers through it the way I always did when she was having a hard night, trying to get over what Justin did to her all those years ago.

She stirs and blinks her emerald eyes open. No woman has prettier eyes than she. Like perfectly flawless gemstones.

"*Cara bonita*, what's your husband going to say when he finds out we've slept together?" My voice is scratchy and thin through the oxygen mask covering my mouth and nose.

She smiles huge as tears fill her eyes. "He'll say it was an exceptional experience sleeping with two women."

Of course, my girl would remember the joke I told her the night I found her sleeping by my side after the fire. I glance across the room and see Chase asleep in a chair far too small for his large size.

"That man will never leave your side."

"Or yours."

"W-w-where's Eli?" I ask, alarm filling me with spikes of fear.

She pats my hand. "Getting stitched up. When the real ambulance came after the crash, he refused medical assistance. Told the paramedic to glue his wound shut, tape it up, and he'd be on his way."

"He didn't?" I lift my hand to my mouth in an attempt to remove the mask over my face.

Pain roars through me with the movement.

Gillian hisses. "Honey, don't move anything. You're all jacked up. Dr. Dutera says you've broken your clavicle, a couple ribs, opened the wound on your shoulder, have new gashes they stitched up, glass they picked out of your hands and arms, and that's not to mention the repeated drowning. Your lungs are so bad from the water you inhaled, you need the oxygen mask for a while. Just breathe and heal. I'll check on him and tell them you're awake."

I nod and breathe in blessed air and then remember the car crash before being taken by Antonio and his sister. "Bree and the baby? Phillip?" I attempt to sit up, and Gillian gently pushes me back down.

A huge smile breaks across her face. Relief the size of a house lifts off me. "She was taken straight in to have an emergency C-section. Phillip is banged up with bumps and bruises, the gash to his head was stitched up, and he has a concussion. The baby was born a few hours ago. Dannica Brielle Parks. Twenty inches long. Seven pounds even. Had the baby made it to full term, she'd have been huge!" She laughs quietly.

I thank the good Lord above for the miracle He brought to our lives. Dannica Brielle. Our newest little angel.

Gillian moves over to Chase and taps his shoulder. "Baby, she's awake. Keep her company while I check on Eli."

Chase stands abruptly. "You're not going anywhere without me." He looks at her and then at me. I can see from his facial features he's at war with what he wants to do and what he should do.

"Antonio is dead, and his sister is detained and going to jail for kidnapping and conspiracy to commit murder. We're okay now. Stay with Maria," Gillian reminds him.

Antonio is dead? Who killed him? How did they find me? I have so many questions, but the pounding in my head is loud, unrelenting, and preventing me from asking anything right now.

Chase frowns and walks to the door with his take-no-prisoners gait. He snaps his fingers and Austin pops into view. "Go with Mrs. Davis. Not out of your sight." His voice is stern and straightforward.

"Yes, sir." Austin lifts his chin.

Gillian shakes her head. "We're going to talk about this overprotective streak later. This is not going to fly, mister." She points at his chest.

Ouch. I know how much that chest pointy thing she does with her bony finger hurts. I've been on the receiving end a time or two.

He grabs his wife around the waist and plasters her to his

chest. "My wife. My children. My job to keep you safe. End of. Nonnegotiable."

Gillian's eyes turn into slits. "We *will* talk about this."

"Nonnegotiable." He smiles and then kisses her hard and fast.

She lets him, turning into a noodle in his arms. When he sets her back on her feet, she has that dreamy in-love look in her eyes. Then she snaps out of it, as if realizing she's been played, and tightens her mouth. "Ugh! Infuriating man."

He turns around toward me. "Yeah, but you love me."

Gillian storms out of the room, Austin following close behind. "*Hey loca. ¿Cómo te va?*" Chase finally addresses me.

"Crazy? You're calling me crazy? I was assaulted. Soooo not my fault. And I'm okay. How's everyone, really?"

"Fine." He sets his hand on top of mine. It's a rare occurrence when Chase reaches out physically, but when he does his intention is clear. "Bree, Phillip, and the baby are going to be okay. Sure, they've been knocked around, but everything came out fine. Had Jack been driving any faster, it could have been worse. If he hadn't been knocked out by the hit and the airbag, things would have been easier."

"I'm sorry."

Chase's brow furrows. "You have nothing to be sorry for. Sick and twisted people are to blame for all that has happened to you and my wife and our family. We're strong. We'll get through it together. Just rest."

"Thank you."

He leans forward and kisses my forehead. "Get better quick. It takes a village to raise a child, and I'm having two. We'll need all the help we can get." He winks.

I can't hold back the laughter even though it hurts.

"You done kissing my woman, or do I need to give you more time?" A deep rumbly sound I know so well comes from behind Chase. I can't see Eli, but I can feel his presence with the energy shift in the room.

"That would be my cue." He moves away from the bed.

"Chase..."

He turns around and taps my foot. "Yes?"

"I love you, brother."

Chase offers me a rare uninhibited smile. His blue gaze pierces straight through mine when he says, "I love you, too, *hermana.*"

Eli and Chase clap shoulders as Chase leaves.

"Seems like that was a pretty powerful moment between the two of you. Should I be worried?" He grins and sits next to me, taking my hand.

"Of a brother type? I don't think so, *Cazador.*"

He kisses the top of my hand, each finger, and finally the center of my palm. "I thought I'd lost you. Scooter tapped into all the security cams tracking the ambulance all the way to where they were holding you. When we entered the boathouse near the docks, you were still being held underwater. By the time Dice subdued the sister, I had Antonio on the ground. I broke his neck, killing him instantly. Dice pulled your body out of the tub, and you weren't moving or breathing." His voice is shaky, and he squeezes my hand in both of his.

Tears fill his eyes, and his mouth purses, his jaw hardening. "All I could think is I had the best thing in my entire fucking life gone in an instant. We didn't have enough time. I wanted more time with you. So I pounded on your chest, babe. Willed you to breathe. Blew air into your lungs. Even when Dice told me you were gone, I kept trying."

"Take the mask off?" I ask, my voice damaged and unrecognizable.

He grimaces as if he's debating. "Only for a minute. Then back on. You need the oxygen until your oxygen sats come back up," he says before pushing it down around my neck.

"Thank you for not giving up on me," I whisper.

"I'll never give up on you. On us. I love you so much it hurts."

"Me too," I say, pain lacing my tone.

"I know." His eyes are soft and sweet.

"No, you're crushing my hand in your giant man hands." I hiss, the pain bone-crushing for a moment.

He lightens his hold and smiles huge. Then he settles around me, both hands to my sides. Once he's positioned over me, he kisses my lips. "Spicy as fuck."

I smile. "But you love me," I whisper against his lips.

"Yes, I love you."

★ ★ ★

A few days later I'm resting comfortably, nestled in our big California king-size bed. Whoever came up with the giant bed was a genius, because having a man the size of mine, it's necessary. I'm a total convert.

Eli is taking a shower, the door open. I glance at his naked form as he showers, my libido kicking in even after he's spent the last thirty minutes going down on me until I came three times by his mouth and fingers. Then he hovered over me so I could suck him off without hurting my healing clavicle. Just watching him shower makes me want to suck on him again. *Jesucristo,* my man is sexy. Water runs down his toned body, and he moves his large, talented hands, following it with soap. I lick my lips.

"I can feel you eye-fucking me over there, Spicy. Cut it out before I fuck your face again," he warns, taunting me.

"Bring it on, *Cazador*! You don't scare me!" I yell back.

He laughs but continues his shower. *Fine. Suit yourself.* I open the bedside drawer to pull out the book I'd started, and my fingertips scrape against something pointy. I maneuver my fingers to pull out the unknown item.

A white envelope with my name on the front of it in Tommy's handwriting.

I gasp and drop the letter in my lap. I'd forgotten all about it.

Now the letter sits, waiting to be opened. With shaky fingers, I undo the flap by sliding one digit across it. I take a deep breath, setting my resolve, and unfold the letter.

My dearest Maria,

If you are receiving this letter then it means I'm gone. To start, I want to tell you I'm sorry I left. I would never have willingly left you in a million years. Since the day I met you, you were a bright star in my life. A cop's life is never an easy one to grasp. I know I was gone more of our relationship than I was able to be home, but knowing you were there, only a phone call away, made me want to work hard to come back to you.

By now, you've learned I have a twin brother. I never told you about EJ because of the rift between us. I didn't want that to be the focus of any future relationship we'd have when I did get the chance to introduce you. For me, it's one of my biggest regrets. I wish you could have known him before. He's the best brother, and an admirable man.

Maria, I know you cared for me. Maybe even loved me in your own way. At least that's what I convinced myself. But I want you to get out there and find the love of your life. As much as I loved you, you need to find a man that has a similar fire as yours. That unquenchable thirst for life you have should not be contained.

It may sound stupid, but I see the type of man you could love in my brother. He's everything I'm not and everything you need to be happy. All I ever wanted was to make you happy. Please don't cut yourself off from finding the one. He's there, maybe even closer than you think.

Take care of yourself above all things, and know my last thoughts on this earth were of you.

All my love,

~Tommy

A single tear drops down on the letter. The bed next to me dips down. I glance at Eli, and his eyes are sad. He probably recognized the handwriting. I hand him the letter silently and wipe at my eyes. He sits back and reads for a couple minutes, and then folds up the letter, leans back, and sighs.

"I was twenty-five when everything went to shit." His voice is low and filled with an immeasurable amount of pain. "Shelly Ann was my girlfriend. A woman both Thomas and I wanted. We'd always had the same taste in women. The exact same." He smiles sadly and looks out the window. "I was in the shower, back home from patrolling all night with Thomas. We were partners. The precinct thought it was great to pair us up, and we agreed." He half-laughs and sighs. "We even lived across the breezeway from one another. We were so close."

I put my hand on his forearm. "What happened?"

"Shelly Ann was sleeping, and I was in the shower. When I came out, a man was straddling her, choking her. He wore a mask so I couldn't see him. Of course I jumped him, but he wouldn't let go of whatever he was choking her with. Twine or some shit. It was cutting into her throat, blood pooling in a line around her neck."

"*Dios mio,*" I gasp.

"He wouldn't let go. I punched at him, but he was huge. Way bigger than I was. She stopped moving completely, but he still wouldn't let go. My gun was sitting on the table next to the bed. I reached for it as Thomas broke into the room, yelling for the perp to freeze. But I knew it was already too late. He'd killed her."

"Babe..."

"So even though he let go of the garrote and put his hands up, I pointed my gun at his head and blew a hole in him. His brains splattered across the dresser, mirror, and wall beyond. Then I dropped my gun, and my brother slammed into me, screaming. He kept saying the guy had his hands up, that I murdered him. And he was right."

Eli clasps my hand, and I hold it tight as the tears fall down my face.

"And I didn't care. He murdered the woman I loved. The woman we loved."

"Why her?"

"A simple accident. The wrong girl, the wrong apartment. There was a woman who could have been Shelly Ann's sister. She lived next door. Apparently, she was running from her druggie ex-boyfriend. He saw Shelly Ann come into this house, mistook her for the neighbor, and in his drug-addled mind, decided if he couldn't have her, no one would. That's why he was so strong and determined to kill her. And he did. Murdered her right in front of my eyes. I lost it."

I scoot as close to Eli's side as I can get. "And Tommy?"

"Couldn't handle that I killed the man in what he considered cold blood. The man's hands were up, and I killed him. Thomas lied to the sergeant and internal affairs for me so I wouldn't be charged, but after it was all over he told me he couldn't handle what I did and what he in turn did to save me from life in prison... So I left."

I close my eyes and kiss the ball of his shoulder. "You did what you had to."

"I've never been sorry for the decision I made that night. I did it for Shelly Ann, and I'd do it again. My only regret was losing my brother in the process."

I inhale long and slow, grip his chin, and turn him so he looks directly at me. "According to both of these letters, Tommy regretted the decision he made. He loved you, came to the conclusion on his own that you did what you had to do to ensure justice for Shelly Ann's murder."

"Yeah, I think you're right, babe. He finally got over it, but it was too fucking late." He closes his eyes, his face a mask of sorrow.

"It's never too late to make amends."

★ ★ ★

That day, we visit Tommy's grave. Eli says what he needs to say, as do I. Eli even promises to name our first son after him. I don't agree to that part, but I know I will later. Anything to keep the man I love smiling and happy. At least a middle name...

As we walk back to the car, he holds me close. I ask him

the single burning question that had been plaguing me. "Would you do it all over again? Go through what we went through the last couple months?"

He stops by the side of the car, and turns me at the waist so I face him head on. "I'd do anything to ensure you're in my life. Hunt down criminals. Scale mountains. Spend every dollar in my bank account. Whatever it took to make sure you were mine."

Eli kisses me long, deep, and so wet, I feel it from the roots of my hair to the tingle in my toes. Every last kiss from him is the best kiss I've ever had.

He rests his forehead against mine until we're sharing one another's breath. Then he blows me away with the one thing I've waited twenty-eight years to hear from the man I love.

His breath whisks across my cheeks and tickles my moistened lips as he speaks. "Without you, Maria, the world does not turn, and my days do not change to night. You are my life."

EPILOGUE

Three years later...

"*Cara bonita*, that is one long flight." I pull Gillian into my arms. Her long red hair bounces over my shoulder as she returns the hug. "But thanks for flying us in one of the Davis jets. They treat us like royalty, *mi amiga*."

Eli stands next to me as I lock an arm around his waist.

Chase claps Elijah on the shoulder. "Soup's on."

I pull Elijah in. Usually I take these trips to Bantry, Ireland, alone so he can get some bounty-hunting work done in another state, but I finally got him to agree to come to the Davis Estate. The girls and I have been coming here since Gillian and Chase bought the house and got married in this tiny town across the pond.

We move through the vast home and head to the patio where I can already hear my nieces and nephew playing. Once we get outside, Eli gasps. "Holy fuck," he whispers under his breath.

I look out over the unimpeded view of the cliffs and ocean beyond. The kids run around after one another in the gated-off area under the patio.

Eli tips his chin toward the kids. "That's going to be us one day soon you know."

I elbow him in the gut. "Not until after the wedding. And don't you dare think otherwise."

"When can we get married?" he says into my ear, kissing my neck.

I shrug. "Whenever. Nothing big. Just these people are all I care about having."

"We'll be here for two weeks. I'll fly my parents out. Why not get married here?"

I turn fully toward him and focus on his gaze. His startling green eyes seem brighter today, and the easy smile proves he's not joking.

"Don't play with me, *Cazador*."

He puts an arm around me and brings me up against his body. "Babe, you say when, you say where, and I'm there. Tomorrow works for me. I'm kind of tired after that flight to do it today." He nuzzles my nose.

I kiss him quick and then tug on his hand to introduce him to Rebecca and Colin, the other half of the Davis staff who are more like family now. "Hold that thought. We'll come back to it after we tell the girls."

"Whatever you say, Spicy." He winks and follows me around until it's time to settle at the table for the feast put out before us.

We find our seats and wait patiently while Chase makes a big deal of passing out pink champagne. It has some type of meaning to him and Gigi. I sit back, lean against Eli, and enjoy the comfort of being with my family, all together as one.

"I'd like to start the next two weeks of celebration by reminding my wife of the promise I made to her three years ago today," Chase says, turning Gillian to look at him. "Gillian Grace Davis, I promise to love, cherish, and worship the ground you walk on every day of my life. I'll strive every day to be the man who's good enough for a woman like you."

He continues to share the vows that the rest of us girls never got to hear since they eloped. By the time he's done and sets his hand over her belly, I lose it, weeping into my napkin. Eli cuddles me from behind, pulls my hair to the side and lays several kisses against my neck. "That will be us in three years too, babe. Just you wait."

Gillian speaks up, looking into her husband's face, the love so clear and pure, it hits my heart with a lasso of joy and squeezes. "I give you me. Body. Mind. Soul," she says, and then jumps into his arms, kissing the daylights out of him.

The three of us girls bounce up and hug the two of them. "*Cara bonita*, you are pregnant again?" I ask, putting my hand over her stomach.

"Yes. We found out today. Don't even know how far along." She wipes at the tears trailing down her cheeks.

"I'm so happy for you."

Once we are all sitting at the table chatting it up, Eli stands up. "Maria and I too have an announcement of our own. Babe, get up here." He holds his hand out to me.

Kat, Gillian, and Bree have all eyes on us.

"We're getting married!" I squeal and show them my ring finger.

This time we all squeal and jump up and down hugging one another again.

"Wait a minute. Ladies, you didn't hear the best part." I dangle the juicy nugget of information.

"You're pregnant?" Gillian asks, a hope so strong in her tone I almost wish I was. Almost.

"*Dios mio*, no!"

Eli laughs. "I wish."

All the girls stop hugging me and focus on him. Three pairs of eyes get huge.

"We want to get married while we're here in Ireland," I announce, bringing the topic back to the matter at hand.

Gillian's mouth drops open, and screech of excitement rips through her lungs and deafens all of us. "We can do it here by the cliffs!" she says.

"*Cazador?*" I look at him, and he glances off toward the open plain of brilliant green grass and the stunning ocean view.

"Perfect to me."

"Just. Like. You." I kiss him over and over. He dips me back, licks my lips, and I open for his tongue. He tastes of salt, champagne, and the ocean breeze. I slide my tongue along his, licking deep and rubbing against him. He lifts me up, grabs my ass, and grinds his hardening length against me.

"Um, hello! There are kids in the vicinity. Go to your room." Gillian laughs.

Eli keeps kissing me until we both can't breathe before he pulls away. "I'm so marrying your fine ass, and locking you down for good, Spicy."

I snort. "I'm the one putting a chain around your ankle. My dancer's legs are always free." I grin saucily at my man.

"Speaking of dancing, how's being a free agent and choreographer going?" Kat asks, sipping her champagne. Her long-sleeved shirt must be annoying, but she doesn't often leave the arm bare if the children or anyone else but us girls are around. She's finally got a bit of movement in the arm and can grip on to things and steady herself more with it, but it still looks like a mangled mess of tissue.

"Amazing! Besides the regular dance company and

Broadway stuff, I was recently asked to do the choreography for a hip-hop video for a friend of mine, Anton Santiago."

Bree's eyes widen. "Anton Santiago! He's the biggest and hottest rapper in the business. That's exciting. Is he going to film here? Please tell me he's going to film here!" She holds her hands in prayer position at her chest.

I chuckle and shake my head. "Nope. Once we get home, I leave for Miami in July. Has some type of muse named Mia Saunders who *baila como una mierda*. You know, dances like shit," I whisper so that little ears don't hear.

Bree taps her bottom lip in thought. "I've heard of her. She's dated some pretty well-to-do guys this past year. I've seen her picture in the gossip rags tied to Weston Channing, that moviemaker in LA. The French artist Alec DuBois did some paintings and pictures of her. Last I heard, she was with that baseball player... What's his name?"

When the conversation hits baseball, Phil jumps right in. "Mason Murphy. Now that guy can hit a ball. Best since Babe Ruth."

"Huh, well, get a headshot and an autograph of Anton for me, will ya? I love his music," Bree asks.

"Sure, babe."

"Is the business doing well though, in general?" Gillian asks, fluttering around filling glasses with more wine and being the hostess with the mostess, as usual.

"It is. Ever since Eli suggested it, helped me fund it—and of course, Chase giving me a space in Davis Industries—it's finally making me *mucho dinero*! As you know, it's taken a couple of years, but everyone seems to want an original Maria De La Torre piece. And once this video of Anton's goes live, I'll be hit up by other parts of the music industry. It's a win-win."

"So amazing. It seems like all of us have finally hit our stride. Our little family is growing. I couldn't be happier for each and every one of you," Gigi says, making eye contact with all of us one by one.

When she reaches Kat, she jumps up with her head hanging down. "I, uh, need to go lie down. The alcohol and the sun are hitting me, and I feel the jet lag taking its toll."

She makes a point to hug each one of us, kiss the kids, and head to her designated room.

"Crap." Gigi slumps into her seat.

"Don't beat yourself up, Gigi. She's been hurting for a long time. I'm not sure what more we can do for her," Bree says, misery lacing her tone. She puts her head in her hand and blows out a breath of air.

"We just have to be there for her while she goes through this."

"Anyone heard from Carson?" Bree asks, looking around to make sure Kat's not in earshot.

Chase lifts his glass, takes a sip, and sets it down. "He's got a woman. Started seeing her pretty seriously a month or two ago. He won't talk much about her, but I get the feeling it's more serious than he's letting on."

Gillian frowns. "Well, did you ask him about Kat?"

His lips firm into a hard line. "You know I did, but he says she pushed him away one too many times, and he needed to move on. Says this woman wants him and it feels good to be wanted. I can't blame him for that. Could you?"

His question hits the hearts of everyone at the table. The answer is definitely no, we don't. Three years is a long time to wait for a woman.

"Well, I hope he finds what he's looking for." I lift my glass.

"Toast!"

"Keep it clean, sister," Gigi warns.

"To Chase and Gillian on the new baby and three years of marriage, to Bree and Phillip going strong for two years, to Kat getting back in the design business and doing better than ever, and to Eli and me about to hit the altar... I think we're doing pretty damn well. To friends, family, love, and living a great life. *Salud!*"

All six of us cheer, our glasses together.

"To life, babe," Eli says and kisses me three times behind the ear in the special way that sends tingles rushing through me.

"To a good life." That's all any of us can ever hope for.

THE END

Want more of The Trinity Novels?
Continue with...

Fate
Book Five in *The Trinity Novels.*
Coming Soon!

EXCERPT FROM *FATE*
A TRINITY NOVEL: BOOK FIVE

The second I enter the kitchen, Gigi rushes to me. She wraps an arm around my waist and pulls me out into the hallway.

"I did not invite him here. Apparently, they already had plans to discuss some business venture over breakfast, but I swear to God on my children's lives, I didn't know he'd be here." Gigi speaks so fast she has to lean over and catch her breath when she's done.

"What are you talking about?"

"It's not my fault." She wraps a hand around her belly.

"What's not your fault?" I ask, confused.

"There you two are. Come on, breakfast is already set," Chase says, putting an arm over his wife's shoulders and kissing her temple.

I walk around them to the kitchen. "Gigi was just apologizing to me for something..." I say, and the words fall right out of my mouth when I see who's sitting at the kitchen table eating a cherry-filled crepe.

He stands, looking like a tall drink of water. His blond hair falls across his forehead in sexy layers that say, "I don't give a fuck what my hair looks like," even though it always looks amazing.

His scent wafts across the room. I'm surprised I didn't smell it when I hit the hallway. Only one man I know smells of hay and the sea. A man who surfs as often as he rides his horses. Living directly on the Pacific Ocean on a swath of land that provides everyday access to the beach and farmland gives him that unique odor. And I must say, even now, it hits every single last one of my nerve endings from the roots of my hair down to my toes. Pleasant tingles of awareness and desire sprinkle out each pore, putting a static energy in the room that anyone within a ten-foot radius could feel.

Carson's eyes are crinkled around the edges, more lines around those baby blues than I like seeing. He's tired, worn out...but why?

"Hey, sweet cheeks. Didn't expect to see you here, but always a pleasure." His low rumbled tone zips through me, calling back memories of making love, laughing till the wee hours of the morning, and whispering vows we've since broken.

Sweet cheeks. His nickname for me. Silly name from a silly man, but he loved my ass and told me as often as he groped it. I just loved him. Still do.

"Carson. It's been a while." I clench my teeth and batten down the hatches of my emotions.

He nods, comes around the table, and stands before me. The entire room ceases to exist when he's in it—as if everything around me has gotten smaller, farther away, and all I'm capable of seeing is him. The man I love. The man I'll always love, but can no longer have.

Carson lifts a hand to my face. With his thumb, he traces a path from my temple down to my chin, where he lifts it up and leans forward. He places a featherlight kiss to my lips. I gasp. He hasn't made that gesture in a solid year. I'm so shocked by his nearness, the sheer connection pumping between us, that I don't move a single muscle. He brushes his lips along mine again. I lick my lips, and just the hint of our tongues touch. He groans, and I pop back at the sound.

I lift my hand to my mouth and then shuffle around him. "Um, yes. So, uh, what are you doing here?" Sizzles of recognition and excitement whip along the surface of my skin.

Neither Chase nor Gillian has said a word. Both of them are standing quietly across the kitchen, leaning against the cabinets. Gigi looks like she's been stunned stupid, whereas Chase has the biggest shit-eating grin on his face.

Jesus. Now he's never going to stop hounding me about his cousin.

"Business concept we've been volleying back and forth."

I nod and make myself busy by getting a cup of coffee. Without thinking, I go to grab the carafe with my right hand. I barely get the pot out when it starts to drop. Carson's fast, though. He wraps a hand around mine where I'm holding the handle.

"Let me get that," he says, plastered against my back. Carson never did have space issues, especially when it came to me. *The closer the better,* he'd always tell me.

Together we pour the liquid into two cups that I imagine were left out for us. He leans deeper into my behind. I can feel the outline of his pelvis and package against my ass and the warm strength of his chest against my back. God, I miss this. Being close to him. To a living, breathing person. I close my eyes, soaking in every ounce of his presence into my memory. I'll need it later.

Once he puts the carafe back, he inhales deeply against my neck. Shivers ripple along my spine, and a fire I'd long forgotten about simmers between my thighs.

"Christ, sweet cheeks. I've missed your smell. Only it's different... Sunshine and..." He shifts my hair over to the side and rubs his nose along my neck.

The hairs at my nape stand at attention, and my knees weaken. I brace myself up against the counter, fingers digging into the granite. He wraps both of his hands over mine. The second he touches my scarred flesh, I stiffen.

He breathes against me as if touching my scars doesn't faze him. Stunned, I stand, unmoving.

"Coconuts. You smell of coconuts."

I bite into my lip and pray he steps back before I internally combust or burst into a puddle of tears. "Coconut oil. It's good for the scars."

"Mmm, I like it. Suits you." He trails his nose up my neck once again and kisses me at my temple. Then he grabs his cup of coffee and backs away. I can hear his footsteps getting farther away and then the chair legs skidding across the floor, but the impression of his warm body still simmers against my backside.

I close my eyes and calm my raging heart, allowing my body movement to come back online.

Gillian comes over to me, plops a teaspoon of sugar into my coffee, and pours some of the homemade vanilla creamer Bentley makes especially for her into my cup. The spoon tinkling against the sides of the glass has me jerking to attention.

"So... Over him, are you?" Gigi accuses.

"Yes," I hiss, and sip my coffee. The soothing vanilla and hot coffee ease the lusty beast inside me as I stare at Carson and Chase laughing it up while digging into their breakfast.

"What are you going to do?"

I jolt my head back. "Nothing. It's over. We're over." I remind her as much as myself.

Gigi's eyebrows rise up into her hairline. "You could have fooled me the way he was pressed up against you, sniffing you. My God, that was so hot!"

I shake my head and hide behind my cup. She leans her shoulder against mine. "He's yours for the taking, you know."

If only that were true.

"It's not meant to be," I say with finality.

"Only because you won't let it."

Continue reading in:

Fate
A Trinity Novel: Book Five
Coming Soon!

ALSO BY AUDREY CARLAN

The Calendar Girl Series

January (Book 1)

February (Book 2)

March (Book 3)

April (Book 4)

May (Book 5)

June (Book 6)

July (Book 7)

August (Book 8)

September (Book 9)

October (Book 10)

November (Book 11)

December (Book 12)

The Calendar Girl Anthologies

Volume One (Jan-Mar)

Volume Two (Apr-Jun)

Volume Three (Jul-Sep)

Volume Four (Oct-Dec)

The Falling Series

Angel Falling

London Falling

Justice Falling

The Trinity Novels

Body (Book 1)

Mind (Book 2)

Soul (Book 3)

Life (Book 4)

Fate (Book 5 - *Coming Soon)*

The Lotus House Series

Resisting Roots (Book 1)

Sacred Serenity (Book 2)

Divine Desire (Book 3)

ACKNOWLEDGMENTS

To my husband, Eric, thank you for always letting me be me and loving every damn inch. I'll always love you more.

To my soul sisters, Dyani Gingerich, Nikki Chiverrell, and Carolyn Beasley...the journey continues. Bet you thought you'd seen the end with the trilogy, but you're baaaaaaccccckkk! I love writing characters loosely based off of you and your likeness. I think these books show the incredible bond, love, and trust we share. If my readers have even one friend with which they can share what we share, I know they'll be lucky. I have three, and I'm bursting with gratitude and supreme love in my heart. You will always be a part of my present and my future, and with this Trinity Series, you'll always be a part of my past. BESOS

To my editor Ekatarina Sayanova with Red Quill Editing, LLC... I almost feel like I should apologize for how little time I gave you to edit this novel. So yeah, I'm sorry! I would say I won't do it again but we both know I'd be lying, and I'm a shitty liar. <grin> Each and every time I get my edits from you, I smile. Not all authors can say that. Thank you for being you.

Roxie Sofia, you are quickly becoming my hidden gem! Your final edits to the manuscript and the fun comments you sprinkle throughout give me peace of mind and happiness in my soul. I'm thrilled we're working together!

To my extraordinarily talented #TEAMAC, Heather White (aka Goddess) and my personal assistant Jeananna Goodall, I can't tell you how much it means to me to have you pre-reading these books and sharing your opinions as you go. It lifts me up and keeps me going. Thank you for supporting me in all things. I love you.

Ginelle Blanch, Anita Shofner, Ceej Chargualaf, my fantastic beta readers... I adore you. Thank you for giving me your time and honest feedback. I just don't feel like I could put it out into the world without your sign of approval! Mad love, ladies!

Gotta thank my super awesome, fantabulous publisher, Waterhouse Press. Thank you for being the nontraditional traditional publisher!

To the Audrey Carlan Street Team of wicked hot Angels, together we change the world. One book at a time. BESOS-4-LIFE, lovely ladies.

ABOUT AUDREY CARLAN

Audrey Carlan is a #1 *New York Times, USA Today,* and *Wall Street Journal* bestselling author. She writes wicked hot love stories that are designed to give the reader a romantic experience that's sexy, sweet, and so hot your ereader might melt. Some of her works include the wildly successful Calendar Girl Serial, Falling Series, and the Trinity Trilogy.

She lives in the California Valley where she enjoys her two children and the love of her life. When she's not writing, you can find her teaching yoga, sipping wine with her "soul sisters" or with her nose stuck in a wicked hot romance novel.

Any and all feedback is greatly appreciated and feeds the soul. You can contact Audrey below:

E-mail: carlan.audrey@gmail.com
Facebook: facebook.com/AudreyCarlan
Website: www.audreycarlan.com